THE OXFORD LIBRARY OF FRENCH CLASSICS

General Editor: Robert Baldick

CYRANO DE BERGERAC

OTHER WORLDS

CYRANO DE BERGERAC

OTHER WORLDS

The Comical History of the States and
Empires of the Moon and the Sun

Translated and Introduced by
GEOFFREY STRACHAN

847
c4

London
OXFORD UNIVERSITY PRESS
NEW YORK   TORONTO
1965

OXFORD UNIVERSITY PRESS

AMEN HOUSE, LONDON E.C.4

Glasgow New York Toronto Melbourne Wellington
Bombay Calcutta Madras Karachi Lahore Dacca
Cape Town Salisbury Nairobi Ibadan
Kuala Lumpur Hong Kong

This translation is based on the *Œuvres*,
edited by Georges Ribemont-Dessaignes, and
published by Le Club Français du Livre, Paris,
1957.

Printed in Great Britain by
Richard Clay (The Chaucer Press), Ltd., Bungay, Suffolk

CONTENTS

CONTENTS

INTRODUCTION

by Geoffrey Strachan

*Let us create vessels and sails adjusted to the heavenly ether
and there will be plenty of people unafraid of the empty wastes.*
Kepler 1610
*The proposition that the sun is the centre of the world and does
not move from its place is absurd and false philosophically and
formally heretical, because it is expressly contrary to Holy
Scripture.* The Holy Office 1633

VISITORS to the town of Bergerac on the Dordogne can buy
picture postcards which show a man in a plumed hat with a
bulbous upturned nose. The caption reads: 'Cyrano de
Bergerac, legendary hero'. In such ways the seventeenth century poet's name remains divorced from historical reality;
the man who three hundred years ago portrayed the hazards
of space flight still has to compete for its use with the soft-
centred hero of a late nineteenth-century box office smash hit.

In the two books of *L'Autre Monde* (also known as the
Histoire Comique), written about 1650, the real Cyrano made
himself the hero of two voyages in space, first to the moon and
next to the sun. The exploits of men in space are almost daily
news to us now. Here is Cosmonaut Leonov on 18 March 1965
venturing out of his spacecraft: 'if the lifeline connecting him
with the spacecraft had snapped, he might have continued in
orbit as a human satellite for about two weeks, eventually
burning up as he re-entered the earth's atmosphere' (*The
Guardian*). Such predicaments are actual, yet turning to
Cyrano's book, one can still feel a thrill as he hurtles towards
the sun in his own frail machine, 'following Phaeton's example in the midst of a chariot race which I cannot abandon
and in which, if I make one false move, all nature together
cannot save me'. He is not the first fictional space traveller
and his successors are legion, but it is interesting to find that

his descriptions of voyages to other worlds, in his various flying machines, seem to stand up to competition with the real
thing in the first decade which has been able to make the
comparison, and during which four separate editions of his
book have been published in France.

It is time for Cyrano, who has been here before, in person
perhaps, and certainly in print, to venture across the channel
once more and reclaim his name from Rostand's self-pitying
grotesque.

Little is known for certain about the life of Savinien
Cyrano de Bergerac. Even the reports of his friends contribute as much to legend as to history—he emerges too sober
or too intemperate. He was born Savinien Cyrano in Paris in
1619, the son of an *avocat au Parlement de Paris*, named Abel
de Cyrano. Three years later, the family moved to their estate
near Paris, part of which was the small fief of Bergerac.
Savinien was educated first by a country priest, whose punish-
ments made him resentful and rebellious. At the age of thirteen, he was sent by his father to the Collège de Beauvais in
Paris, but not before he had met at school his lifelong friend
and future literary executor, Henri Le Bret. At the Collège
de Beauvais, the young Savinien studied his classics and fell
foul of the principal, Jean Grangier, a classical scholar of
some standing, but apparently himself of a quarrelsome disposition and a fierce disciplinarian. His various weaknesses,
real and imaginary, were later outrageously burlesqued in
Cyrano's comedy, *Le Pédant Joué*. In 1636 Abel sold his
property at Bergerac and the family moved to Paris once
more, but Savinien was to adopt the name of Bergerac and to
use it throughout his life in various forms: Alexandre de
Cyrano Bergerac, de Bergerac Cyrano, Hercule de Bergerac
and the more familiar Cyrano de Bergerac.

At about eighteen, he left the Collège de Beauvais, having
doubtless acquired a considerable humanist culture, as well
as a deep dislike of arbitrary authority. He mixed with the
literary bohemian world of the period, which included such

people as François Tristan L'Hermite, the playwright. He frequented taverns and indulged in gambling, a pastime his father's fortunes could ill afford. He probably also read widely and voraciously. Henri Le Bret remained his friend and adviser and something of a mediator between Cyrano and his father. It was on Le Bret's suggestion that he enlisted with M. de Carbon de Casteljaloux' company of guards, his admission being facilitated by the noble and Gascon ring of his new name, for both qualifications were required in this company. He was apparently soon involved in many duels and acquitted himself well. He is said to have fought only as a second (the normal custom for seconds then) and never in his own quarrels. He received a musket shot through the body at the siege of Mouzon in Champagne in the bitter winter of 1639, and the following year he was again wounded, this time at Arras and in the throat. Soon after this he abandoned his military career, with a weakened constitution but having won considerable respect from his brother officers.

In 1641 he returned to a life of study at the Collège de Lisieux, perhaps earning his keep as an usher. He attended the classes of Gassendi, the Epicurean philosopher, mathematician and free-thinker, newly arrived in Paris. His pupils included brilliant young men of Cyrano's generation like Molière and Jacques Rohault, the disciple of Descartes, who was to remain a close friend of Cyrano and to guide him in his study of physics.

A number of stories are told about his exploits at this period. Those told by Le Bret (which include routing a band of a hundred hired ruffians in order to protect the poet Lignières) do him credit. Others indicate a preposterously vain and ill-tempered disposition and belong to the burlesque legend built up by less loyal friends, such as the poet Charles Dassoucy, with whom at times he quarrelled. It seems certain that Cyrano mixed intelligent conversation and studies with a fairly dissolute way of life, during which he gambled with Tristan L'Hermite, contracted syphilis, which was never properly cured, helped to impoverish his father, broadened his knowledge of current scientific and philosophical ideas, talked well, and wrote his comedy, *Le Pédant Joué*, from which Molière was to borrow heavily for one of the most famous scenes in *Les Fourberies de Scapin* (1671). He began to write the literary letters later collected together as *Lettres Diverses*, *Lettres Satiriques* and *Lettres Amoureuses*, exercises in elegance, wit, and invective. He may have travelled at this time to England, Italy, and Poland, where some say he observed experiments with a flying machine, a winged dragon that beat its wings. In 1648 he first appeared in print with a preface to one of Dassoucy's poems.

About this time, Le Bret tells us, Cyrano refused the offered patronage of the Maréchal de Gassion—because he wished to remain a free man. He was for the moment somewhat less impoverished, as a result of the death of his father, whom he and his brother, Abel, are alleged to have robbed as he lay dying. He now began to work on *L'Autre Monde* (literally, 'The Other World'). In 1648 there had been published a French edition of Bishop Godwin's *The Man in the Moone*, the fanciful tale of one Domingo Gonsales, who was carried to the moon on a machine borne by a number of large birds. Once in the moon, he made a study of its utopian institutions. The French edition is prefaced by the remarks: 'If, reader, you have ever seen either the *True History* of Lucian, or Thomas More's *Utopia*, or Chancellor Bacon's *New Atlantis*, I have no doubt that you will class with the same type of writing this story, which is no less ingenious than diverting.' Cyrano would know these books, as well as Campanella's rationalist utopia, *The City of the Sun*, and perhaps Kepler's fragmentary *Somnium*, a tale of a trip to the moon. This was envisaged in quite realistic terms, with a light face and a dark face to the moon, and a race of huge reptiles living there. Cyrano's own book was to be broader in scope than any of these.

In 1649 he ventured into print again with a 'mazarinade', an unbridled attack on Mazarin in the manner of the burlesque poets like Scarron. The following year he changed sides and wrote (either for money, or to spite Scarron and the rest) his letter, *Contre les Frondeurs*, an attack on the princes of the Fronde. Meanwhile *L'Autre Monde* (or at any rate the first book of it) was completed. He sent the manuscript of it to his friend, the poet Jean Royer de Prades, who expressed in verse his alarm and his intention of avoiding Cyrano in future:

> Car autant qu'une affreuse mort
> Je crains les gens de 'L'Autre Monde'.

(I fear these people of 'The Other World' as greatly as a dreadful death.) The reaction of other friends is unknown. The manuscript remained unpublished, though its private circulation probably added to his reputation both as a writer and as a dangerous *libertin* (i.e. a free-thinker).

In 1652 he overcame any earlier scruples, driven perhaps both by poverty and by the need for respectability, which would permit him to publish, and obtained the patronage of the dull and vain Duc d'Arpajon. His tragedy, *La Mort d'Agrippine*, was published with a dedication to his new patron and this was followed by a second volume of works, including *Le Pédant Joué. L'Autre Monde* remained unpublished, but the audience which witnessed the first performance of *La Mort d'Agrippine* at the Hotel de Bourgogne evidently came prepared to be shocked by the work of a madman or an atheist or both. Bold tirades against the gods ('which were made by man and did not make man') may have passed unnoticed but a harmless phrase was taken as an insult to the Eucharist (*hostie* can mean both victim and the Host) and an uproar ensued. The play was taken off and the duke sought to rid himself of his embarrassing protégé.

But by this time, fate (or as some biographers have had it, the agents of the Holy Office) had intervened and caused a wooden beam to fall on Cyrano's head as he entered the duke's house. He was now ill and confined to his room. The duke advised him to go to the country. Feeling betrayed, Cyrano left the duke's house for good, and was tended by his aunt, Catherine, and his friends at a house in Paris. Here he worked over the manuscripts of *L'Autre Monde* until they were stolen—or removed by friends in order to save them from destruction at the hands of the pious nuns, who were also in attendance. They later came into the hands of Le Bret, but he, in turn, was robbed of the third book, *L'Étincelle*, which has never come to light. Cyrano moved to the house of his cousin, Pierre de Cyrano at Sannois, where he died in July 1655, at the age of thirty-six, probably of the malady which had kept him away from the opposite sex for the last ten years of his life. Apparently he made a Christian end.

In 1657 Le Bret published the first book of *L'Autre Monde* as the *Voyage dans la Lune*. Himself about to take orders, Le Bret undoubtedly whitewashed his friend in the prefatory account of his life, not merely glossing over the more disreputable aspects of it, but also apologizing for the very idea of presenting the moon as a world. He cites Heraclitus, Gassendi, and others as supporters of the view but praises Cyrano for treating it lightly rather than seriously (this nearly fifty years after Galileo had observed its surface through a telescope and said, 'it is full of irregularities, uneven, full of hollows and protuberances, just like the surface of the earth itself'). Le Bret also cut out all the obviously blasphemous or bawdy passages. The full version of the first book (the second book remains incomplete) was preserved in a manuscript in either Cyrano's hand or that of a friend. This was published in 1920.

Bowdlerized by Le Bret, the book achieved some success as a comical history, and was soon joined in print by the second part, *L'Histoire des États et Empires du Soleil* (the source of the manuscript is unknown). Before the end of the century there were several more editions and two English versions. There was a new edition in 1741 and then Cyrano seems to have been forgotten for almost a hundred years.

In 1838 Charles Nodier in his *Bulletin du Bibliophile* praised Cyrano, as did Théophile Gautier in a highly inaccurate account in *Les Grotesques* (1844). Gautier penned a whimsical description of Cyrano's face, based on the extant portraits. It is vivid and exaggerated. His surprising description of Cyrano's big aquiline nose as 'the highest mountain in the world after the Himalayas' helped, along with some of Dassoucy's insults, to lay the foundations for Rostand's creation. Cyrano's own comments on the subject of large noses appear in *L'Autre Monde*.

New editions appeared in 1855 and 1858. The general picture of Cyrano remained confused, and the success of Rostand's play in 1897 confused matters still more. The free-thinking martyr to clerical fanatics, who had pursued him beyond the grave by destroying copies of his works whenever they came upon them, hardly fitted in with the grotesque hero nursing a broken heart. And did he come from Gascony or did he not? Rostand cannot be blamed for using legends and superficial local colour in order to write good theatre rather than good history. His borrowings from Cyrano's own work, however, now seem rather feeble and his portrayal of the man who satirized the tearful amorous swains of precious literature as one of them himself is rather a cheek.

In 1920 Frédéric Lachèvre published the full text of *L'Autre Monde*, and wrote an account of Cyrano's life which distinguished critically between fact and fiction. He himself shows a curious distaste for Cyrano as a spendthrift, petulant blasphemer. He was of course anxious to give the emphatic lie to all the legends: Cyrano was not a nobleman; he was not the worthy, martyred free-thinker of innocent nineteenth century myth—any more than Galileo was an uncomplicated Resistance hero who quipped 'and yet it moves' as he signed away the Copernican theory. A little of Lachèvre's distaste was perhaps shared by Richard Aldington, who translated the book into English for the first time since 1754 shortly after Lachèvre's edition was published. Aldington praises the liveliness of the book, but one feels he might have preferred Cyrano to have omitted his physics and his travesties of myth and scripture, to have been more logical, more classical, more

Swiftian. But he rightly defends Cyrano against the irrelevant charge of plagiarism. Again the nineteenth century had misunderstood Cyrano's originality: it was not that of the scientist or philosopher. It was that of a poet who listened to their talk and used it for his own ends. The value of this has been perceived more recently.

The revival of interest in Cyrano during the past ten years may perhaps be related to that in a more modern fantastic writer, Alfred Jarry (also a rebellious schoolboy who pilloried his teacher in a play, who mated a passion for physics with a belief in the paramountcy of the imagination to produce 'pataphysics', his science of impossible solutions, and who made *L'Autre Monde* one of the twenty-seven 'equivalent books' of his own voyager through space-time, Dr Faustroll). Our age has outgrown the sweetly reasonable straitjacket of classicism and the heroic individualism of the romantics. Cyrano can speak to us directly now as a voice from an age of fragmented culture, like our own, in which there are many authorities demanding subservience but no one Authority; in which the physical world is seen to be governed by huge forces we observe at work but cannot quite fathom; and in which solid matter melts away into infinitesimal particles as we try to define it.

Cyrano de Bergerac was an accomplished writer in at least three standard genres of his time. His letters show elegance, wit, pungent rhetoric, and a feeling for nature. His comedy shows Rabelaisian verve, with its larger-than-life characters and satire on pedantry. It contains many sallies at the expense of the literary rules of classicism, including those of comedy. ('I should have riddled this rogue's belly with holes already, but I was afraid of breaking the rules of comedy by spilling blood upon the stage.') His tragedy, however, shows considerable formal discipline and Cornelian eloquence. It was only in *L'Autre Monde* that Cyrano found a genre which gave full scope to his gifts and to the diversity of his experience. He did not invent the genre but rather developed it from an

manipulate

existing one. *The Man in the Moone* had combined the elements of the utopian tradition, space fiction, and the tall story (Lucian and Rabelais). To these Cyrano added a flavour of Montaigne's speculation, the burlesque taste for old myths travestied, and satire, both fierce and oblique.

It might have been an indecipherable hotch-potch, like the culture it reflected; a book so full of allusions that only a scholar could relish it. One may indeed study it for its mechanical inventions, for its classical allusions, for its use of other men's utopian ideas (both right way up and upside-down), for its expression of Gassendi's and Descartes' conflicting theories. Or one can just sit back and enjoy it; for the story of Cyrano's two voyages with its fourth dimension of speculation and its alienation effect of leg-pull is written for the layman. The author has borrowed left and right and the book contains a number of witty, oblique acknowledgements to people whose ideas he borrows, embellishes, or burlesques: Gassendi, Godwin, Sorel, Campanella. It all forms part of his graceful, inexhaustible conversation piece. It is the work of a man who delights in speculating and cherishes the freedom to speculate and to believe whatever he chooses.

Cyrano, Le Bret relates, noted the diversity of the opinions of the philosophers and therefore scorned any man who took a single one of them as his gospel. Diversity fascinated him. Given his support for the thesis that the moon is a world, one may marvel at the perversity of the fancies that go with it. But the work of a man like Kepler, who helped to usher in the Newtonian revolution, was itself a mixture of astronomical observation and mathematical mysticism. His chores included casting horoscopes for princes. It was a culture which had not yet created the classical compartments. In arguing more than one side to a case, and in alternating between common sense and lunatic logic, Cyrano was writing—amusingly—of what he heard and read round about him. His book is a poem from an age when poetry, physics, metaphysics, and astronomy could all still exist side by side in one book, albeit a fantastic one. In 1687 Newton's *Principia* appeared. The mystery of those 'influences' exerted by bodies on one another, which so fascinated men's minds, Cyrano's included, was formulated as the law of gravity. The sun was no longer a spirit, a god; it became an engine, the heart of the great clockwork universe which Swift was to inhabit. Drawing much from *L'Autre Monde*, Swift was to give it quite a new emphasis, to write a more forceful, more earth-bound, more perfect book, banking his fires, and suiting it to his age of reason.

Cyrano lived in a fantastic age. The fantastic delights him, whether it be a new theory, an ingenious device, or the folly of a bigot. He thumbs his nose not only at bullying authority, but at all literal-minded dogmatists. His book is full of inconsistencies, even in the narrative occasionally, but this is the point. From them, unified by his lively, throwaway style and his burning enthusiasm for the idea that all things are possible in nature, arises the delight.

*　　*　　*

I AM indebted to the editors of the recent French editions of *L'Autre Monde*: Frédéric Lachèvre; Georges Ribemont-Dessaignes; Claude Mettra and Jean Suyeux; and Willy de Spens, and also to *The Sleepwalkers* by Arthur Koestler.

There is a break in the original text at the end of Chapter 2.

The titles of Chapters 15 and 16 are taken from the original text. All other divisions and chapter titles are my own.

THE STATES AND EMPIRES
OF THE MOON

I

Journey to the moon

THE moon was full, the sky was cloudless, and it had already struck nine. We were returning from Clamard, near Paris, where the younger Monsieur de Cuigy, who is the squire there, had been entertaining myself and several of my friends. Along the road we amused ourselves with the various speculations inspired by this ball of saffron. All our eyes were fixed on the great star. One of our number took it for a garret window in heaven, through which the glory of the blessed could be glimpsed. Another, convinced by the fables of the ancients, thought it possible that Bacchus kept a tavern up there in the heavens and that he had hung up the full moon as a sign. Another assured us that it was the round, copper ironing board on which Diana presses Apollo's collars. Another that it might be the sun itself, having cast off its rays in the evening, watching through a peep-hole to see what happened on earth in its absence.

'And as for me,' I told them, 'I will gladly add my own contribution to your transports. I am in no way diverted by the ingenious fancies with which you flatter time, to make it pass more quickly, and I believe that the moon is a world like ours, which our world serves as a moon.'

Some of the company treated me to a great outburst of laughter. 'And that, perhaps,' I said to them, 'is just how someone else is being ridiculed at this very moment in the moon for maintaining that this globe here is a world.'

But although I informed them that Pythagoras, Epicurus, Democritus, and, in our own age, Copernicus and Kepler had been of the same opinion, I merely made them laugh more heartily.

Nevertheless this notion, the boldness of which matched the humour I was in, was only fortified by contradiction and lodged so deeply in my mind that for all the rest of the day I remained pregnant with a thousand definitions of the moon of which I could not be delivered. As a result of upholding this fanciful belief with half-serious arguments, I had almost reached the stage of yielding to it, when there came the miracle—the accident, stroke of fortune, chance (you may well name it vision, fiction, chimera or, if you will, madness)— which afforded me the opportunity that has engaged me upon this account.

Upon my arrival home I went up to my study, where I found a book open on the table, which I had certainly not put there myself. It was that of Girolamo Cardano[1] and, although I had had no intention of reading from it, my eyes seemed to be drawn to the particular story which this philosopher tells of how, when studying one evening by candlelight, he observed the entry, through closed doors, of two tall old men. After he had put many questions to them, they replied that they were inhabitants of the moon and at the same moment disappeared. This left me in such amazement —as much at seeing a book which had transported itself there all by itself, as at the occasion when it had happened and the page at which it had been opened—that I took the whole chain of incidents to be a revelation sent in order that men should know that the moon is a world.

'How now,' I said to myself, 'here have I been talking about one thing all day, and now does a book, which is perhaps the only one in the world where this matter is so particularly dealt with, fly from my library to my table, become capable of reason to the extent of opening itself at the very place where just such a marvellous adventure is described, pull my eyes towards it as if by force, and then furnish my imagination with the reflections and my will with the intentions which now occur to me?

'Doubtless,' I continued, 'the two ancients who appeared to that great man are the very same who have moved my book and opened it at this page, in order to spare themselves the

[1] *De subtilitate rerum* by Girolamo Cardano (1501–76), doctor, mathematician, philosopher, and alchemist.

trouble of making me the speech they had already made to Cardano.

'But'—I added—'how can I resolve this doubt without going the whole way up there?

'And why not?' I answered myself at once. 'Prometheus went to heaven long ago to steal fire there. Am I less bold than he? And have I any reason not to hope for an equal success?'

After these outbursts, which may perhaps be called attacks of delirium, came the hope that I might successfully accomplish so fine a voyage. In order to make an end of it, I shut myself away in a comparatively isolated country house where, having gratified my daydreams with some practical measures appropriate to my design, this is how I offered myself up to heaven.

I had fastened all about me a quantity of small bottles filled with dew. The sun beat so violently upon them with its rays that the heat which attracted them, just as it does the thickest mists, raised me aloft until at length I found myself above the middle region of the air. But the attraction made me rise too rapidly and, instead of it bringing me nearer to the moon, as I had supposed it would, this now seemed to me more distant than at my departure. I therefore broke several of my phials, until I felt that my weight was overcoming the attraction and that I was descending towards the earth again.

My supposition was correct, for I fell to earth some little time afterwards and, reckoning from the hour at which I had left, it should have been midnight. However, I perceived that the sun was now at its zenith and that it was midday.

I leave you to picture my astonishment. It was very great indeed, and not knowing how to explain this miracle, I was insolent enough to imagine God had favoured my daring by once more nailing the sun to the heavens in order to illuminate an enterprise of such grandeur. I was further astonished by the fact that I completely failed to recognize the country where I found myself. For it seemed to me that, having gone straight up into the air, I should have come down in the place I had left from. However, accoutred as I was, I made my way towards a kind of cottage where I could see some smoke, and I was barely a pistol shot away from it when I found myself surrounded by a large number of stark naked men. They seemed greatly surprised to have encountered me for I was, I believe, the first person dressed in bottles they had ever seen. What still further confounded all the interpretations they might have put upon my harness was to see that I hardly touched the earth as I walked. What they did not know was that at the least impulse I gave to my body, the heat of the noonday rays lifted me up with my dew and if my phials had not been too few in number I could quite easily have been carried away on the winds before their eyes.

I was going to address them but they disappeared in an instant into the near-by forest, just as if fright had turned them all into birds. However, I managed to catch one of them, whose legs had doubtless betrayed his feelings. I asked him with some difficulty (for I was quite out of breath) what the distance was reckoned to be from there to Paris; since when, in France, people went about stark naked, and why they ran away from me in such alarm. The man to whom I was speaking was an olive-skinned ancient who first of all threw himself at my knees and then clasped his hands in the air behind his head, opened his mouth and closed his eyes. He mumbled between his teeth for a long time but I did not notice that he was articulating anything and took his talk for the husky babbling of a mute.

Some time later I saw a company of soldiery arriving with beating drums and observed two of them emerging from the ranks to investigate me. When they were near enough to be heard I asked them where I was.

'You are in France,' they answered me. 'But what devil has put you in that state and how comes it that we do not know you? Have the ships arrived? Are you going to inform my Lord the Governor? And why have you divided up your brandy into so many bottles?'

To all this I retorted that the devil had certainly not put me in the state I was in; that they did not know me for the reason that they could not know all men; that I knew nothing of the Seine carrying ships to Paris; that I had no message for my Lord the Marshal of the Hospital, and that I carried no brandy at all.

'Oho,' they said, taking me by the arm, 'so you want to play the clown. My Lord the Governor will know you all right!'

They led me towards their troop, where I learned that I was indeed in France—in New France. Some little time later I was presented to the Viceroy, who asked me my country, my name, and my quality. I satisfied him by relating the happy outcome of my voyage and, whether he believed it or only pretended to do so, he had the goodness to arrange for me to be given a room in his house. My joy was great at meeting a man capable of lofty reasoning, who was not at all surprised when I told him that the earth must have revolved during the course of my levitation, since I had begun my ascent two leagues away from Paris and had come down almost perpendicularly in Canada.

In the evening, as I was going to bed, he came into my room and said to me, 'I should not have come to disturb your rest if I did not believe that a person who can discover the secret of covering so much ground in half a day must also possess that of avoiding all fatigue.

'But you do not know what an amusing argument I have been having with our Jesuit Fathers about you,' he added. 'They absolutely insist that you are a sorcerer and the greatest compliment you can expect from them is not to be considered an imposter. Indeed, this motion, which you attribute to the earth, is a somewhat ticklish paradox. To be frank with you, the reason I do not share your opinion is that even if you left Paris yesterday, you could still have arrived in this country without the earth having revolved at all. For if the sun lifted you by means of your bottles, would it not have brought you here, since, according to Ptolemy and the modern philosophers, it travels in the direction you attribute to the earth? What great semblance of truth makes you judge the sun to be motionless when we can see it travelling? And is it likely that the earth revolves at such speed, when we can feel it to be firm beneath us?'

'Sir,' I answered him, 'here are the reasons, more or less, which oblige us to presume it to be so.

'Firstly, it is common sense to believe that the sun has its place at the centre of the universe, since all the bodies which exist in nature have need of this fundamental source of heat. It dwells in the heart of the kingdom so that it may swiftly satisfy the needs of each region. The first cause of all life is situated at the very centre of all bodies in order to function with equity and with greater ease. Wise nature has located the genital organs in man after the same fashion, pips at the centre of apples and stones in the middle of their fruit. The onion likewise protects, under the shield of the hundred skins which surround it, the precious seed whence ten million others must draw their essence. For the apple is a little universe in itself, wherein the pip, warmer than the other parts, is a sun giving off the heat which preserves the rest of its sphere, and the onion seed, according to this theory, is the little sun of its own little cosmos, which warms and nourishes the vegetative salts of this little body.

'If one supposes this, then I would claim that the earth, being in need of the light, heat, and influence of this great fire, revolves about it in order to receive in all its parts an equal measure of the virtues which conserve it. For it would be as ridiculous to believe that this great luminous body revolved round a speck, which is useless to it, as to imagine when we see a roast lark, that the hearth has been revolved about it in order to cook it. Otherwise, if the sun had to perform this task, it would seem as if the medicine needed the sick man, the strong should yield to the weak, the great serve the small and, instead of a ship sailing along the shores of a province, the province would have to be navigated round the ship. And if you find it difficult to understand how such a heavy mass can move, I pray you tell me if the stars and the heavens, which you would have so solid, are any lighter? Since we are certain of the rotundity of the earth, it is easy for us to deduce its motion from its shape. But why should you suppose the sky to be round, since you cannot know for sure? And if, out of all the possible shapes, it does not happen to possess this one, it is certain that it cannot move.

'I am not going to reproach you for your *eccentrics*, your *concentrics*, and your *epicycles*, all of which you could only explain very confusedly and from which I have rescued my own system. Let us simply discuss the natural causes of this motion. *You* are all forced to fall back on intelligences which move and govern your spheres. But I, on the other hand, do not disturb the repose of the Supreme Being, who doubtless created nature all perfect, and who is wise enough to have accomplished the task in such a way that, having made it complete in one respect, He did not leave it defective in another. I, I tell you, find in the earth itself the virtues which make it move. I maintain that the rays and influences of the sun fall upon it as they circulate and make it revolve (just as we make a globe revolve by striking it with our hands); or equally that the vapours continually evaporating from its heart on the side visible to the sun are repelled by the cold of the middle region of the air and fall back upon it, and, of necessity only being able to strike at an angle, thus make it pirouette.

'The explanation of the other two motions is even less complicated. Pray you, consider a little. . . .'

At these words the Viceroy interrupted me: 'I would prefer,' he said, 'to spare you the trouble, since I have read several books by Gassendi on this subject, but on condition that you listen to the reply given me one day by one of our Fathers who was upholding your opinion. "Indeed," he said, "I am convinced that the earth revolves, not for the reasons alleged by Copernicus, but because the fires of hell, as the Holy Scriptures tell us, are enclosed in the centre of the earth and the damned, seeking to escape the burning flames, clamber up the vault in order to avoid them and thus cause the earth to revolve, as a dog turns a wheel when it runs enclosed within it." '

We spent some time praising this notion as a pure fruit of

9

the good Father's zeal, and finally the Viceroy told me he was much astonished, seeing how improbable Ptolemy's system was, that it should have been so generally accepted.

'Sir,' I replied to him, 'the majority of men, who only judge things by their senses, have allowed themselves to be persuaded by their eyes, and just as the man on board a ship which hugs the coastline believes that he is motionless and the shore is moving, so have men, revolving with the earth about the sky, believed that it was the sky itself which revolved about them. Added to this there is the intolerable pride of human beings, who are convinced that nature was only made for them—as if it were likely that the sun, a vast body four hundred and thirty-four times greater than the earth, should only have been set ablaze in order to ripen their medlars and to make their cabbages grow heads!

'As for me, far from agreeing with their impudence, I believe that the planets are worlds surrounding the sun and the fixed stars are also suns with planets surrounding them; that is to say, worlds which we cannot see from here, on account of their smallness, and because their light, being borrowed, cannot reach us. For how, in good faith, can one imagine these globes of such magnitude to be nothing but great desert countries, while ours, simply because we, a handful of vainglorious ruffians are crawling about on it, has been made to command all the others? What! Just because the sun charts our days and years for us, does that mean to say it was only made to stop us banging our heads against the walls? No, no, if this visible god lights man's way it is by accident, as the King's torch accidentally gives light to the passing street-porter.'

'But,' he said to me, 'if, as you affirm, the fixed stars are so many suns, one could conclude from this that the universe is infinite, since it is likely that the peoples of one of these worlds going round a fixed star can themselves observe other fixed stars, farther above them, which we cannot make out from here, and so on, to infinity.'

'Without a doubt,' I replied. 'Just as God could make the

soul immortal, so He could make the universe infinite, if it be true that eternity is nothing but an endless duration of time and infinity a limitless stretch of space. Besides, if the universe were not infinite, God Himself would be finite, since He could not exist where there was nothing. In that case, He could not increase the size of the universe without adding something to His own dimensions and beginning to exist where He had not been before. One must therefore believe that, just as we can see Saturn and Jupiter from here, if we were on one or other of them we should discover many worlds which we cannot now perceive, and that the cosmos is constructed in this way to infinity.'

'Upon my soul!' he replied to me, 'it is no use your talking so. I shall never understand this infinity.'

'Why! tell me,' I countered, 'do you understand the nothingness beyond the end of space? Not at all! For when you think about this nothingness, at the very least you imagine it like wind, or like air—and that is something. But even if you do not understand infinity as a whole you may at least conceive of it in parts, since it is not difficult to picture, beyond the earth, air, and fire which we can see, more air and more earth. And infinity is really nothing but a limitless texture of all that. And if you ask me in what manner these worlds were made, seeing that the Holy Scripture tells us only of the one which God created, I reply that it only speaks of ours for the reason that it is the only one which God wished to take the trouble of making with His own hands, while all the others we see, or do not see, suspended amidst the azure of the cosmos, are nothing but the dross of suns purging themselves. For how could these great fires subsist if they were not attached to some matter which feeds them? So, just as fire expels the cinders which choke it, and gold, when it is refined in the crucible, divides from the marcasite which weakens its carat, and we vomit to free our hearts of the indigestible humours which attack them, so these suns disgorge and purge themselves every day of the remains of the matter which is the fuel for their fire. But when they have burned up all the matter which sustains them, they will scatter in every direction, you need have no doubt, in search of fresh nourishment, and they will attach themselves to all the worlds they formerly created, particularly the nearest to hand. And so these great fires will mix all the bodies up together again and then drive them out everywhere pell-mell, as before, and, having little by little purified themselves, they will begin to serve as suns for other little worlds, which they engender by expelling them out of their own spheres.

'And that is doubtless what made the Pythagoreans predict universal conflagration. This is not a ridiculous fancy: New France, where we are, provides a convincing example of it. This vast continent of America forms a half of the earth which, despite our ancestors having sailed the ocean a thousand times, had never been discovered. It is evident that it was not yet there; nor were many of the islands, peninsulas, and mountains which have since appeared on our globe, when the dross from the sun, as it purged itself, was driven far enough and condensed in clusters heavy enough to be attracted by the centre of our earth—possibly little by little, in tiny particles, perhaps all at once in a mass. This theory is not so unreasonable that Saint Augustin would not have applauded it, if the discovery of this continent had been made in his time, for this great man, whose genius was enlightened by the Holy Spirit, affirms that in his time the earth was as flat as a pancake and floated upon the water like half a sliced orange.

'But if ever I have the honour of seeing you in France, I will show you, with the aid of an excellent spy-glass, that certain obscurities, which look like spots from here, are worlds in formation.'

My eyes were closing as I finished this speech and the Viceroy was obliged to leave me. On the next day and the days following we had conversations of a similar nature. But when some time later the pressure of the affairs of the province called a halt to our philosophizing, I returned even more eagerly to my intention of ascending to the moon.

As soon as it rose I would go off through the woods, dreaming of the conduct and success of my enterprise; and, finally, one Eve of St. John, when a council was being held at the Fort to determine whether help should be given to the local savages against the Iroquois, I went off all alone behind our house to the top of a small hill and here is what I carried out. I had built a machine which I imagined capable of lifting me as high as I desired and in my opinion it lacked nothing essential. I seated myself inside it and launched myself into the air from the top of a rock. But because my preparations had been inadequate I tumbled roughly into the valley. Covered with bruises as I was, I nevertheless returned from there to my room without losing heart, took some marrow of beef and anointed my whole body with it, for I was battered all over from head to foot. After fortifying my courage with a bottle of a cordial essence, I returned to look for my machine. I did not find it, however, for some soldiers, who had been sent into the forest to cut wood to build a fire for the feast of St. John, had chanced upon it and brought it to the Fort, where several explanations of what it could be were advanced. When the device of the spring was discovered, some said a quantity of rockets should be attached to it, so that when their speed had lifted them high enough and the motor was agitating its great wings, no one could fail to take the machine for a fire dragon.

Meanwhile I spent a long time searching for it, but at last I found it in the middle of the square in Quebec just as they were setting fire to it. My dismay at discovering my handiwork in such danger so excited me that I ran to seize the arm of the soldier who was setting light to it. I snatched the fuse from him and threw myself furiously into my machine to destroy the contrivance with which it had been surrounded, but I arrived too late, for I had hardly set my two feet inside it when I was borne up into the blue.

The horror which overcame me did not destroy my presence of mind so completely as to make me incapable of recalling later what happened to me at that moment. When the fire had consumed one row of the rockets, which had been arranged six by six, the device of a fuse, fixed at the end of each half dozen, set off another layer and then another, so that the saltpetre caught fire and gave me a fresh lease of life, at the same time as it carried me farther into danger.

However, when the supply was all used up, the contrivance failed and I was resigning myself to leaving my crown upon that of some mountain when (without my making any movement at all) I felt my levitation continuing. My machine took leave of me and I saw it falling back towards the earth. This extraordinary occurrence filled my heart with a joy so uncommon that in my delight at seeing myself delivered from certain disaster, I had the impudence to philosophize upon it. As I was thus exercising my eyes and my brain to seek out the cause, I noticed my swollen flesh, still greasy with the marrow I had smeared upon myself for the bruises from my tumble. I realized that the moon was on the wane and, just as it is accustomed in that quarter to suck the marrow out of animals,[2] so it was drinking up what I had smeared upon myself, and with all the more strength because its globe was nearer to me, so that its vigour was in no way impaired by the intervention of clouds.

When, according to the calculations I have since made, I had travelled much more than three quarters of the way from the earth to the moon, I suddenly found myself falling head first, although I had not somersaulted in any fashion. I would not, indeed, have noticed this, if I had not felt my head taking the weight of my body. I was, in fact, quite certain that I was not falling back towards our world, for although I found myself between two moons, I could clearly observe that the farther I went from one, the nearer I came to the other, and I was convinced that the larger one was our globe, since, after I had been travelling for a day or two, the reflected light of the sun grew more distant and gradually the distinctions between different land masses and climates became blurred and it no

[2] It was popularly believed that, when the moon was on the wane, the bones of animals contained little or no marrow, since it was sucked out of them by the moon.

longer seemed to me like anything other than a great disc of gold. This made me think I was coming down towards the moon and this supposition was confirmed when I came to remember that I had only begun to fall after three quarters of the way.

'For,' I said to myself, 'this body, being smaller than our earth, must have a less extensive sphere of influence and in consequence I have felt the pull of its centre later.'

At last, after I had been falling for a very long time—or so I presumed, for the violence of my precipitation made observation difficult—the next thing I can remember is finding myself under a tree, entangled with two or three large branches which I had shattered in my fall, and with my face moist from an apple which had been crushed against it.

2

The earthly paradise

FORTUNATELY this place was the earthly paradise, as you will soon find out, and the tree upon which I fell turned out to be the Tree of Life itself. So you can easily judge that, but for this stroke of luck, I should have been killed a thousand times over. I have often reflected since then upon the popular belief which claims that when one falls from a great height, one is suffocated before making contact with the ground, and I have concluded from my own experience that this is false—unless the vital juice of the fruit which had trickled into my mouth actually recalled my soul before it had gone far from my corpse, while this was still warm and disposed to the functions of life. In fact my pain departed as soon as I reached the ground and before it had even left its mark upon my memory, while the hunger, which had greatly tormented me during my journey, gave way to only the faintest recollection that I had lost it.

When I got up, I had hardly had time to observe the

broadest of four great rivers, which flow together to form a lake, before the invisible essence of the herbs which exhale their fragrance over this country came to delight my nostrils and I discovered that the stones were neither hard nor uneven and that they were careful to soften themselves when one walked on them. I came first to a cross-roads where five avenues met, in which the trees were so exceedingly tall that they seemed to be holding a garden of foliage aloft in the sky. As I lifted my eyes from the roots to the topmost branches and let them fall from the summit to the foot, I began to wonder whether the ground supported them or if they did not themselves carry the ground suspended from their roots. Their crowns, proudly aloft, also seemed as if they were bowed down under the weight of the celestial spheres, so that one would think they sustained their load only with groaning limbs. Their boughs, uplifted to embrace heaven, showed how they prayed to the stars for the purest benignity of their influences and received them before any of their innocence had been lost in the bed of the elements.

On all sides there the flowers, which have no other gardener than nature, exhale a breath so sweet, though they are wild, that it both pricks and satisfies the nostrils. There, neither the crimson of a rose on the briar nor the brilliant azure of a violet beneath the brambles leave one any freedom of choice, for each enforces the judgement that it is lovelier than the other. There the spring makes up all the seasons. No venomous plant germinates there, whose preservation is not betrayed by its very birth. The streams recount their travels in a pleasant murmur to the pebbles. A thousand little feathered throats make the woods there ring with the sound of their melodious songs and the fluttering assembly of these divine musicians is so ubiquitous that it seems as if every leaf in the woods had adopted the shape and tongue of a nightingale, and even the echo takes so much pleasure in their tunes that, to hear her repeating them, you would think she desired to learn them by heart.

Beside this wood there are two meadows to be seen. Their

uninterrupted bright green offers an emerald expanse as far as the eye can see. Such is the confused mixture of colours with which spring paints the hundred little flowers, that their various shades are lost in one another in an agreeable confusion, and when these flowers are stirred by a gentle zephyr one cannot tell if they are not chasing one another, rather than flying to escape the caresses of the wanton breeze. One could even take this meadow for an ocean, since it is like a sea which offers no shore. My eyes, alarmed at travelling so far without discovering the edge, swiftly dispatched my mind after them. My mind, unwilling to believe it was the end of the world, sought to reason that perhaps the charms of the place had compelled heaven to join on to the earth.

Through the middle of this carpet, which is so broad and pleasant, there runs, amidst silver bubbles, a rustic spring, whose banks are clothed in turf which is adorned with creeping crow-foot, violets, and a hundred other tiny flowers, that seem to jostle one another to see their reflections in it. It is still in its cradle there, for it has only just been born, and its young, smooth face does not show a single wrinkle. The great circles it travels in, winding back on itself a thousand times, reveal how unwilling it is to leave its birthplace. As if it were ashamed to see itself caressed near to its mother's side, it repulsed my hand with a murmur when I sought to touch it. The animals that came to quench their thirst there, being more reasonable than those of our world, betrayed surprise at seeing that it was broad daylight above the horizon, although they could see the sun at their feet in these antipodes, and they did not dare to lean over the brink, for fear of falling into the firmament of heaven.

I must confess to you that at the sight of so many objects of beauty, I felt myself tickled by those pleasant pains which the embryo is said to feel at the infusion of its soul. My old hairs fell out and gave place to a new head of hair, finer and more luxuriant. I felt my youth rekindle, my face become ruddy, my natural warmth gently mingle once again with my bodily moisture; in short, I went back on my age some fourteen years.

I had made my way half a league through a forest of jasmine and myrtle, when I perceived something lying in the shadows that stirred. It was a youth, whose majestic beauty almost compelled me to adoration. He rose to prevent me.

'Nay, it is not to me,' he cried, 'but to God, that you owe this homage!'

'You see before you a person,' I answered him, 'amazed by so many miracles that I do not know where my admiration should begin. For, coming from a world which you here doubtless take for a moon, I thought I had landed in another, which the men of my country also call the moon; and now I find myself in paradise at the feet of a god who will not be adored, a stranger who speaks my own language.'

'Apart from your ranking me as a god,' he replied, 'when I am merely one of His creatures, what you say is true. This earth is the moon which you see from your globe and this place you walk in is paradise, but it is the earthly paradise, where only six human beings have ever set foot: Adam, Eve, Enoch, myself, being old Elijah, St. John the Evangelist, and yourself. You are well aware of how the first two were banished from here, but you do not know how they reached your world. Know, then, that when both had tasted of the forbidden fruit, Adam, who was afraid that God, angered by his presence, might increase his punishment, decided that the moon, your earth, was the only refuge where he might seek shelter from the sanctions of his Creator.

'Now in those days man's imagination was so powerful (for it had not yet been corrupted by debauchery, coarse foods, or debilitating diseases) that when it was aroused by his violent desire to reach this asylum, the ardour of his transports made his body light. He was levitated up there in the same way as philosophers, whose imagination was powerfully concentrated on something, have been observed to be lifted into the air by raptures which you would call *ecstatic*. Eve, whom the infirmity of her sex rendered more feeble and less ardent, would doubtless not have had a powerful enough imagination to overcome the weight of her matter by the force of her will, but since she was only recently taken from the body of her husband, the affinity which still bound this part to its parent carried her towards him as he went up—like a straw drawn to amber, or the loadstone turning towards the regions of the north, whence it has been wrested—and he attracted this portion of himself, just as the sea attracts rivers, which originated in it.

'Once arrived upon your earth, they made their dwelling between Mesopotamia and Arabia. The Hebrews knew him under the name of Adam and the idolaters under that of Prometheus. The poets made up the story that he had stolen fire from heaven, because he begot descendants endowed with souls as perfect as the one with which God had filled him. Thus, in order to people your world, the first man left this one uninhabited. But it was not the will of the All-Wise God that so happy an abode should remain without inhabitants. A few centuries later He allowed Enoch to grow weary of the company of men, whose innocence was becoming corrupted, and to desire to leave them behind. However, this holy man did not judge any refuge secure from the ambitions of his kinsmen, who were already cutting one another's throats over the sharing out of your world, other than that blessed land of which Adam, his grandfather, had told him so much. But how was he to go there? Jacob's ladder had not yet been invented!

'The grace of the Most High made up for this by inspiring Enoch to reflect that the fire of heaven descended upon the burnt offerings of the just and of those who were pleasing in the sight of the Lord and, according to the words of His mouth, "The odour of the sacrifices of the just has risen to my nostrils." One day when this divine fire was rushing down to consume a victim he was offering to the Eternal One, he filled two great jars with the fumes which it gave off, sealed them hermetically with clay and attached them to himself under his armpits. The vapour tried to rise straight up towards God, and since it could only have penetrated through the metal by a miracle, it immediately drove the jars upwards and in this way they carried the holy man up with them. When he had risen as high as the moon, he was apprised by an almost super-natural access of joy that this was the earthly paradise, where his grandfather had once lived.

'He promptly unfastened the vessels, which he had tied round his shoulders like wings and was lucky enough to be barely eight yards in the air above the moon when he parted company with his floats. This was still a great enough height for him to have been severely injured, had it not been for the vast spread of his robe, which was filled with wind, as well as the ardour of the Fire of Charity, which combined to support him until he had set foot upon the ground. As for the two jars, they continued to rise until God set them in the Firmament, where they have remained; and they are what you call the Sign of the Balance, and daily demonstrate to us that they are still filled with the odours from the sacrifice of a just man, by the favourable influence they have upon the horoscope of Louis the Just, who was born when the Balance was in the ascendant.

'But Enoch was still not in this garden; he only arrived here some time afterwards. It happened at the time when the Flood was unleashed, for the waters which engulfed your world rose to so prodigious a height that the Ark was drifting about in the heavens near the moon. The humans perceived our globe through the window, but the reflected light from this great opaque body had become weak, since they were near enough to share in it, and they all believed it was part of the earth which had not been submerged. Only one of Noah's daughters, called Achab—perhaps because she had noticed that the higher the ship rose, the nearer they drew to this star —clamorously maintained that it was without doubt the moon. In vain it was put to her that when soundings were taken they had only found four fathoms of water. She replied that the sounding-lead must have struck a whale's back, which they had mistaken for the earth and that, for her part, she was certain it was the moon itself where they were about to land. In the end, as everyone adopts the opinions of their fellows, all the other women persuaded themselves of this too. And now, though forbidden by the menfolk, they begin to let down the boat into the sea. Achab was the most daring of them and wanted to be the first to brave the dangers. She flung herself nimbly into it and all her sex would have joined her if a wave had not separated the boat from the ship.

'Vainly they shouted after her, calling her "lunatic" a hundred times and protesting that she would be the cause of all women being one day reproached for having a quarter of the moon in their heads: she merely laughed at them. And so she floated away from the world. The animals followed her example, for the majority of the birds, who felt their wings strong enough and were impatient with the first prison in which anyone had ever restrained their liberty, made their way there. Even the bravest of the quadrupeds began swimming. Nearly a thousand had got away before Noah's sons could close the stable doors, which were being held open by the multitude of escaping animals. Most of them reached this new world. As for the skiff, it came to rest on a very pleasant shore where the great-hearted Achab landed. Happy to have recognized that this land was indeed the moon, she had no desire to go back to her boat and rejoin her brothers. She dwelt for some time in a cave and as she was walking one day, considering whether she should be vexed at having lost the company of her kinsfolk or glad of it, she caught sight of a man knocking down acorns. Overjoyed by this encounter, she flew to embrace him. She received as good as she gave, for it was even longer since the old man had seen a human face. This was Enoch the Just.

'They lived together, and if the impious nature of his children and the arrogance of his wife had not driven him to seek refuge in the woods, they would have spun out the thread of their days together in all the sweetness with which God blesses the marriages of the just. There, in the wildest retreats of those dreadful solitudes, the good old man used every day to offer up to God a purified spirit and his heart as a sacrifice, until one day an apple fell from the Tree of Knowledge, which is in this garden, as you know, into the river beside which it is planted and was carried out of paradise by the current to a place where poor Enoch was fishing in order to keep body and soul together. The fine fruit was caught in the net. He ate it. At once he knew where the earthly paradise was and, thanks to secrets such as you could not conceive, unless, like him, you had eaten of the Apple of Knowledge, he came to live here.

'But now I must tell you the manner in which I came here myself. You have not, I think, forgotten that my name is Elijah, for I told you this just now. Know then, that I used to live in your world and that I dwelt with Elisha, a Hebrew like myself, on the banks of the Jordan. There among my books I lived a life pleasant enough for me not to regret it, although it is over. However, the more enlightenment my mind acquired, the greater my awareness became of that which I did not possess. Not once did our priests remind me of the illustrious Adam without the memory of his perfect philosophy making me heave a sigh. I had despaired of ever being able to attain to it, when one day, after I had sacrificed to expiate the frailties of my mortal being, I fell asleep and the Angel of the Lord appeared to me in a dream. As soon as I awoke I undertook every one of the tasks he had prescribed for me. I procured about two cubic feet of loadstone, which I put into a furnace. When it was well purged, precipitated, and melted, I drew off the calcinated magnet and reduced it to about the size of a middling cannon ball.

'Following these preparations, I had an extremely light iron chariot built, and several months later, when all my contrivances were completed, I entered my ingenious wagon. You may perhaps ask me what all this paraphernalia was for. But you must know that the Angel had told me in my dream that if I wished to acquire a science as perfect as I desired, I must go up to the moon, where I should find the Tree of Knowledge in Adam's paradise. Once I had tasted of its fruit, my soul would be enlightened with all the truths which one of God's creatures is capable of comprehending. So this was the voyage for which I had built my chariot.

'At length I climbed into it and, when I was well and truly

settled upon the seat, I hurled the ball of loadstone very high into the air. Now the iron machine, which I had expressly forged heavier at the centre than at its extremities, was at once lifted up in perfect equilibrium because it was always impelled faster at this point. So every time I arrived where the loadstone had drawn me, I immediately threw my ball into the air above me again.'

'But how,' I interrupted him, 'did you manage to throw your ball so straight above your chariot that it never went to one side?'

'I can see no cause for wonder in this occurrence,' he told me. 'For once the loadstone had been thrown up into the air, it drew the iron straight up towards itself and it was consequently impossible for me ever to come up to one side of it. Let me tell you, furthermore, that even when I held the ball in my hand I did not stop rising, because the chariot continued to pursue the loadstone which I held above it: but the iron leaped so violently after my ball that it bent my body in half and I only dared to try this novel experience once.

'It was truly a most astonishing spectacle to behold, for the steel of this flying house, which I had polished with great care, reflected the light of the sun so vividly and brilliantly from every side that I thought I was all on fire. At last, when I had done a great deal of hurling and flying after my throw, I arrived, as you did, at a stage where I was falling towards this world. Since at that moment I had my ball clasped firmly in my hands, my machine, whose seat pressed against me in order to draw close to its magnet, did not leave me. The only danger I had to fear was that of breaking my neck, but to preserve myself from this I threw up my ball from time to time so that the machine should be held back by its magnet, and slowed down in its fall and my descent made less rough. And this is how it turned out: for when I saw that I was some five or six hundred yards from the ground, I threw my ball in all directions at the same level as the chariot, now to one side, now to the other, until my eyes had picked out the earthly paradise. At once I threw it above me, my machine followed it and I left it and let myself fall to one side as gently as I could upon the sand, so that my fall was no more violent than if I had fallen my own height. I will not describe to you the astonishment which took hold of me at the sight of the marvels here, since it more or less resembled your own consternation, which I have just witnessed.

'I will simply tell you that on the following day I discovered the Tree of Life, by means of which I prevented myself from growing old. It quickly burnt up the serpent and purged it in a puff of smoke.'

At these words I said to him, 'Venerable and holy patriarch, I should be very glad to know what you mean by this *serpent*, which was burnt up.'

With a smile he replied to me as follows: 'I was forgetting, O my son, to reveal to you a secret of which you cannot have been informed. You must know that when Eve and her husband had eaten of the forbidden apple, God punished the serpent which had tempted them, by imprisoning it in a man's body. Since then no human creature has been born who does not, in punishment for the crime of his first father, nourish a serpent in his belly, descended from this first one. You call them guts and believe them necessary to the functions of life. Learn that they are nothing else but serpents, doubled upon themselves in many coils. When you hear your entrails complaining, it is the serpent hissing and—in accordance with its gluttonous temperament, which once made it incite the first man to take a bite too many—asking to be fed in its turn. For in order to punish you, God desired to make you mortal like the other animals and had you plagued with this insatiable beast, so that if you should give it too much to eat, you would choke yourselves and if you should deny it its pittance, when it is starving and gnawing at your stomach with invisible teeth, it would scream, rage, disgorge that venom which your doctors call *bile* and heat you up so much with the poison it injects into your arteries, that you would swiftly be consumed by it. And for the ultimate proof that your guts are a serpent inside your body, remember that such were found in the tombs of Aesculapius, of Scipio, of Alexander, of Charles the Hammer and of Edward of England, still feeding off the corpses of their hosts.'

'Yes indeed,' I said, interrupting him, 'I have noticed how, as this serpent is always trying to escape from man's body, you can see its head and neck emerging at the bottom of our bellies. Furthermore, God does not suffer man alone to be tormented by it: it was His will that it should rise up against woman to inject its poison into her and that the swelling should last for nine months after the bite. And the proof that I speak according to the word of the Lord is that He curses the serpent, saying that in vain will it cause woman to stumble by hardening itself against her, for in the end she will bruise its head.'

I would have continued with these trifles, but Elijah prevented me. 'Consider,' he said, 'that this place is holy.'

Then he fell silent for a time, as if to recall the point he had reached, after which he spoke these words: 'I only partake of the Fruit of Life once in every hundred years. Its juice has a taste whose character is somewhat akin to that of wine. I believe it was the apple Adam ate which made our forefathers live so long, because something of its energy had passed into their seed, until it was finally extinguished in the waters of the Flood. The Tree of Knowledge is planted opposite. Its fruit is covered with a rind which induces ignorance in whoever tastes it. The intellectual virtues of this learned food are conserved beneath the thickness of this peel. In the days when God had driven Adam out of this blessed land, He rubbed his gums with the peel for fear that he might find his way back. From that moment his wits wandered for more than fifteen years and he forgot everything to such a point that neither he nor any of his descendants until Moses even remembered the Creation. But the remaining effects of this sluggish rind were finally dissipated by the warmth and the brilliance of the genius of that Great Prophet.

'By happy chance I addressed myself to one of these apples which was ripe enough to have shed its skin and hardly had

25

my saliva moistened it when I was enveloped by universal philosophy. It seemed to me that an infinite number of little eyes plunged into my head and I knew how to speak to the Lord.

'When I have since reflected upon my miraculous ascent here, I have readily believed that I could not have overcome the vigilance of the seraphim which God has commanded to guard this paradise, simply by means of the hidden virtues of a natural body; but because He is pleased to make use of secondary causes, I came to believe that He inspired me to think of this means of entry, even as it was His will to use Adam's ribs to make him a wife, although He could have made her out of clay just as well as him.

'I spent a long time walking in the garden, but since the Angel Doorkeeper of the place was my chief host, I had a desire to greet him. My journey was accomplished in an hour's walking, for at the end of this time I arrived in a country where the conjunction of a thousand flashes of lightning produced a brilliance so blinding that one could only see darkness.

'I had not properly recovered from this occurrence when I beheld a handsome youth in front of me. "I am the Archangel you are seeking," he told me. "I have just read in God that He suggested to you the means of coming here, where He desires you to await His will." He spoke to me about many subjects and told me, among other things, that the light which seemed to have alarmed me was nothing to be afraid of. It could be seen almost every evening when he was making his rounds, because, to avoid being surprised by the sorcerers who enter invisibly everywhere, he was obliged to brandish his flaming sword all round the earthly paradise and this brilliance came from the flashes of lightning produced by his blade.

' "Those which you observe from your world," he added, "are caused by me. If you sometimes notice them from a long way off, it is because the clouds in a distant clime are disposed so as to receive their impression and reflect these faint images of fire down to you, just as a vapour situated in a different way is disposed to produce a rainbow. I will instruct you no further, for the Apple of Knowledge is not far from here; as soon as you have eaten of it you will be as learned as I am. But above all beware of taking the wrong one: the majority of the fruits which hang upon this plant are covered with a rind which, if you taste it, will cause you to sink lower than the lowest man, while the inside will raise you to the level of the angels." '

Elijah had reached this point with the instructions the Seraph had given him when a little man came up to join us. 'Here is that Enoch about whom I was telling you,' my guide told me in a low voice. As he spoke these words Enoch presented us with a basket filled with some unknown fruits, like pomegranates, which he had just discovered in a secluded grove the same day. I had crammed several of them into my pockets as Elijah instructed me when Enoch asked him who I was.

'His adventure is one which deserves a longer conversation,' replied my guide. 'This evening when we have retired, he will tell us himself the miraculous details of his voyage.'

As he finished speaking we found ourselves in a kind of hermitage made of palm branches, ingeniously interwoven with myrtles and orange trees. In a small nook I caught sight of piles of a kind of gossamer so white and so fine that it could have been taken for the very essence of snow. I also saw some distaffs scattered here and there and asked my guide what they were used for.

'For spinning,' he replied. 'When the good Enoch wishes to relax from his meditations he sometimes cards this tow, sometimes he spins thread from it and sometimes he weaves cloth which is used to make shifts for the eleven thousand virgins. At some time in your world you must have come across something white floating in the autumn air round about seed time: the country people call it "Our Lady's Cotton" and it is, in fact, the flock which Enoch combs out from his flax when he is carding it.'

27

We hardly stayed a moment before taking leave of Enoch, whose cell this hut was. What compelled us to go so soon was the fact that he prays every six hours and it was at least that since he had last done so.

On the way I begged Elijah to finish telling me the story of the assumptions to paradise on which he had embarked, saying that I believed he had reached that of Saint John the Evangelist. 'Then since you have not the patience,' he said, 'to wait for the Apple of Learning to teach you all these things better than I can, I am willing to inform you of them. You must know that God . . .'

At this point the devil somehow interfered and I could not prevent myself interrupting him with a quip: 'I remember now,' I told him. 'One day God noticed that this evangelist's soul had become so disembodied that he could only hold on to it by clenching his teeth. Meanwhile the time when it was foreseen that he would be transported here had almost come. Not having time to prepare a machine for him, God simply had to cause him to *be* here all of a sudden, without having the leisure to make him *come* here!'

Throughout this speech Elijah regarded me with looks which could have killed me, if I had been in a state to die of anything else but hunger. 'Abominable!' he said, drawing back. 'You have the impudence to jest about sacred things. But you would not go unpunished if the All-Wise God did not wish to leave you to the nations as a famous example of His mercy. Go from hence, impious man, and publish abroad in this little world and in the other—for you are predestined to return there—the irreconcilable hatred which God bears towards atheists!'

He had hardly come to the end of this imprecation when he laid hold of me and led me roughly towards the gate. When we had arrived near a great tree whose branches were laden with fruit and bowed down almost to the ground, he said to me: 'Here is the Tree of Learning, whence you would have derived inconceivable illumination if it had not been for your impiety.'

Before he had finished these words, I pretended to faint from weakness and let myself fall against a branch, from which I adroitly stole an apple. Only a few more strides were needed for me to step outside this delicious park. However, my hunger tormented me so violently that it made me forget I was in the hands of an enraged prophet. I pulled out one of the apples I had crammed into my pocket and plunged my teeth into it. But instead of my taking one of the ones Enoch had given me, my hand fell upon the apple I had plucked from the Tree of Knowledge and from which, unfortunately, I had not removed the rind.

I had scarcely tasted it when a thick cloud enveloped my mind: I no longer saw anyone beside me and I could not discover a single trace of the road I had taken anywhere on this side of the horizon, but for all that, I did not lose the memory of everything that had happened to me. When I have since reflected on this miracle, I have surmised that the rind of the fruit I had bitten into did not altogether stupefy me because my teeth had gone right through it and tasted a little of the juice which lay beneath it; and the energy of this had dissipated the ill effects of the rind. I remained surprised to find myself alone in the middle of a country I did not know at all. In vain I cast my eyes about me and scrutinized the landscape; they could pick out no creature to console them. Finally I resolved to continue walking until fortune brought me face to face either with beasts of some kind or else with death.

She hearkened to me, for at the end of half a mile I encountered two very large animals, one of which stopped in front of me while the other fled nimbly to its lair, at least so I presumed; for some time after that I saw it returning, accompanied by more than seven or eight hundred of the same species, which surrounded me completely. When I could observe them from close to, I discovered that they had bodies and faces like ours. This occurrence reminded me of the tales I had once heard from my nurse about sirens, fauns, and satyrs. From time to time they raised hootings so furious, doubtless caused by their amazement at seeing me, that I

29

almost thought I must have turned into a monster. Finally one of these man-beasts, picked me up by the scruff of my neck as wolves do when they carry off sheep, flung me over his shoulder and took me to their town, where I was even more astonished than before (realizing now that they were in fact men) not to come across a single one who did not walk on all four legs.

When this people saw that I was so small (for the majority of them are eighteen feet long) and that my body was only supported on two legs, they could not believe that I was a man. For they held that since nature has given man two legs and two arms like the beasts, he should use them as they do. And in fact, pondering upon it since, I have reflected that this body position was by no means fantastic. I recalled that while children are still schooled by nature alone, they walk on four legs and only get up on to two as a result of attentions of their nurses, who stand them in little chariots and attach straps to them, to stop them falling back on all fours, which is the only posture in which bodies shaped like ours are naturally inclined to come to rest.

3

The friendly demon

THEY then said (according to the interpretation which was later given to me) that I was without a doubt the female of the Queen's little animal. So in this or some other capacity I was taken straight to the Town Hall, where I observed that, judging from the murmurs and gesticulations of the people and the magistrates, they were discussing what I could be. When they had conferred together for a long time, a certain citizen who kept rare beasts begged the aldermen to commit me to his care until the Queen should send for me to be brought to live with my male. No objection was made and the mountebank took me to his house where he taught me to act like a puppet, turn somersaults and make faces. And after dinner he collected a certain price at the door from those who wanted to see me.

But heaven was softened by my wretchedness and angered to see the temple of its Master profaned and one day brought it to pass that when I was attached to the end of a rope, with which the charlatan was making me prance to divert the gaping mob, one of the spectators, after considering me very attentively, asked me in Greek who I was. I was greatly astonished to hear someone in that country speaking as men do in our world. He questioned me for some time. I answered his questions and then told him the whole story of the adventure and the outcome of my voyage. He comforted me, and I remember him saying to me: 'Well, my son, now at last you are tasting the distress which is caused by the follies of your own world. There is a common herd here, as there is there, which cannot tolerate the thought of anything to which it is not accustomed. But you must realize that you are only being given some of your own medicine, for if anyone from this earth went up to yours and had the effrontery to call himself a man, your learned doctors would have him stifled as a monster or an ape possessed of the devil.'

He then promised me that he would notify the court of my misfortune and added that as soon as he had heard the news going round about me, he had come to see me and recognized me as a man from the world whence I said I came. My country was the moon and I was from Gaul, for he had once travelled there and had lived in Greece where he was known as the Demon of Socrates. Following the death of this philosopher he had governed and instructed Epaminondas at Thebes. Then he had gone to live among the Romans where justice had attached him to the cause of Cato the Younger and, after his death, he had given his services to Brutus. Since all these great men had left nothing in their place in that world but the ghosts of their virtues, he and his companions had withdrawn to temples and lonely places.

'At last,' he added, 'the people of your earth became so stupid and gross that I and my companions lost all the pleasure we had formerly taken in instructing them. You cannot have failed to hear us spoken of, for they called us Oracles, Nymphs, Genii, Fairies, Household Gods, Lemures, Larvae, Lamias, Naiads, Incubi, Shades, Manes, Spectres, and Phantoms. We abandoned your world during the reign of Augustus, shortly after I had appeared to Drusus, son of Livia, who was invading Germany and had forbidden him to go any further.

'I have recently returned from there for the second time, for a hundred years ago I was commissioned to make another journey there. I travelled about Europe a great deal and conversed with people you may possibly have known. Among others, I appeared to Girolamo Cardano,[1] one day as he was studying; I taught him a number of things and in recompense he promised me that he would bear witness to posterity from whom he learned the miracles he intended to set down. I saw Doctor Agrippa de Nettesheim,[2] Abbot Johannes of Trittenheim,[3] Doctor Faustus,[4] La Brosse,[5] and César de Nostradamus[6] there and a certain cabal of young men, known to the common herd under the name of "Rosicrucians", whom I instructed in a number of sleights of hand and secrets

---

[1] Cardano claimed that much of his work was dictated by a familiar demon from Venus.

[2] Henri-Corneille Agrippa de Nettesheim (1486–1535), doctor and occult philosopher, reputed to have a black dog as a familiar.

[3] 1462–1516: as Abbot at Spanheim his erudition and study of magical practices earned him a reputation as a sorcerer.

[4] Sorcerer and charlatan, already a legendary figure in Germany in his own lifetime (c.1480–c.1540). His familiar spirit was Mephistopheles.

[5] A man of this name was hanged as a sorcerer under Louis XIII. But Guy de La Brosse was a doctor, natural scientist, and bohemian of the early seventeenth century who followed a kind of pagan cult of nature.

[6] Early seventeenth century adventurer who claimed to have a familiar spirit called Sophocles.

of nature which will doubtless have made them pass for great magicians among the people!

'I also knew Campanella.[7] It was I who advised him, when he was at the Inquisition in Rome, to copy with his own face and body the habitual attitudes and expressions of those whose minds he wished to know, so as to excite in himself, by imitating them, the thoughts which the same behaviour had evoked in his adversaries—for if he knew them from the inside he would be able to deal with them better. And it was at my request that he began a book which we called *De Sensu Rerum*. I was similarly acquainted with La Mothe Le Vayer[8] and Gassendi in France. The latter is as much a philosopher in his writing as the former is in his life. I have known a number of other people whom your century treats as divine, but I have found nothing in them save much hot air and much arrogance.

'Finally, when I crossed over from your country to England to study the way of life of its inhabitants, I met a man who was a disgrace to his country—for it is a real disgrace that the great ones of your state can discern in him the virtue of which he is the seat, but do not worship it. To cut his praises short, he is all intellect and all heart, and possesses all those qualities, a single one of which would have sufficed to mark him as a hero in the old days; this was Tristan l'Hermite.[9] I should have avoided naming him, for I am sure he will never forgive me for this blunder, but as I do not ever expect to return to your world, I want to offer this testimony of my conscience to the truth. And I must admit, frankly, that when I saw such

---

[7] Tommaso Campanella (1566–1639), philosopher and author of *The City of the Sun*. His rejection of Aristotle's scientific teaching helped to earn him many years of imprisonment, interrogation and, torture.

[8] François de La Mothe Le Vayer (1588–1672): traveller, libertine, friend of Gassendi (1592–1655), the sceptical philosopher. His son was a friend of Cyrano.

[9] François Tristan l'Hermite (1601–55), poet and tragedian, a friend of Cyrano.

lofty virtue, I was afraid that it would go unrecognized. That is why I tried to make him accept three phials: the first one was filled with oil of talc, the next with powder of projection, and the last with potable gold, in other words, the vital essence from which your chemists promise eternal life. But he refused them with a scorn more noble than that with which Diogenes received Alexander's compliments, when he came to visit him in his barrel. I can add nothing, finally, to my eulogy of this man, save that he is the only poet, the only philosopher, and the only free man among you. These are the people with whom I conversed who are worthy of note. All the rest, at least of those I knew, are so sub-human that I have seen beasts somewhat superior to them.

'I should add that I am not a native of your earth at all, nor of this one: I was born in the sun. But because our world sometimes becomes over-populated, on account of the longevity of its inhabitants and the almost total lack of wars and diseases, from time to time the magistrates send out colonists into the neighbouring worlds. As for myself, I was ordered to go to yours and proclaimed leader of the population they sent with me. I have since then moved to this one for the reasons I gave you; and what induces me to stay here at the moment is the fact that men here are lovers of truth. There is not a pedant to be seen. Philosophers only permit themselves to be convinced by reason and neither the authority of a scholar, nor that of the majority can outweigh the opinion of a thresher on the farm, when his arguments are as good as theirs. In this country, briefly, only logic-choppers and tub-thumpers are reckoned to be mad.'

I asked him how long his kind lived. He told me three or four thousand years and continued in this way: 'In order to make myself visible, as I am at present, when I feel that the carcass I inhabit is almost worn out or that the organs are no longer performing their functions perfectly enough, I breathe myself into a young body recently dead.

'Although the inhabitants of the sun are less numerous than those of this world, the sun is often overcrowded with them, since, being of a very fiery temperament, the people are restless and ambitious and have great appetites.

'What I am telling you should not seem surprising, for although our globe is very vast and yours is small, although we die only after four thousand years and you after half a century, you must know that, all the same, there are not so many stones as there are grains of earth, nor so many plants as stones, nor so many animals as plants, nor so many men as animals. It follows that there should not be so many demons as men, because of the difficulties encountered in the generation of so perfect a composite being.'

I asked him if they had bodies, like us. He replied yes, they had bodies, but not like ours, nor like anything which we considered as such, because we commonly only call a body what we can touch. There was, in any case, nothing in nature which was not material; and although they themselves were, when they wanted to make themselves visible to us, they were forced to assume shapes commensurate with what our senses are capable of perceiving. This was doubtless what had caused many of us to think that the stories which were told about them were no more than the products of feeble-minded people's dreams, since they only appeared at night. He added that as they were obliged to be hasty in manufacturing themselves the bodies they had to use, they very often lacked the time to make them perceptible to more than one of the senses. Sometimes this would be hearing, as with the voices of oracles; sometimes sight, as with jack o'lanterns and spectres; sometimes touch, as with incubi and nightmares. Since their bodies were nothing but air thickened in one way or another, this was destroyed by the warmth of light, just as one sees light dissipating a fog by dilating it.

He explained so many fine things to me that I was curious to question him about his birth and his death, to know whether individuals in the country of the sun saw the light of day by way of procreation and if he died through the disorder of his constitution or the rupture of his organs.

'There is too little relation,' he said, 'between your own

senses and the explanation of these mysteries. You men imagine that what you cannot understand is either spiritual or else does not exist, but this conclusion is quite false. The proof of this is the fact that there are perhaps a million things in the universe which you would need a million quite different organs to know. Myself, for example, I know from my senses what attracts the loadstone to the pole, how the tides pull the sea, and what becomes of an animal after its death. Except by an act of faith, you men could no more attain to such lofty conceptions—because you lack the senses proportionate to these marvels—than a blind man could imagine what makes up the beauty of a landscape, the colouring of a picture, or the nuances of the rainbow, unless he imagined them as something palpable like food, as a sound, or as a scent. In exactly the same way, if I sought to explain to you what I perceive with the senses which you do not possess, you would picture it to yourself as something which can be heard, seen, touched, smelt or tasted, and it is, in fact, none of these things.'

He had reached this point in his discourse when my mountebank perceived that the company were beginning to tire of my jargon, which they did not understand and took for inarticulate grunting. He began pulling at my rope harder than ever, so as to make me leap about, until the spectators had debauched themselves with laughing and insisting that I was almost as clever as the beasts in their country, and each returned to his home.

Thus, the cruelty of the ill-treatment I received from my master was alleviated by the visits which this obliging demon paid me. For, as to conversing with those who came to see me, apart from the fact that they took me for an animal well and truly rooted in the category of the brutes, I did not know their language and they did not understand mine and you can judge now what similarity there was between the two. For you must know that only two idioms are used in this country, one which serves the great and the other which is peculiar to the common people.

That of the great ones is nothing else but a variety of non-articulated notes—more or less like our music when the words are not added to the melody—and it is certainly an invention which is at once most useful and most agreeable. For when they are weary of speaking or when they scorn to prostitute their throats for this purpose, they take up either a lute or some other instrument, which they can use just as well as their voices to communicate their ideas to one another. Thus sometimes a company of as many as fifteen or twenty will meet together and dispute a point of theology or the intricacies of a lawsuit in the most harmonious concert one could possibly devise to charm the ear.

The second language, which is in use among the common people, is expressed by the shaking of the limbs, but perhaps not quite as you might imagine it, for certain parts of the body signify a complete speech. For example the agitation of a finger, a hand, an ear, a lip, an arm, an eye, or a cheek will each separately convey a peroration or a sentence with all its parts. Other movements serve only to express words, such as a wrinkling of the brow, the twitching of various muscles, the reversal of the hands, a stamp of the foot and contortions of the arms. Thus when they speak, with the habit they have adopted of going about stark naked, the movements of their limbs, which are well practised in gesticulating their ideas, come so thick and fast that it seems less like a man talking than a body trembling.

The demon came to visit me almost every day and his marvellous conversation permitted me to endure the harshness of my captivity without distress. At length, one morning, I saw a man coming into my little cell whom I did not know at all. After licking me over for a long time he gently picked me up in his mouth by the armpit. With one of his feet he supported me, for fear of my being injured, and tossed me on to his back, where I felt myself so comfortable and so much at ease that, with the distress I felt at being treated like a beast, I had no desire to escape. Besides, these men who walk on all fours move at quite a different speed from us. The heaviest of them can catch stags by outrunning them.

I was extremely upset, however, at having no news of my courteous demon and on the evening of the first stage, when we had reached our shelter for the night, I was walking about in the inn yard waiting for the meal to be ready, when this very young and tolerably handsome man came up and laughed in my face and threw his two front feet about my neck. After I had examined him for sometime he said to me in French: 'What? Do you not recognize your friend any more?'

I leave you to imagine how I felt then. Indeed my amazement was so great that I now believed that the whole globe of the moon, all that had happened to me on it and everything I could see there must be nothing but an enchantment. The man-beast, who was in fact the one who had just served me as a mount, went on to address me in these words: 'You promised me that the services I might render you would never slip your memory, but now one would think you had never seen me before!'

But he saw that I was still as perplexed as ever. 'To cut a long story short,' he added, 'I am the Demon of Socrates.'

This remark increased my astonishment, but he came to my rescue and went on: 'I am the Demon of Socrates who entertained you during your imprisonment and in order to continue to be of service to you, I reclothed myself in the body on which I have carried you during the past day.'

'But how can all this be possible,' I interrupted, 'seeing that yesterday you were extremely long in the body and today you are very short, yesterday you had a feeble, quavering voice and today you have a clear, vigorous one, in fact yesterday you were a grey-haired ancient and today you are no more than a youth? How's this? Instead of travelling from birth towards death, as they do where I come from, do the animals here progress from death to birth and become rejuvenated as they grow older?'

'As soon as I had spoken to the Prince,' he said, 'and

received the command to bring you to court, I set out to find you, but, having brought you here, I felt that the body I was inhabiting was so enfeebled with weariness that all the organs were refusing to perform their normal functions for me. I therefore inquired the way to the hospital, where I went in and found the body of a young man who had recently given up the ghost as the result of an extremely strange accident, yet an extremely common one in this country. I drew near to him, pretending that I could make out some movement in him still and protesting to those who were present that he was not dead at all and that the state they feared had robbed him of his life was no more than a simple coma. Thus, without anyone noticing, I brought my mouth close to his and went in through it like a breath of air. Then my old carcass fell to the ground and I got up as if I were the young man and came away to look for you, leaving the bystanders there crying out that it was a miracle.'

At this point they came and summoned us to sit down at table and I followed my guide into a room which was magnificently furnished but in which I could see no preparations for a meal. This complete absence of any victuals, when I was dying of hunger, compelled me to ask him where supper had been laid. I did not listen to his reply, however, for three or four young boys, children of the host, came up to me at this moment and undressed me down to my shirt with great civility. This new ceremony astounded me so much that I did not even dare to ask my fair attendants the reason for it and I do not know how my guide (who was asking me what I would like to begin with) managed to elicit from me the two words: 'A soup.' But I had hardly uttered them when I smelt the aroma of as succulent a brew as ever tickled the nostrils of a rich villain. I began to get up from my place to track down this delightful vapour to its source, but my former steed prevented me.

'Where are you going?' he said. 'We shall be going for a walk in a minute but now is the time to eat. Finish your soup and we will send for something else.'

'But where the devil is the soup?' I answered him, almost in a rage. 'Have you made a wager to tease me for the whole of today?'

'I thought,' he replied, 'that in the town you have come from you would have seen your master or somebody else taking his meals. That is why I did not tell you the way they feed themselves here. But since you are still ignorant of this, you must know that here they live solely upon vapours. Their culinary art consists in enclosing in great vessels, especially moulded for the purpose, the exhalation which comes off meats when they are cooking. When several of various kinds and different flavours have been collected, they uncork the vessel in which a particular odour has been gathered to suit the appetites of those who are being served. After that they uncover a second and so on until the company is satisfied. Unless you have already lived in this way you would never believe that the nose, without assistance from the teeth or the gullet, could do the mouth's job in feeding a man, but I should like to show you by experience that this is so.'

As soon as I had finished speaking, I felt so many agreeable and nourishing vapours entering the room in succession that, in less than ten minutes, I felt myself completely gorged. When we had risen he said: 'This is not something which should cause you much surprise, since you cannot have lived so long without observing that in your world cooks, pastry-cooks, and roasters, who eat less than people from any other walk of life, are nonetheless much fatter. Where do you think their corpulence comes from, if not from the vapour in which they are incessantly enveloped and which penetrates and nourishes their bodies? In this way the people in this world enjoy much more constant and vigorous good health, because their food produces hardly any excrement, which is the origin of almost all diseases. You were possibly surprised at being undressed before the meal, as this custom is not observed in your country, but here it is the fashion and they follow it so that the body should be more accessible to the vapour.'

'Sir,' I returned, 'what you say is highly probable and I have just verified it myself to some extent, but I must admit that, being unable to debrutalize myself as quickly as this, I should still be glad to feel a solid morsel between my teeth.'

He promised me that I should, but only on the following day, for the reason, he said, that to eat so soon after a meal would give me indigestion. We conversed for some time more and then went up to our rooms to rest. At the top of the stairs a man introduced himself to us and, after staring at us attentively, led me into a chamber where the floor was covered with orange blossom to a depth of three feet, and my demon into another filled with carnations and jasmine. Seeing how surprised I looked at this magnificence, he told me that these were the beds of the country. Finally we lay down, each in our own cell. When I was stretched out upon my flowers I saw by the light of thirty large glow-worms enclosed in a glass (for they use no other kind of candles), the three or four young boys who had undressed me at supper. One of them began to tickle my feet, another my thighs, another my sides, another my arms—and all with so many caresses and with such a delicate touch that in less than a moment I felt myself dozing off.

Next day I saw my demon coming in with the first rays of the sun. 'Now I want to keep my word to you,' he told me. 'You will breakfast more solidly than you supped yesterday.'

At these words I got up and he led me by the hand behind the garden of the hostelry, where one of the host's children was waiting with a weapon in his hand almost like one of our guns. He asked my guide if I wanted a dozen larks, because barbary apes (he took me for one) feed upon this meat. Hardly had I replied that I did when the hunter fired a shot and twenty or thirty larks fell at our feet, ready roasted.

'This,' I thought to myself, 'is what they mean by that proverb in our world about a land where the larks fall ready roasted.' Doubtless someone had returned from here.

'All you have to do is eat,' said my demon. 'They are diligent enough here to mix a certain compound with their powder and shot which kills, plucks, roasts, and seasons the game.'

I gathered up and ate several of them, as he told me to, and truly I have never tasted anything so delicious in all my life.

After this breakfast we made ourselves ready to leave, and with a thousand grimaces such as they employ when they want to display affection, the host took a paper from my demon. I asked him if it was a bond for the amount the bill came to. He retorted that it was not, that the account was now settled and that it was some verses.

'How do you mean, verses?' I rejoined. 'Are the innkeepers here connoisseurs of rhymes, then?'

'It is,' he said, 'the currency of the country, and the expenses we have just incurred here finally added up to a stanza of six lines, which is what I have given him. I was not afraid of running short, for even if we feasted here for a week, we should not be able to run through a sonnet and I have four of them on me, as well as two epigrams, two odes, and an eclogue.'

'Well to be sure,' I said to myself, 'this is just the currency which Sorel makes Hortensius use in *Francion*, I remember. Doubtless this is where he got it from: but who the devil could have told him about it? It must have been his mother, for I have heard tell that she was a lunatic.'

'And would to God,' I said aloud, 'that it were the same in our world! I can think of many honest poets there who are starving to death and who would live like fighting cocks if innkeepers were paid in this coin.'

I asked him if these verses continued to be legal tender provided one copied them out again. He replied that they did not and went on: 'When some have been composed, the author brings them to the Court of the Mint, where the Jury of Poets of the Realm hold their sessions. There these Officers of Versification put the pieces to the test and if they are judged to be of good alloy, they are taxed not according to their weight but according to their wit, that is to say a sonnet is not always worth one sonnet: it depends upon the merit of the piece. Thus when someone starves to death it is never anyone but a blockhead and witty people always live off the fat of the land.'

While I was lost in rapturous admiration for the judicious government of that country, he continued in this manner: 'There are, in addition, other people who run their houses in a very different way. When you leave their premises they ask for an acquittance for the other world equivalent to the costs and when you have given it to them they make an entry in a great ledger, which they call God's Account Book, more or less on these lines: "Item, the value of so many lines of verse, delivered on such and such a day to so and so, which God must reimburse from the first available credit on receipt of acquittance." Then when they feel in danger of dying, they have these ledgers chopped into pieces and swallow them, because they believe that unless they were digested in this way, God would not be able to read them, and it would profit them nothing.'

4

The little Spaniard

THIS conversation did not hinder our progress, that is with my carrier on all fours beneath me and myself astride his back. I will not go into any further detail about the adventures that delayed us on our journey, which we at length completed in the town where the King has his residence. As soon as I arrived there, they conducted me to the palace, where the great ones received me with more restrained amazement than the common people had shown when I passed through the streets. But the great ones reached the conclusion that I was doubtless the female of the Queen's 'little animal', as had the common people. That was how my guide interpreted it to me, although he could not understand the enigma himself, not knowing what this little animal of the Queen's could be. But we were soon enlightened, for some time after the King had

43

examined me, he commanded that it should be brought; and half an hour later, in the midst of a troop of monkeys, all dressed in ruffles and breeches, I saw a little man coming in, almost completely like myself, for he walked on two legs. As soon as he caught sight of me, he greeted me with a '*Criado de vou estra merced!*' [1] I returned his salutation in more or less similar terms. But alas! they had no sooner seen us talking together than they found their prejudice confirmed and indeed this conjecture could scarcely produce any other result, for even the one among those present whose opinion favoured us the most protested that our conversation was a grunting which the joy of being reunited made us give voice to by natural instinct.

The little man informed me that he was a European, a native of old Castille: he had found a means of having himself borne aloft by birds to the world of the moon, where we now found ourselves. He had fallen into the hands of the Queen, who had taken him for a monkey, for the reason that in this country they happen to dress up monkeys in the Spanish fashion and having found him clothed in this style, she had not doubted that he belonged to the same species.

'It must be admitted,' I replied, 'that after trying all kinds of costume on them, they could not find any more ridiculous, and that is the only reason why they fit them out in this fashion, since they keep these animals solely for their amusement.'

'That,' he rejoined, 'is to deny the dignity of our nation, on behalf of which the universe produces men, uniquely in order to provide us with slaves, the only one for whom nature could create objects of mirth.' He then begged me to tell him how I had come to dare risk an ascent to the moon with the machine I had described to him. I replied that it was because he had already taken the birds, upon which I had been thinking of riding. He smiled at this joke and about a quarter of an hour later the King ordered the keepers of the monkeys to take us

[1] i.e. 'your servant, sir.' Domingo Gonsales, a Spaniard, was the hero of *The Man in the Moone* by Francis Godwin.

off, with an express command to make us sleep together, the Spaniard and myself, so that our species should multiply within his realm. The will of the Prince was executed in all particulars, and I was very glad of this because of the pleasure I derived from having someone to talk to during the solitude of my brutification.

One day my male (for they took me to be the female of his species) told me that what had really driven him to flee across the face of the earth and finally to abandon it for the moon, was the fact that he had not been able to find a single country where even the imagination was at liberty. 'You see,' he told me, 'unless you wear a hood, whatever fine things you may say, if they are against the principles of the doctors of the cloth, you are an idiot, a madman, and something worse besides. They wanted to bring me before the Inquisition in my country because I told the pedants to their beards that there are vacuums in nature and that I knew of no substance in the world heavier than any other.'

I asked him what evidence he had to support an opinion which was so little accepted.

'In order to prove the point,' he replied, 'one must suppose that there is only one element; for although we may see water, earth, air, and fire in separation from one another, they can never be found in so completely pure a state that they are not still combined together. For example, fire, when you examine it, is not fire, but merely air greatly distended; air is only water greatly dilated; water is only molten earth, and earth itself is nothing else but water greatly contracted. From a serious investigation of matter, therefore, you would discover that it is all one, but that, like an excellent actor, it plays all kinds of roles in this life, in all kinds of disguises. Otherwise you would be forced to admit that there are as many elements as there are kinds of body. And if you ask me why fire burns and water cools, seeing that it is all merely a single substance, I reply to you that this substance behaves sympathetically according to the situation in which it finds itself at the time of its activity. Fire, which is nothing but earth even more

45

rarefied than when it constitutes air, tries to transform into itself by sympathy everything it encounters.

'Thus the heat from coal, being the most refined form of fire, and the best suited to penetrating a body, first slips between the pores in our bodies and then makes us give off sweat because we are being filled with a new substance. This sweat, dilated by the fire, is converted into vapour and becomes air; this air, still further diffused by the heat of the reaction, or by the neighbouring bodies, is called fire, and the earth, abandoned by the cold and humidity which bind all the parts together, falls back to earth. Water, on the other hand, although it only differs in substance from fire in that it is more compact, does not burn us, because, being compact, it seeks to make more compact by sympathy the bodies it encounters. The cold which we feel is nothing else but the effect of our flesh drawing in upon itself, as a result of the proximity of the earth or the water, which makes us imitate them. That is why dropsical people convert all the food they consume into water. That is why bilious people convert into bile all the blood which their livers produce. Thus if we suppose that there is one single element, it is most certain that all bodies, each according to its nature, are equally attracted towards the centre of the earth.

'Now you will ask me why it is that iron, the metals, earth, and wood fall towards this centre more quickly than a sponge —if it is not because the latter is full of air, which naturally tends upwards. Well that is not the reason at all, and here is how I reply to you. Although a stone falls more quickly than a feather, both have the same inclination towards their journey. But if a cannon ball, for example, found the earth pierced right through, it would hurtle to the centre more swiftly than a bladder filled with air; and the reason is that the mass of metal consists of a lot of earth forced into a small space, while the air is a very small amount of earth occupying a lot of space. All the particles of matter contained in the iron, being fused together as they are, derive increased strength from their unity. Having closed their ranks, they find they are many fighting against few, seeing that a parcel of air equal in size to the cannon ball is not equal in numbers. The air therefore yields to the weight of troops more numerous than its own and equally impetuous, and allows itself to be thrust aside to let them pass.

'Without going into a whole string of arguments to prove this, I will ask you how it comes about, by your faith, that we can be wounded by a pike, a sword, or a dagger, if it is not because steel is a substance in which the particles are closer and more compact than your flesh—the pores and softness of which show that it contains a very little matter spread over a large space—and because the point of the weapon which pierces us consists of an almost incalculable quantity of matter opposed to a very small amount of flesh and forces it to yield to the stronger, just as a squadron in close order easily breaches a battalion which is less closely drawn up and more spread out. For why is glowing steel from the furnace hotter than a burning tree trunk if it is not because there is more fire in the steel, contained in a small space—since there is some attached to all the particles of the metal—than in the stick of wood, since this is very spongy and consequently contains a considerable amount of vacuum—which is nothing but an absence of substance and cannot take on the form of fire?

' "But then," you will object to me, "you postulate the existence of a vacuum as if you had proved it, and that is what we are arguing about!" Very well, I will prove it to you, and though this difficulty be the sister of the Gordian knot, I have a strong enough arm to be its Alexander.

'Let him now answer me, I beg him, this common blockhead who will not even believe he is a man until a learned doctor tells him so! Supposing there is only one substance, as I believe I have sufficiently proved, how does it come about that, by condensing itself, a lump of earth can turn into a stone? Are the particles of this stone fitted inside one another so that where one grain of sand is already located, another can occupy the same space? Such a thing would be impossible, even according to their own principles, since bodies do not penetrate one another—and yet this matter must have been drawn together and, if you like, abridged. The particles have therefore occupied some space which was not occupied before.

'You may say it is incomprehensible that there should be nothingness in the universe, that we should be partly composed of nothing. Well, why ever not? Is not the whole universe surrounded by nothingness? And since you grant me this much, confess, then, that it is just as easy for the universe to have nothingness within it as around it.

'Now I am well aware that you are going to ask me why a vessel of water bursts when the water freezes and contracts, if it is not to prevent a vacuum being created. But my answer is that it only happens because the air above it, which is drawn towards the centre of the globe, just as much as earth and water, encounters a vacant hostelry on its path through this territory and goes in to lodge there. If it finds the portals of this vessel—that is to say the channels leading to the pocket of vacuum—too narrow, long and tortuous, it satisfies its impatience to reach its berth sooner by smashing it open.

'But without amusing myself by replying to all these objections, I will venture to state that, if there were no vacuums, there would be no movement, or else it would be necessary to admit that bodies penetrate one another. For it would be ridiculous to believe that when a fly pushes a parcel of air aside with its wings, this parcel makes another recoil in front of it, and this second one yet another, and that in this manner the agitation of a flea's little toe produces a hump on the other side of the world!

'When these people are hard pressed to explain this, they have recourse to rarefaction. But when a body becomes rarefied how, in good faith, can one particle of its mass move farther from another particle without leaving emptiness in between them? Otherwise would not the two particles which have just moved apart have to have occupied the same space as a third one—and thus all three would have penetrated one another? I expect you will ask me how, in that case, we can make water rise upwards, against its inclination, by means of a tube, a syringe, or a pump. My answer is that it is raped. It is not fear of a vacuum that obliges it to change direction but, being fused with the air in an imperceptible nuance, it rises when the air is drawn up, since this clutches it in a tight embrace.

'That is not a very thorny point to grasp when you understand the perfect cycle and subtle interconnection of the elements. For if you examine attentively the slime that makes the marriage between earth and water, you will find that it is at this stage neither earth nor water but the honest broker making a contract between these two enemies. Similarly, water and air each send one another a mist, which partakes of the characters of both and makes peace between them, and air is reconciled with fire by means of a mediating exhalation which unites them.'

I believe he would have continued speaking; but they brought us our food and, because we were hungry, I closed my ears to his speeches, the better to open my stomach to the meats they had set before us.

I remember that another time, when we were philosophizing (for we both had little taste for conversation upon low topics), he said to me: 'It distresses me deeply to see a mind of the stamp of yours infected with the errors of the common herd. You must know that despite the pedantry of Aristotle, with which your classrooms in France today resound, everything is in everything. That is to say, for example, that in water there is fire and in fire, water; air contains earth and earth, air. Although this opinion may make the academics open their eyes as wide as saucers, it is, in fact, easier to prove it than it is to convince them. For I ask them, first of all, if water does not engender fish. If they deny me this, let them dig a ditch and fill it with the juice of the water jug (which they may also pass through a sieve, to avoid the objections of the blind); and if they find no fish there after some time, I am willing to drink all the water they poured into it. But if they do find any, as I have no doubt they will, it is a conclusive proof that it contains salt and fire.

'It follows that it is not a very difficult undertaking now to discover water in fire. Even if they choose the form of fire which is the most detached from matter, such as comets, there is still always a great deal of water in them. For if the oily humour from which they are created, reduced to sulphur by the heat of the reaction which sets them alight, did not meet some resistance to its violence in the cold humidity which tempers and combats it, it would swiftly be consumed like a flash of lightning.

'That there is air in earth they will not now deny—or else they have never heard of the terrible earthquakes which so recently convulsed the mountains of Sicily. Apart from this, we can see that earth is completely porous, down to the grains of sand which compose it. However, no one has yet said that the holes are filled with nothing, so they will not find it improper for the air to make its dwelling there. It remains for me to prove that there is earth in the air, but it is hardly worth my while to take the trouble, since it is demonstrated to you every time you see the legions of atoms falling on your heads which are so numerous that they smother arithmetic.

'But let us turn from simple to composite bodies. These will offer me much more common examples and will show that all things are contained in all things and do not change into one another, as your peripatetics are always babbling. For I will tell them to their beards that the principal substances combine, separate, and combine again in such a way that what was created water by the Maker of the world in His wisdom will always remain water.

'Unlike them, I do not assume any proposition I cannot prove. I therefore invite you to take a log or some other combustible matter and set fire to it. When it is burning they will say that what *was* wood has *become* fire, but I tell them no. There is no more fire in it when it is in flames than before you set a match to it. The fire which lay hidden in the log and which the cold and the damp prevented from spreading and being active, has been succoured by the newcomer. Rallying its forces against the phlegm which had it by the throat, it has stormed the field that was occupied by its enemy, and can now show itself freely as it triumphs over its gaoler. Do you not see the water running away at both ends of the tree stump, still hot and smoking from the fight it has put up?

'The flame which you observe above it is the most refined fire, the most disengaged from the matter, and the soonest ready, in consequence, to return to its home. But it holds together in a pyramid up to a certain height, in order to force its way up through the dense humidity of the air which resists it. Then, as they rise, the particles of fire gradually become disengaged from the violent company of their fellows. Finally they take their leave of one another because they encounter nothing further which is hostile to their passage. This carelessness is very often the cause of a second imprisonment, for, travelling separately, they sometimes get lost in a cloud. If they meet one another at other times in sufficiently large numbers to hold their own against the vapour, they join forces; they rumble; they thunder, and they flash. And the animated rage of these inanimate objects often causes the death of innocent people. But if a particle of fire finds itself held fast by this oppressive unrefined matter of the middle region and is not strong enough to defend itself, it abandons itself to the mercy of its enemy, which forces it, by its weight, to fall back to earth. The unfortunate, enclosed in a drop of water, will find itself perhaps at the foot of an oak tree, whose animal fire will call to the poor wayfarer to lodge with it. And thus we behold it returning to the same state as it left several days before.

'But let us consider the fate of the other elements of which our log was composed. The air retires to its home district, but still mingled with vapour, which the fire, in all its wrath, has brusquely expelled hither and thither. Now we can see it serving as a football to the winds, supplying the breathing of the animals and filling the vacuum made by nature. It is possible, in addition, that a particle of this air, engulfed in a drop of dew, will be sucked in and digested by the thirsty leaves of the tree in which our fire has also come to rest.

'The water which the flames drove out of the log, raised by the heat as high as the cradle of the meteors, is as likely to fall back as rain on to our oak tree as on to any other.

'And the earth from it, turned into ashes and then cured of its sterility—either by the nourishing heat of a dunghill it has been thrown on, or by the vegetative salts of neighbouring plants, or by the fertile water of streams—may well end up near the oak tree, be attracted by the warmth of its seed, and become absorbed as a part of the whole.

'Thus we observe the four elements all suffering the same fate and returning to the state they were in some days before. Therefore one can say that there is everything in a man that it takes to make a tree, and everything in a tree that it takes to make a man. In this way all things ultimately meet in everything, but we lack a Prometheus to draw from the bosom of nature and make perceptible to us what I would call *primary matter*.'

5

On trial

SUCH, more or less, were the matters with which we passed the time, for the little Spaniard had a pretty wit. Our conversations only took place at night, however, since from six in the morning until the evening we should have been distracted by the great throng of people that came to stare at us in our house. Some of them threw stones at us, some of them nuts and some of them grass. There was no talk of anything but the King's beasts. They served us with food every day at our meal times and the Queen and King themselves quite often took the trouble to feel my belly, to see if I was not filling out at all, for they were consumed with an extraordinary desire to start a breed of these little animals. I do not know if it was from being more attentive to their grimaces and their sounds than my male, but I learned quicker than he to understand their language and to murder it a little, which made them consider us in quite a different way from before.

The news at once ran through the kingdom that two wild men had been found, smaller than the rest of them (on account of the poor nourishment we had taken in our isolated state) and, thanks to a failing in their fathers' seed, with front legs too weak to carry their own weight.

This belief would have spread and taken root, if the priests of the country had not made a stand against it, saying that it was shocking impiety to believe that not merely beasts, but monsters could belong to their species. 'Even our domestic animals,' added the more dispassionate of them, 'would be much more likely to share in humanity's privilege of immortality—for they are born in our country—than a monstrous beast that says it was born heaven knows where in the moon. And then consider the visible difference between us and them: we walk upon four feet, because God would not entrust something so precious to a less secure posture. He was afraid of some misfortune befalling man if he walked in any other way: that is why He took the trouble to set him upon four columns, so that he could not fall. But, scorning to interfere with the construction of these two brutes, He abandoned them to the whim of Nature, who had no fears about the loss of something so trivial, and placed them upon two paws only.

'Not even the birds,' they said, 'have been so ill used as these. At least they have been given feathers to compensate for the feebleness of their legs, so that they can launch themselves into the air when we drive them from our houses; while nature, in taking away two of these monsters' feet has rendered them incapable of flight from our justice.

'And apart from this, just take a look at how they have their heads turned towards heaven! It is the paucity of God's gifts to them which makes them stand in this way. Their suppliant attitude shows that they are complaining to heaven about their Maker and begging leave to be fitted out with what is left over from us. We, on the other hand, carry our heads bowed down in contemplation of the good things of which we are the masters, for in our happy condition there is nothing in heaven for us to gaze at with envy.'

Every day I heard the priests spinning these yarns or similar ones near my lodgings. By this means they finally gained such a hold over people's minds on the subject that it was decreed that, at the very most, I must not rank as more than a parrot without feathers; for they could point out to their converts the fact that I had only two legs—no more than any bird has. I was consequently put into a cage by express order of the Supreme Council.

The Queen's fowler took the trouble to visit me there every day and whistle the language to me, as we do here to starlings, and I was indeed happy in that I did not go short of food. Moreover, in the midst of the trivialities with which the on-lookers assailed my ears, I learned to speak like them, so that when I was sufficiently practised in the idiom to express the greater part of my notions, I gave some account of the best of them. The neatness of my epigrams and the esteem in which my wit was held had already become the sole topic of conver-sation in company. Things went so far that the Council was obliged to publish a decree prohibiting the belief that I was endowed with reason. All persons of every quality and degree were expressly commanded to believe that whatever witty accomplishments might be mine, my behaviour was purely instinctive.

However, the question of defining what I was divided the town into two factions. The party which supported my in-terest was growing from day to day and, in spite of the ana-thema and excommunication with which the prophets tried to frighten the people, my partisans finally demanded an assembly of the Estates in order to resolve this stumbling-block to religion. They took a long time to agree on the choice of who should give their opinions, but the judges pacified the opposition by balancing the numbers of interested parties and the latter ordered that I should be brought into the assembly, as was done. There I was treated as severly as it is possible to imagine. The examiners questioned me, among other things, on the subject of philosophy. I explained to them, in complete good faith, what my tutor had once taught me about it, but they had little trouble in refuting what I said with many likely and convincing arguments. Finding myself totally defeated in debate, I cited the principles of Aristotle as a last resort, but these served me no better than sophisms, for they revealed the falseness of them to me in a couple of words.

'This Aristotle,' they told me, 'whose science you make so much of, doubtless made his principles fit his philosophy, instead of fitting his philosophy to basic principles. But even then he was under an obligation to prove they were at least more reasonable than those of the other sects, which he could not do. And that is why the good Lord will not find fault with us if we bid him adieu.'

When they finally saw that all I could jabber was that they were no more learned than Aristotle and that I had been forbidden to argue with anyone who denied his principles, they all unanimously concluded that I was not a man but possibly some type of ostrich, seeing that like these birds I carried my head erect, walked upon two legs, and indeed, apart from a trifling amount of down, wholly resembled them. They therefore ordered the fowler to take me back to my cage.

I spent my time there pleasantly enough, for now I had mastered their language correctly, all the Court delighted to make me chatter. Among others, the Queen's ladies-in-waiting would always thrust some titbit into my basket. The most good-natured of them all conceived some fondness for me and she was so transported with joy when I revealed to her in secret the mysteries of our religion, particularly when I told her about our bells and our holy relics, that she protested to me with tears in her eyes that if ever I found myself in a position to fly back to our world, she would follow me with all her heart.

Early one morning I woke up with a start to see her beating

a tattoo on the bars of my cage. 'Take heart,' she said to me, 'Yesterday in the Council they decided to declare war on King ▦▦▦▦. Amid the confusion of preparations, while our monarch and his subjects are away, I hope to find an occasion to rescue you.'

'Did you say war?' I interrupted her. 'Do quarrels arise between the princes of this world here, as they do between those of ours? Why then, tell me, I beg you, about their manner of fighting.'

'When the umpires,' she went on, 'elected according to the liking of the two sides, have designated the amount of time to be allowed for arming and marching, the number of combatants and the day and place for the battle, and all so fairly that there is not a single man more in one army than in the other, the crippled soldiers are all drawn up into a company on the one hand, and when the fighting begins the field officers are careful to expose them to cripples. Giants, on the other hand, are pitted against colossi, fencers against nimble swordsmen, valiant men against brave, weak against feeble, indisposed against sick, robust against strong and if anyone ventures to strike a man who is not his allotted enemy, unless he can prove that he did it by mistake, he is condemned a coward. After the battle is over they count the wounded, the dead and the prisoners—for as to deserters there are none. If the losses prove to be equal on either side, they draw lots for which shall be declared victorious.

'But though a kingdom may defeat its enemy in a fair fight it has gained almost nothing, for there are other armies, small in numbers, composed of scholars and men of wit, upon whose disputations the triumph or subjection of states entirely depends.

'One scholar is opposed to another scholar, one wit to another, one wise man to another. Moreover, a triumph won by a state in this manner counts the same as three conquests by brute force. After the proclamation of the victory the whole assembly is broken up and the winning side choose as their King either the enemy's or their own.'

I could not help laughing at this scrupulous way of fighting battles and, as an example of a more effective policy, I cited the general practice in our own Europe, where a monarch takes care not to neglect any advantage which will secure a victory. This is how she replied.

'Tell me,' she said to me, 'do not your princes excuse their resort to arms on the ground that might is right?'

'Quite so,' I answered her, 'but also by the justice of their cause.'

'In that case,' she continued, 'why do they not select umpires who are above suspicion to negotiate an agreement between them. And if it emerges that each has as much right on his side as the other, let them stay as they were or play a hand of piquet for the town or province under dispute. For while the heads of four million better men than they are being broken on their behalf, they merely sit at home and jeer at the slaughter of these idiots! But it is wrong of me to find fault with the valour of your brave subject peoples in this way: they are quite right to die for their country. It is an important matter, for it is a question of whether to be the vassal of a king who wears a ruff or of one who wears a lace collar.'

'But as for you,' I countered, 'why all this circumstance in your manner of fighting? Is it not enough for the armies to have the same number of men?'

'You have little judgement,' she replied. 'By your faith, if you had conquered your enemy in the field in single combat, would you consider you had vanquished him in a fair fight if you were in armour and he were not; if he had only a dagger and you a sword; in short if he were one-armed and you had two arms? For despite all the fairness you are always recommending to your gladiators, they are never evenly matched. One will be tall, the other short; one will be skilled, the other will never have wielded a sword before; one will be robust, the other a weakling. And even if these discrepancies are evened out and they are each as skilful and as strong as the other, they would still not be equals, for one of the two may have more courage than the other. So this impulsive man, shielded by the fact that he disregards the danger, that he has a fiery temper, more blood and a firmer heart, with all these qualities which make for courage—and are they not just as good as a sword, a weapon his enemy does not possess?—rouses himself to charge recklessly at, to frighten and to take the life of a poor man who foresees the danger, whose natural warmth is choked with phlegm, and whose heart is too dilated to summon up the spirits needed to dissipate that icy chill known as *poltroonery*. Thus you praise a man for killing his enemy when the advantage was on his side, and in praising him for his daring you are in fact praising him for a sin against nature, since his daring spurs him on towards his own destruction.

'On this subject, by the way, I can tell you that a remonstrance was made to the Council of War some years ago, urging them to bring a more circumspect and conscientious ruling into battles. And the philosopher who gave this opinion spoke as follows:

' "You imagine, gentlemen, that you have properly evened out the handicaps between two adversaries when you have chosen them both tall, both skilful, and both full of courage; but that is still not enough, since the winner must finally triumph through cunning, strength, or good luck. If he does it through cunning, it means he must have struck his enemy in a place where he did not expect it, or more quickly than seemed likely; or, pretending to take him on one side, he assailed him from the other. But to do all that is to be subtle, it is to deceive, it is to betray—and the renown of a truly noble man should not be founded upon deception and betrayal.

' "If he triumphs through strength, do you consider his enemy vanquished merely because he has been overpowered? No, of course not, any more than you would say that a man has lost a victory when he has been crushed by a falling mountain, because he was not strong enough to get the better of it! It is likewise true that this man has not been defeated, because at the given moment he was not in a position to be able to resist the violence of his adversary.

' "And if it is by good luck that our man brings his enemy to the ground, why then it is fortune and not he who ought to be crowned; he has contributed nothing. In short, the loser is no more to blame than the dice thrower who sees his seventeen points beaten by eighteen."

'They admitted to him that he was right, but that it was not humanly possible to regulate this, saying that it was better to submit to a small inconvenience than to leave oneself exposed to a hundred others of greater significance.'

This time she conversed with me no further, because she was afraid of being found alone with me so early in the morning. It is not that immodesty is a crime in that country, on the contrary, apart from convicted criminals, every man has the right to possess every woman, and a woman, similarly, can take a man to court if he refuses her. But she did not dare to visit me often in public, she told me, because at the last sacrifice the priests had preached that it was chiefly women who were spreading the story that I was a man, using this pretext to conceal the abominable lust which consumed them to have intercourse with the beasts and shamelessly to commit with me sins against nature. This was the reason why I was left for a long time without seeing her or any of her sex.

Someone must have stirred up the embers of the controversy about what I was, however, for just when I was looking forward to nothing so much as dying in my cage, they came and fetched me once more to give me a hearing. I was questioned on several points of physics in the presence of a large number of courtiers. My replies, I believe, gave no satisfaction, for the one who presided explained his opinions on the structure of the universe to me at great length. They seemed ingenious to me and if he had not passed on to its origin, which he claimed was 'eternal', I would have found his philosophy much more reasonable than ours. But as soon as I heard him upholding a fantasy so contrary to what our faith teaches us, I asked him what answer he had to the authority of Moses, for this great patriarch had expressly said that God created it in six days. The ignoramus merely laughed instead of replying, and I was driven to tell him that since they had come to that, I was beginning to believe that their world was nothing but a moon.

'But,' they all said to me, 'you can see earth here, rivers and seas. What could they all be?'

'Never mind!' I retorted. 'Aristotle assures us that it is only the moon, and if you had said the opposite in the classes where I did my studies, you would have been hissed.'

At this there was a great outburst of laughter. There is no need to ask whether this was due to their ignorance, but at all events they led me back to my cage.

The priests, however, were more outraged than this assembly had been. When they learned that I had dared to say that the moon I came from was a world and that their world was only a moon, they believed that this furnished a good enough pretext for having me condemned to the water, which is their method of exterminating atheists. To this end they went in a body to make their complaint to the King who promised them justice and commanded that I should be put in the dock.

So there I was, uncaged for the third time. The most ancient of them took the floor then and pleaded against me. I do not remember his speech because I was too alarmed to make out the elements of his voice without confusion and also because he used an instrument for declaiming, the sound of which quite deafened me. It was a trumpet which he had deliberately chosen so that the violence of its martial sound might excite a desire for my death in their minds and so that this emotion should prevent their reason from performing its office, as happens in our armies where the hurly-burly of trumpets and drums keeps the soldier from reflecting upon the importance of his life. When he had spoken, I rose to plead my case, but I was spared this by an adventure which will surprise you. Just as I had opened my mouth, a man who had had great difficulty in penetrating the throng came and fell at the King's feet and dragged himself about on his back in front of him for a considerable time. This behaviour did not surprise me, for I knew that it was the posture they adopted when they wished to speak in public. I simply pocketed my own speech and here is the one we had from him:

'Just men, hear me! You cannot condemn this man, this ape, this parrot, for having said that the moon is a world whence he came. For if he is a man—even if he has not come from the moon—since all men are free, is he not also free to imagine what he chooses? How's this? Will you put constraint on him for not sharing your own visions? Of course you can compel him to say that the moon is not a world, but none the less he will not believe what he says, because for him to believe something, certain possibilities must be presented to his imagination, which seem more likely than not. Unless you offer him this likelihood, or it springs to his mind of its own accord, he may well tell you that he is convinced, but for all that he will remain incredulous.

'I now have to prove to you that he should not be condemned if you place him in the category of the beasts.

'Supposing he is an animal devoid of reason, would you then be reasonable to accuse him of sinning against it? He has said that the moon was a world, but beasts only act by natural instinct, *ergo* it is nature speaking and not him. To believe that wise nature, who made the world and the moon, should not know what it is herself, while you—who possess no knowledge which is not derived from her—know better, would indeed be ridiculous.

'But even if passion led you to renounce your principles and to suppose that nature does not guide the beasts, at least you should blush at the anxieties caused you by the caprices of one of them. Truly, gentlemen, if you encountered a grown man policing an anthill, now cuffing an ant for knocking down its comrade, now imprisoning one for stealing a grain of corn from its neighbour, now bringing another to justice for abandoning its eggs, would you not consider him mad to be busying himself with these things so far beneath him and striving to make creatures submit to reason which have not its use? Then what name, venerable pontiffs, would you give the concern you show about the caprices of this little animal? Just men, I have spoken.'

As soon as he had finished, the whole room resounded with a sort of music of applause, and after their opinions had all been debated for a good quarter of an hour, the King pronounced that I should be regarded henceforward as a man, and as such given my freedom, and that the punishment of being drowned should be altered, in mitigation, to that of making Ignominious Amends (for in that country they have no such thing as 'Honourable Amends'). In doing this I should publicly retract my claim that the moon was a world, on account of the shock that the novelty of this opinion might give to the souls of the weak.

This decree pronounced, they took me out of the palace; they dressed me with great splendour as a mark of shame; they made me ride on the platform of a magnificent chariot, drawn by four princes who were yoked to it, and here is what they made me announce at every cross-roads in the town:

'People, I declare unto you that this moon here is not a moon, but a world; and that that world down there is not a world but a moon. Such is what the priests deem it good for you to believe!'

After I had cried the same thing in the five great squares of the city, I perceived my advocate offering me his hand to help me down. When I looked into his face I was greatly astonished to recognize that it was my demon. We were a whole hour embracing one another.

'Now come along to my house,' he said to me, 'for if you returned to the court after making Ignominious Amends you would not be looked on with favour. Moreover, I must tell you that you would still be with the monkeys like your friend the Spaniard, if I had not published the vigour and force of your wit everywhere in company, and intrigued in your favour for the protection of the great ones against the prophets.'

The end of my thanks saw us entering his house. He entertained me until the meal was ready by telling me of the devices by means of which he had forced the priests to abandon such an unjust persecution, despite all the highly specious scruples they had used to win over the consciences of the people. But when they informed us that dinner was served, he told me that to keep me company that evening he had invited two professors from the Academy of that town to come and dine with us. 'I will draw them out,' he added, 'on the philosophy which they teach in this world and at the same time you shall also see my host's son. He is as intelligent a young man as I have ever come across. He would be a second Socrates if he could control his brilliance, refrain from smothering in vice the graces with which God continually visits him, and cease affecting to be a libertine, as he does with a fantastic ostentation and an ambition to acquire the reputation of a man of wit. I have taken lodgings here so as to seek out opportunities for instructing him.'

He fell silent, as if to leave me free to speak in my turn. Then he made a sign that I should be divested of the shameful ornaments with which I was still resplendent.

6

Dinner with two philosophers: youth, age, and vegetables

THE two professors we were expecting entered almost at once and we went to sit down at the table which was laid, where we found the young man he had mentioned, already eating. They greeted him with great salutations and treated him with a respect as profound as a slave's for his master. I asked my demon the reason for this and he replied that it was on account of his age, since the old in that world showed every kind of respect and deference to the young. Moreover, fathers obeyed their children as soon as they had reached what the Senate of Philosophers considered to be the age of discretion.

'You may be surprised,' he went on, 'at a custom so contrary to that of your own country, but it is in no way repugnant to common sense. For tell me, in all conscience, is not a hot young man, who still has the power to imagine, judge, and act, more capable of ruling a family than an infirm sixty-year-old—a poor dullard, his imagination chilled by the snows of sixty winters, guided only by what you call his experience of successful achievements (which were in fact the simple effects of chance, contrary to all the rules governing human prudence)?

'As for judgement, he has little enough of it, although the common herd in your world make it an attribute of old age. But if they want the truth, they should realize that what is called "prudence" in an old man is no more than a panic apprehension, a wild fear which obsesses him of undertaking anything at all. So when he refuses to take a risk, in a situation where a young man comes to grief, it is not that he has foreseen the young man's fate, but merely that he lacked sufficient fire to spark off those noble impulses which make us dare to act. The young man's boldness, on the other hand, was like a pledge for the success of his enterprise, because it was the ardour which makes for speed and facility in performance that prompted him to undertake it.

'As for the matter of action, I should be insulting your intelligence if I offered proofs to convince you. You know that youth alone is suited to deeds. But even if you are not wholly persuaded of this, tell me, I pray you, when you respect a courageous man, if it is not because he can take revenge on your enemies or your oppressors? And is it from any other consideration than pure habit that you have regard for him, once a battalion of seventy Januaries has chilled his blood and frozen to death all that noble enthusiasm for justice which fires young people? When you defer to a man stronger than yourself, are you not making him indebted to you for a victory which you could not contest? Why then submit to

him, when idleness has softened his muscles, enfeebled his
arteries, evaporated his spirits and sucked out the marrow
from his bones? If you worship a woman, is it not on account
of her beauty? Then why continue your genuflections after age
has made her a spectre which threatens the living with death?
When, lastly, you have loved a clever man, it was surely
because his lively genius could fathom and unravel a confused matter; his brilliant talk held the attention of assemblies of the highest alloy; he could digest whole sciences in a
single thought. And yet you continue to honour him, when
his worn-out organs render his head foolish, ponderous, and
importunate in company and when he bears more resemblance to the figure of a household god than to that of a
reasonable man.

'You may fairly conclude from all this, my son, that it is
better for young people to be entrusted with the government
of families than old men. All the more because, according to
your maxims, Hercules, Achilles, Epaminondas, Alexander,
and Caesar, who almost all died this side of forty, would not
have merited any honours, being, by your reckoning, too
young. Yet their youth alone was the sole cause of their fine
actions, which a more advanced age would have rendered in-
effective. They would then have lacked the fire and agility, to
which they owed their great successes.

' "But," you will say, "all the laws of our world are careful
to resound with the respect due to old men." True, but then
the lawgivers were old men, who were afraid the young would
rightly dispossess them of their extorted authority and so, like
the legislators of false religions, they have made a mystery of
what they could not prove.

' "Yes," you will say to me, "but this old man is my father,
and heaven promises me a long life if I honour him." If your
father, O my son, orders you nothing contrary to the inspira-
tions of the Almighty, I grant you this. Otherwise, walk upon
the belly of the father that begot you! Trample upon the
breast of the mother that conceived you! For as to your
imagining that this cowardly respect which vicious parents

have wrung from your weakness is so pleasing to the heavens that they will prolong your lease of life for it, I see little likelihood of this. What! Does doffing your hat to flatter and nourish the arrogance of your father lance the abscess in your side or correct your bodily moisture? Does it cure you of a stoccado through your stomach? Does it break up the stone in your bladder? If these things are so, then your doctors are all wrong. Instead of the infernal potions with which they plague the lives of men, why do they not prescribe for the smallpox three curtsies on an empty stomach, four *thank you very kindly*s after dinner, and twelve *goodnight father and mother*s before going to sleep?

'You will reply to me that but for your father you would not exist. That is true, but neither would he have ever existed without your grandfather, nor your grandfather without your great-grandfather; and without *you* your father could not have a grandson. When nature brought him into the world it was on the condition that he pay back what she lent him. So when he begot you he gave you nothing, he was merely paying off a debt! And besides, I should very much like to know if your parents were thinking of you when they made you. Alas, not at all! And yet you think yourself obliged to them, all the same, for a gift they granted you without thinking about it. How's this! Just because your father was so lustful that he could not resist the charms of some fair creature and signed a contract for her, to gratify his passion, and you were the edifice that arose from them pawing one another, you reverence this voluptuary as one of the seven sages of Greece! What! Because another man, a miser, purchases his wife's riches by means of a child, may this child only speak to him on bended knees? Oh yes, your father did well to be a lecher and the other man to be avaricious, for otherwise neither you nor this child would ever have existed. But I should very much like to know whether, even if he had known for sure that his pistol would beget a rat, he would not still have fired his shot. Just God! I wish the people of your world could be made to see it!

'All you have from your mortal architect is your body: your

soul comes from the heavens. It is only by chance that your father was not your son, as you are his. How do you know that he did not even prevent you inheriting a coronet? Your soul may have left heaven, destined to animate the King of the Romans in the belly of the Empress and only chanced to meet your embryo on the way and stayed there in order to cut its journey short. No, no, even if your father had died as a little boy, God would not have struck you off his plans for mankind. But who knows if today you might not have been the handiwork of some valiant captain, who would have shared his glory with you as well as his property. So perhaps you are no more in your father's debt for the life he has bestowed on you, than you would be in a pirate's, who put you in chains because he wanted to keep you as his slave.

'And even supposing he had engendered you a prince or a king, a gift nevertheless loses its value when the one who receives it has no choice. Death was given to Caesar: it was also given to Cassius. Cassius was indebted to the slave at whose hand he received it, yet Caesar was not to his murderers, because they forced it upon him. Did your father consider your wishes when he took your mother in his arms? Did he ask you if you would like to see this century or if you would rather wait for another one? Whether you would be content to be the son of a fool or if you would long to spring from a brave man's loins? Alas! you, whom the matter alone concerned, were the only one not to be consulted. Perhaps if you had been, and instead of being in the matrix of nature's ideas, you had actually been shut up somewhere with an option on your birth, you would have said to the Fate: "My dear lady, take up another man's spindle. I have been in the void for a very long time and I should much prefer to remain non-existent for another hundred years, rather than come into being today, only to repent of it tomorrow." Nevertheless you were forced to make the transition. In vain you howled to return to the long, dark house whence they had snatched you: they pretended to think you were asking for suck.

'These, O my son, are more or less the reasons for the

respect which fathers have for their children. I am well aware that I have been more biased on the side of the children than justice required, and that in favouring them I have gone a little against my conscience. But I wanted to correct the arrogance with which some fathers defy the weakness of their little ones, and I was compelled to act like those who, in order to straighten out a lopsided tree, pull at it from the other side, so that between opposing tensions it grows straight and even. In making fathers restore the deference which they had tyrannically usurped, I have robbed them of much that was theirs, so that next time they might be content with their due. I know for certain that I will have shocked all old men with this apology. But let them remember that they were children before they were fathers and a good deal of what I have said must also have been in their favour, since they were not found under heads of cabbages themselves. Whatever happens in the end, even if my adversaries were to make war on my friends, I should be bound to win, for I have served the whole of mankind well and only done disservice to half of them.'

With these words he fell silent and our host's son took up the conversation as follows: 'Permit me,' he said to my demon, 'since, thanks to the trouble you have taken, I am acquainted with the origin, history, customs, and philosophy of the world of this little man, to add something to what you have said and to show that children are in no way indebted to their fathers for their birth, because their fathers were obliged by their consciences to beget them.

'The very narrowest philosophy in their world admits that it is better to die—since in order to die one must have lived—than never to exist at all. Therefore since, if I do not give substance to this nonentity, I put it into a state worse than death; in not bringing it into the world I am committing a worse crime than killing it. Now if you had cut your son's throat, O my little man, you would consider yourself guilty of unforgivable parricide. It would indeed be monstrous, but it is even more execrable not to give any existence at all to someone who could have received it. For this child, whom you thus permanently deprive of the light of day, would at least have had the satisfaction of enjoying it for a space of time. Of course we know that he is only deprived of it for a few centuries, but then if you maliciously prevent these poor little nothings (out of which you might have made your King forty good soldiers) from coming into the world and leave them corrupting in your loins, you run the risk of an apoplexy which will choke you.

'Let no man answer by singing the praises of virginity; this honour is just so much empty vapour. For despite all the veneration with which it is idolized by the mob, it is still no more than a recommendation, even among your own people. But not to kill and not to make one's son (by not making him at all) more wretched than a dead man—these are commandments. For this reason I am greatly astonished, seeing that in the world you come from continence is held to be preferable to carnal intercourse, that God has not arranged for you to be born from the dew in the month of May like mushrooms, or at least, like crocodiles, from the greasy slime of the earth in the heat of the sun. None the less He only sends eunuchs among you by accident. He does not snatch away the genitals from your monks, your priests, nor your cardinals. You will tell me that they were given them by nature. Yes, but He is the Lord of nature, and if He had regarded this part as dangerous to their salvation He would have commanded it to be cut off, just as He commanded the Jews to do with their foreskins in the ancient law.

'But such fancies are too ridiculous! I ask you, is there any place upon your body more sacred or more accursed than any other? Why do I commit a sin when I touch myself on the part in the middle and not when I touch my ear or my heel? Is it because of the titillation I feel? Then I should not relieve myself at the privy either, for that cannot be done without a certain kind of pleasure. Nor should the devout lift themselves up to the contemplation of God, for their imagination enjoys great delight in this. Indeed, when I see how much the religion of your country is against nature and jealous of all the gratifications of men, I am astonished that your priests have not made it a crime for you to scratch yourselves, on account of the agreeable pain you feel in doing it.

'For all that, I have noticed that far-sighted Nature has given all great men, the valiant and the clever, an inclination towards the delights of love, as witness Samson, David, Hercules, Caesar, Hannibal, Charlemagne. Was it in order that they might reap the organ of this pleasure from themselves with a blow of a bill-hook? Alas, she even found a way under a wash tub and debauched Diogenes, thin, ugly and lousy as he was, and constrained him to heave sighs, reeking of carrots, for Lais. Doubtless nature treated him in this way because she feared there was a shortage of honest men in the world.

'Let us conclude from all this that your father was compelled by his conscience to allow you to see the light of day, and though he might think he had greatly obliged you by making you, while gratifying himself, he has in essence given you no more than an ordinary bull gives the cows ten times a day for his own pleasure.'

'You are wrong,' my demon then broke in, 'to want to regulate the wisdom of God. It is true that He has forbidden us the excess of this pleasure, but how do you know He did not want it this way, so that the difficulties we encounter in fighting this passion might make us worthy of the glory He has in store for us? Or how do you know His purpose was not to whet our appetites? How do you know He did not foresee that if the young were abandoned to the impulses of the flesh, over-frequent coition would weaken their seed and bring the world to an end with the great-great-nephews of the first man? How do you know He was not seeking to prevent the earth's fertility being exhausted by the needs of so many hungry mouths? How do you know, lastly, if He did not wish to make it appear quite unreasonable in order to reward just those who had faith in His Word contrary to all semblance of reason?'

This reply did not satisfy the young host, so far as I could judge, for he wagged his head at it three or four times. But our common mentor fell silent because the meal was impatient to take flight.

We stretched ourselves out upon very soft mattresses covered with vast carpets. A young serving man took the elder of our philosophers and led him into a separate little room. My demon called out to him that he must come back and join us as soon as he had eaten.

This whim of eating apart made me curious to ask the reason for it. 'He has no taste for the odour of meat,' he told me, 'or even that of vegetables, unless they have died a natural death, because he believes them capable of feeling pain.'

'I am not so surprised,' I replied, 'at his abstaining from flesh and all things that have once been sentient beings, for in our world the Pythagoreans and even some anchorite saints have adopted this regimen. But not to dare to cut a cabbage, for example, for fear of hurting it, seems to me totally ridiculous.'

'And I,' replied my demon, 'find his opinion very plausible.

'For tell me, is not this cabbage you mentioned just as much one of God's creatures as you? Are not God and necessity equally father and mother to both of you? Has not God throughout all eternity had His mind taken up with the question of its birth just as much as with yours? He would even appear to have provided more surely for that of the vegetable than for that of the reasoner, since he has entrusted the generation of a man to the caprices of his father, who can beget him or not as he likes—a hazard to which He did not, however, wish to subject the cabbage. Far from leaving the fertilization of sons to the discretion of their father, He seems to have feared the extinction of the race of cabbages more than that of the human race. He makes them give birth to one another willy nilly, unlike men, who only beget offspring when the fancy takes them and cannot produce more than a score at the most, while cabbages can produce four hundred thousand per head.

'To say that none the less God loves mankind more than cabbages is simply tickling ourselves to make ourselves laugh. Being incapable of passion, He can neither hate nor love anyone, and if He were capable of love He would have more tenderness for this cabbage you have in your hand, which cannot offend Him, than for this man, whose offences against Him He can already foresee and who would destroy Him if he could. Furthermore, a man cannot be born without crime, for he is a part of the first criminal: but we know very well that the first cabbage did not offend its Creator in the earthly paradise. It may be said that we are made in the image of the Sovereign Being whereas the cabbage is not. But even if this is true, in tarnishing our souls, which are what we resemble Him by, we have destroyed the likeness, since there is nothing more contrary to God than sin. And if our souls are no longer portraits of Him, we do not resemble Him any more with our feet, our hands, our mouths, our foreheads, and our eyes than the cabbage does with its leaves, its flowers, its stalks, its stem, and its head.

'Truly if this poor plant could speak, do you not think it would say when it is being cut: "Man, my dear brother, what have I done to you to deserve death? I only grow in your gardens. You will never find me growing wild in places where I could live in safety. I scorn to be the work of other hands than yours. Hardly am I sown in your garden when to show you my goodwill, I flourish, I stretch out my arms to you, I offer you my children in seed and yet as a reward for my courtesy you have my head cut off!"

'That is the speech this cabbage would make if it could express itself. But what happens? Because it cannot complain, does that mean we have the right to do it all the harm it cannot prevent? If I find a wretch in bonds, may I kill him without committing a crime just because he cannot defend himself? On the contrary, his impotence would make my cruelty worse, for, however poor and deprived of all our advantages this wretched creature may be, it does not deserve death. What! Of all the blessings of existence the only one it enjoys is that of vegetating and we deprive it of this! The sin of massacring a man is not so great—for one day he will live again—as that of cutting a cabbage and taking its life, since it cannot hope for any other. You are destroying the soul of a cabbage when you make it die, whereas by killing a man you merely make his soul change its abode.

'I will go further: since God, the common Father of all things, cherishes all His works equally, it would surely be reasonable for Him to have shared His benefits equally between us and the plants, so it is only just to consider them as our equals. It is true that we were born first, but in God's family there is no right of seniority. Therefore if cabbages were given no share in the fief of immortality along with us, they were doubtless endowed with some other gift which made up for its transience by its greatness. This may be a universal intellect, a perfect understanding of the causes of all things; and it may well be why the wise Mechanic did not fashion them organs like ours—which only produce mere reasoning, feeble and often misleading—but others, more ingeniously formed, more powerful and numerous, which serve them in conducting their speculative conversations. Now you may ask me what they have ever communicated to us of these great thoughts. But then what, pray, have the angels ever taught you, any more than these? Just as there is no correspondence, connexion, nor harmony between the imbecile faculties of man and the ones of those divine beings, so any attempt on the part of these intellectual cabbages to make us grasp the occult causes of all the wonders of the world would also be vain: we lack the senses capable of such lofty perception.

'Moses, the greatest of all philosophers, who drew his understanding of nature from the source of nature itself, pointed out this truth when he spoke of the Tree of Knowledge. He doubtless wanted to teach us, by means of this enigma, that plants are in possession of the perfect philosophy, to the exclusion of ourselves. Remember then, O most arrogant of all animals! that although the cabbage you cut may not utter a word, it is thinking just the same. The unfortunate vegetable has no organs suited to yelling like you; it has none for writhing, nor for weeping. But it has them, none

73

the less, for lamenting the wrong you do to it, and for bringing down the vengeance of heaven upon you.

'And if, in conclusion, you insist on asking me how I know that cabbages have these fine thoughts, I ask you how you know that they do *not*. How do you know that when one of them closes in the evening it does not say, in imitation of yourself: "I am, Sir Curly Kale, your most humble servant, Garden Cabbage"?'

7

Dinner with two philosophers: bodies great and small

HE had come to this point in his speech, when the young lad who had taken our philosopher out brought him back again.

'What's this! finished dinner already?' my demon called to him. He replied that he had, or almost, because the physiognomist had given him permission to have a taste of ours.

Our young host did not wait for me to ask him to explain the mystery. 'I can easily see,' he said, 'that this way of life surprises you. But you should know that although you are more negligent with your health in your world, our regimen here is not to be despised.

'In every house there is a physiognomist, supported at the public expense, who is more or less what would be called a doctor, where you come from, apart from the fact that he only looks after healthy people and only judges the various ways in which we must be treated from the proportion, shape, and symmetry of our limbs, the lineaments of our faces, the colouring of our flesh, the delicacy of our skin, the agility of our bodies, the sound of our voices, and the shade, strength, and hardness of our hair. Did you notice quite a short little man studying you just now? He is our physiognomist here. You may be certain that he varied the odours of your dinner in accordance with his diagnosis of your complexion. Look how far the mattress you were given to lie on is from our beds. Doubtless he judged you to be of a temperament far removed from ours, since he was afraid that the odour which arises from these little taps under our noses might spread across to you, or that yours might waft over to us. This evening you will see him choosing the flowers for your bed with the same circumspection.'

Throughout this discourse I was signalling to my young host for him to try and make the philosophers turn to some chapter of the science which they professed. He was too good a friend not to create the opportunity at once. In view of this, I will not recount to you the speeches and prayers which solicited the following treatise, since the nuance between parody and seriousness was too subtle for it to be possible to imitate it. At all events, reader, the most recently arrived of these learned doctors, after dealing with various matters, continued in this way:

'. . . It remains for me to prove that there are infinite worlds within an infinite world. Picture the universe, therefore, as a vast organism. Within this vast organism the stars, which are worlds, are like a further series of vast organisms, each serving inversely as the worlds of lesser populations such as ourselves, our horses, etc. We, in our turn, are also worlds from the point of view of certain organisms incomparably smaller than ourselves, like certain worms, lice, and mites. They are the earths of others, yet more imperceptible. So, just as each single one of us seems to this tiny people to be a great world, perhaps our flesh, our blood, and our minds are nothing but a tissue of little animals, nourishing themselves, lending us their movement, allowing themselves to be driven blindly by our will (which acts as their coachman), carrying us about, and all together producing that activity which we call life.

'For do you find it hard to believe that a louse should take your body for a world, or that, when one of them travels from one of your ears to the other, his friends should say that he has voyaged to the ends of the earth, or that he has journeyed from pole to pole? Why, doubtless this tiny people take your hair for the forests of their country, your pores full of sweat for springs, your pimples for lakes and ponds, your abscesses for seas, your streaming nose for a flood; and when you comb your hair backwards and forwards they think this is the ebb and flow of the ocean tides.

'Does not the itch prove my point? The mite which produces it is surely none other than one of these little animals, which has broken away from civil society and set itself up as a tyrant in its own country. If you ask me how such creatures come to be larger than the rest of their imperceptible fellows, I will ask you why elephants are bigger than us and Irishmen bigger than Spaniards. As for your blister and your scab, whose origins are unknown to you, they must either result from the rotting carcasses of enemies slaughtered by these little giants, or else a plague (caused by the lack of foodstuffs upon which the rebels have gorged themselves) has left behind heaps of corpses, or else the tyrant has driven away all his neighbours, whose bodies stopped up the pores in our own, thus making a passage for the phlegm, which then escapes from the bloodstream and becomes corrupted.

'It may be asked why one mite produces so many others. But this is not difficult to conceive, for just as one revolt produces another, so these little peoples are roused by the bad example of their seditious companions and each aspires to take command, enflaming war, massacre, and famine all around.

' "But," you will tell me, "some people are much less subject to the itch than others, although all of them are equally filled with these little animals, since it is they—you say—who make up life." This is true, but let us also observe that phlegmatic people are less a prey to scratching than choleric people, for the reason that, in accordance with the climate they inhabit, the peoples in a cold body are more lethargic than those heated by the temperature of a homeland which crackles, shifts, and cannot remain in one place. Thus the choleric man is much more delicate than the phlegmatic, because he is animated in many more parts of his body, and as his being is made up of the action of these little beasts he is sensitive in all the places where their herds are stirring. On the other hand the phlegmatic man is not hot enough to make this mobile population active, save in a few places, and is therefore only sensitive in a few places.

'As further proof of this universal mite-system, you need only consider how when you are wounded the blood runs to the wound. Your doctors say that it is guided by nature seeking to help the weakened parts, but that is just a pretty fantasy, for in that case there would have to be a third intellectual substance in us, apart from mind and soul, with separate functions and separate organs. That is why I find it much more plausible to say that these little animals, finding themselves attacked, send word to their neighbours to ask for help. When they are gathered together from all sides, the country is unable to support so many and they either die of hunger or are suffocated in the throng. These deaths occur when the abscess is ripe and the fact that the rotten flesh goes numb proves that these creatures are stifled then. If the bleeding, which is prescribed to divert the flow, does very often take effect, this is because the little animals have already lost many of their number through the opening they were trying to block and now refuse to assist their allies, having barely the strength to defend themselves, each on their own ground.'

He had concluded in this way when the second philosopher found all our eyes focused upon his, exhorting him to speak in his turn.

'Men,' he said, 'seeing that you are interested in teaching this little animal, our fellow creature, something of the science which we profess, I shall be very pleased to supply him with a treatise which I am now dictating, on account of the illuminating light it sheds on our physics: it is an explanation of the eternal origin of the world. But I am in a hurry to start my bellows working, as the town is leaving tomorrow without delay, so I hope you will excuse me for the moment, with the promise, however, that as soon as it arrives at its destination, I will satisfy you.'

At these words the host's son called his father to know what time it was, but when the latter replied that eight o'clock had struck, he flew into a rage and asked him why he had not notified them when it was seven, as he had commanded him to do: he knew very well that the houses were leaving next day and the town walls had done so already.

'My son,' replied the good man, 'an express prohibition has been published while you were at table, forbidding anyone to leave until the day after tomorrow.'

'That makes no difference,' retorted the young man. 'You should obey me blindly, without trying to understand my orders, and only remember what I have commanded. Quickly now, go and fetch your effigy!'

When it was brought he seized it by the arm and whipped it for a good quarter of an hour. 'Now, sir, you good-for-nothing,' he went on, 'as a punishment for your disobedience I will make a laughing-stock of you today, for all to see, and to this end I command you to walk upon two legs only for the rest of the day.'

The poor old man went out in floods of tears and his son continued: 'Gentlemen, I must ask you to excuse the knaveries of this hot-headed fellow. I had hopes of making something of him, but he has abused my indulgence. For my part, I believe the rascal will be the death of me. To tell you the truth, I have been on the verge of cutting him off with my curse ten times already.'

I found it very difficult, although I bit my lips, to keep myself from laughing at this topsy-turvy world. So, in order to have done with his burlesque of discipline, which would doubtless have ended by making me guffaw, I begged him to tell me what he meant by this journey of the town's he had mentioned just now, and whether the houses and walls actually travelled.

He replied to me: 'Among our towns, dear stranger, there are both mobile and sedentary ones. The mobile ones, like the one we are in now, for example, are made in the following manner. The architect constructs each mansion of a very light wood, as you can see; underneath it he installs four wheels; in the thickness of one of the walls he sets ten large pairs of bellows, whose nozzles lie in a horizontal line across the top storey from gable to gable, so that when we want to drive the towns somewhere else (for they have a change of air for each of the seasons) everyone unfurls a quantity of large sails on one of the sides of his house in front of the bellows. Then when a mechanism has been wound up to make them work, in less than a week their houses can be transported over a hundred leagues, if it is desired, by the constant blasts vomited from these wind-monsters.

'As for those which we call "sedentary", the dwellings there are very like your towers, except that they are made of wood and have a huge and powerful screw running through the centre of them from cellar to roof, so that they can be raised and lowered at discretion. A hollow is dug out of the earth, as deep as the building is high, and the whole is constructed in this way so that, as soon as the frosts begin to chill the heavens, they can lower their houses into the earth, where they remain in shelter from the inclemencies of the air. But immediately the gentle breezes of spring arrive to soften it, they come up into the light by means of the great screw I have told you of.'

I begged him, since he had already shown me so much kindness and the town was only leaving on the following day, to tell me something of that eternal origin of the world, which he had mentioned to me some time before. 'And I promise you,' I said to him, 'that in recompense, as soon as I return to the moon from whence my tutor (I indicated my demon) will bear witness to you that I have come, I will spread your reputation there, by recounting the fine things which you have told me. It is easy to see that this promise makes you laugh, because you do not believe that the moon I speak of is a world or that I am an inhabitant of it; but I can also assure you that the peoples of that world, who take this one for a mere moon, will make fun of me when I say that your moon is a world with landscapes and inhabitants.'

To this he merely replied with a smile and then spoke these words: 'Since, when we want to come at the origin of this great Whole, we are bound to run up against three or four absurdities, it is reasonable enough to take the road which makes us stumble the least. I say, then, that the first obstacle standing in our way is the eternity of the universe. Since men's minds were not powerful enough to conceive of this and were not capable, moreover, of imagining how this great cosmos, so beautiful and so well ordered, could have made itself, they have had recourse to the idea of Creation. But like the man who plunges into a river for fear of being soaked by the rain, they escape from the clutches of a dwarf only to find themselves at the mercy of a giant. Besides they do not escape: this eternity of which they rob the universe, because they fail to understand it, they then give to God—as if He needed the gift, and as if it were easier to conceive of in the one than in the other! So this absurdity, or this giant I spoke of, is their Creation. For tell me truly, has anyone even been able to imagine how something could be made from nothing? Alas! there is such an infinite difference between nothing and a single atom that the sharpest brain could not fathom it. In order to escape this inexplicable labyrinth, you have to admit the eternity of matter as well as God, and then it is no longer necessary to admit a God because the universe could have existed without Him.

' "But," you will say, "supposing I grant you the eternity of matter, how did this chaos order itself on its own?" Aha! I will explain to you.

'One must, O my little animal, first mentally divide every tiny visible body into an infinity of tiny invisible bodies and think of the universe as being composed of nothing but these infinite atoms, which are quite solid, quite incorruptible and quite simple and some of which are cubic, some parallelogrammatic, some angular, some round, some pointed, some pyramidal, some hexagonal, some oval—all behaving diversely, each according to its shape. Now if you take a round ivory ball and place it upon a very flat surface, at the slightest touch you give it, it will roll for seven minutes without stopping: and let me add that if it were as perfectly round as some of these atoms I am speaking of, and the surface on which it was placed were completely flat, it would never stop. If art, therefore, is capable of making a body inclined to perpetual motion, why should we not believe that nature can do it? It is the same with the other shapes: ones like the square seek a state of perpetual repose, others a sideways motion, others quiver in a partial movement: and when one of the round ones, whose essence is to move, comes into conjunction with one of the pyramidal ones, it may well be that they produce what we call "fire", because fire not only moves restlessly, it also pierces and penetrates easily. Apart from this, the flame behaves differently, according to the type and size of the angles made between the pyramid and the sphere: so the flame produced by pepper, for example, is quite a different thing from a sugar flame: sugar produces a different one from cinnamon, cinnamon from cloves, and this last differs from the flame of a burning faggot.

'It is fire, the builder and designer of both the parts and the whole of the universe, which has drawn together and assembled in this oak tree the quantity of shapes needed to compose it. "But," you will say to me, "how can all the elements needed to produce this oak tree be gathered together in one place by chance?" My reply to you is that it is no marvel for the matter thus arranged to have formed an oak tree, although it would have been a great marvel if the matter were arranged thus and an oak tree had not been produced. A few less of some shapes and it would have been an elm, a poplar or a willow. A few less of certain others and it would have been a *mimosa pudica*, an oyster in its shell, a worm, a fly, a frog, a sparrow, an ape, a man. When you throw three dices upon a table and a triple two comes up, or three, four, and five, or two sixes and a one, you will say: "Oh, what a miracle! The same number has come up on all the dice, although so many numbers could have done!" "Oh, what a miracle! three consecutive numbers have come up!" "Oh, what a miracle! Just two sixes have come up and the opposite side of the other six!"

'But no, I am sure that being a man of intelligence, you will never make such exclamations, since the numbers on the dice are limited and it is impossible for one of them not to come up. Yet you are still astonished at the way this matter, mixed up pell-mell at the whim of chance, could have produced a man, seeing how many things were necessary for the construction of his person. Are you not aware that this matter has stopped a million times on its way towards the formation of a man, sometimes to make a stone, sometimes a lump of lead, sometimes coral, sometimes a flower, sometimes a comet? All this happened because there were more or less of certain shapes, which were necessary, or certain shapes, which were superfluous to the design of man. Hence it is no marvel that they should have come together, from among an infinity of substances which are shifting and changing incessantly, to make the few animals, vegetables, and minerals which we see, any more than it is a marvel for a triple number to come up in a hundred throws of the dice, since it is impossible for this movement not to produce something. And a fool will always marvel at this thing, not knowing how near it came to not being made.

'If the great river of ⸺ turns a mill and drives the mechanisms of a clock, while the little stream of ⸺ does nothing but flow along, sometimes hiding underground, you would not say that the river has great intelligence, because you know that it simply meets in its path the devices put there to produce all these masterpieces of artifice. Were the mill not situated on its course, it would not grind any wheat. Had it never encountered the clock, it would not tell the time. And if the little stream I mentioned had had the same encounters, it would have performed the same miracles. It is just the same with this fire, which moves by itself. Where it has met organs suited to the kind of vibration necessary for reasoning, it has reasoned. Where it has found those suited only to feeling, it has felt. Where it has found them suited for vegetating, it has vegetated. Morevoer, if one puts out this man's eyes, which the fire of his soul causes to see, he will no longer see, just as our great clock will cease to mark the hours if you break the mechanism.

'Lastly, these primary and indivisible atoms offer us a wheel on which the most problematical difficulties of physics will run smoothly. There is nothing, not even the operation of the senses, which I cannot easily explain by means of these little bodies. Let us begin with sight, which, as the most mysterious of them, is worthy of our first attempts.

'To my way of thinking, this occurs when the outer coats of the eye, which have openings in them similar to those in glass, send out the fire dust known as sight-rays and it is stopped by some opaque matter which makes it rebound back to its home. On its way this dust meets the image of the object that repulsed it, which consists of nothing but an infinite number of tiny bodies continually and evenly given off by the subject observed, and it drives them back to our eye. You are sure to object to me that glass is an opaque body and very compact, yet nevertheless, instead of repulsing the first little bodies, it allows itself to be penetrated by them. But my answer to you is that the pores in glass are the same shape as the atoms of fire which pass through it: just as a wheat sieve is no good for sifting oats, nor an oats sieve for sifting wheat. Similarly a deal box, although it is thin and lets sounds through, is not penetrable to sight; whereas a piece of crystal is transparent and penetrable to sight, but one cannot touch things through it.'

I could not help interrupting him here. 'A great poet and philosopher of our world,' I told him, 'following Epicurus, who followed Democritus, has spoken of these little bodies

almost in the way you have, so your discourse does not surprise me at all. Please tell me, when you continue, how you
can explain by these principles the way one's image is reflected in a mirror.'

'That is quite easy,' he replied. 'You must picture these fires
from your eye passing through the glass, encountering behind
it a non-diaphanous body, which repulses them, and returning the way they came. Meeting more of these little bodies
travelling evenly towards the mirror, they call them back to
our eyes, from whence our imagination, being warmer than
the other faculties of our soul, draws the most subtle of them
and from them makes itself a portrait in miniature.

'The operation of hearing is not more difficult to conceive
and for the sake of brevity let us simply consider the case of
the notes of a lute touched by the hands of a virtuoso. You
will ask me how I can possibly perceive something so far away
from me and which I cannot see at all. Does a sponge come
out of my ears and soak up this music in order to bring it to
me? Or does the musician beget another little musician inside
my head with a little lute and instructions to sing the same
tunes to me like an echo? No; the miracle is due to the fact
that the plucked string strikes the air which is composed of
little bodies and drives it into my brain, gently piercing it
with these little bodily nothings. If the string is taut the note
is high, because it drives the atoms more vigorously and once
the organ is thus penetrated it furnishes my imagination with
sufficient of them from which to make its picture. If it is not so
taut, it happens that when our memory has not yet completed
its image, we are obliged to repeat the same sound to it; so
that, for example, from the materials furnished by the
measures of a saraband, it takes enough to complete the portrait of this saraband.

'But this operation is by no means as wonderful as those by
which we are moved now to joy, now to anger with the aid of
the same organ. This occurs when in the course of their movement the little bodies meet others inside us which are moving
in the same manner, or whose own shape makes them suscep-

tible to the same type of vibration. The new arrivals excite their hosts to imitate their motion and in this way when a violent tune encounters the fire of our blood, it makes it take up the same dance and excites it to thrust itself outwards, and that is what we call "the ardour of courage". If the sound is sweeter and has only the strength to raise a lesser, more quavering flame, by causing this to travel along the nerves and membranes and through the apertures in our flesh, it excites that tickling sensation which we call "joy". The other passions are aroused in the same way, according to the greater or lesser violence with which these little bodies are hurled at us, according to the motion resulting from their contact with other impulses and according to the mobility they find in us. So much then for hearing.

'The demonstration of the sense of touch is now no more difficult, if one imagines that there is a perpetual emission of little bodies from all palpable matter and that when we touch it, still more of them evaporate off it because they are squeezed out of the object—just like water from a sponge when we press it. The hard ones come to the organ of touch to make a report of their solidity, the supple ones of their softness, the rough ones, etc. Moreover, when our hands are worn with work they are no longer so sensitive to touch, for the thick callosity, being neither porous nor animated itself, only transmits these vapours of matter with great difficulty.

'Does someone desire to learn where the sense of touch has its seat? For my part I think it is spread over all the surfaces of the body, seeing that this can feel with all its parts. I do believe, however, that the closer the organ we feel with is to our heads, the quicker we can make things out. This can be tested by closing our eyes and feeling something with our hands, for we can guess what it is more easily than if we felt it with our foot instead, when we should have some difficulty in recognizing it. This is due to the fact that, our skin being riddled all over with little holes, our nerves, whose substance is no more compact, lose many of these little atoms on the way, through the tiny gaps in their fabric, before they have reached the brain which is their destination. It remains for me to speak of smell and of taste.

'Tell me now, when I taste a fruit, is it not the heat of my mouth that makes it melt? Admit to me that, since there are salts in a pear which split up, when they dissolve, into little bodies of a different shape from those which make up the taste of an apple, they are bound to pierce our palate in a very different fashion. In the same way the wound made by the blade of a pike going through me is not like the blow from a pistol bullet, just as the pain from a pistol bullet is different from the one imprinted by a lozenge of steel.

'Of smell I have nothing to say, since your philosophers themselves confess it to be produced by a continual emission of little bodies.

'On this principle I am now going to explain to you the Creation, the harmony and influences of the celestial globes, and the immutable variety of the meteors.'

8

Some lunar customs and inventions

HE was going to continue, but at this point the old host came in, which made our philosopher think of retiring. Our host was carrying glass vessels filled with glow-worms to illuminate the room. But as these little insect-fires lose much of their brilliance when they are not freshly gathered, this collection, being ten days old, shed hardly any light at all. Without waiting for the company to be inconvenienced by this, my demon went up to his chamber and came down at once with two balls of fire so brilliant that everyone was astonished he did not burn his fingers.

'These incombustible torches,' he said, 'will serve us better than your bunches of worms. They are rays of the sun, which I have purged of their heat, otherwise the corrosive properties of its fire would have damaged your eyes by dazzling them. I have trapped their light and enclosed it in these transparent balls which I have here. This should give you no great cause for amazement since it is just as easy for me, a native of the sun, to bottle its rays, which are the dust of that world, as it is for you to gather up the dust or atoms which are the pulverized earth of this one.'

Our host then dispatched a servant to escort the philosophers, because it was dark, with a dozen globes of worms suspended from his four legs. As for the rest of us (to wit, my preceptor and myself), we went to bed according to the physiognomist's orders. This time he put me in a chamber of violets and lilies and sent them to tickle me as usual. At nine the following day I saw my demon coming in and he told me

he had come from the palace, where ▬▬▬▬▬, one of the

Queen's ladies-in-waiting, had begged him to go and visit her. She had inquired after me, vowing that she still firmly intended to keep the promise she had given me, namely that she would cheerfully follow me if I would take her with me to the other world.

'What greatly edified me,' he continued, 'was to learn that the principal motive for her journey was to become a Christian. I therefore gave my word to assist her scheme to the extent of my powers and for this purpose to invent a machine capable of holding three or four persons, in which you can travel up there together this very day. I am going to apply myself seriously to the execution of this undertaking and so for your entertainment, while I am not with you, here is a book, which I will leave with you. I brought it back from my native land long ago. It is entitled: *The States and Empires of the Sun*, together with the *History of the Spark*. I am giving you this one besides, which I regard much more highly. It is *The Great Works of the Philosophers* composed by one of the best brains upon the sun. In it he proves that all things are true and states how the truths of all contradictions may be reconciled physically, such as for example that white

is black and black is white; that one can be and not be at the
same time; that there can be hills without valleys; that
nothingness is something and that everything, which is, is not.
But take note that he proves all these unheard-of paradoxes
without any fallacious or sophistical reasoning.

'When you are tired of reading, you can take a walk or converse with our host's son. His wit is quite delightful: what dis-
pleases me in him is his impiety. If he should chance to
scandalize you or to undermine your faith with any of his
arguments, you must not fail to come and put it to me at once
and I will resolve the difficulties for you. Anyone else would
order you to leave his company, when he desires to philosophize on such matters, but as he is extremely vain I am
certain that he would take your flight for defeat and begin to
imagine that our beliefs were not founded upon good reasons
if you refused to listen to his. Reflect how you may live
freely!'

With these words he left me, for in that country they are the
valediction with which one takes leave of someone, just as
'good day' or 'your servant, Sir,' is expressed by this compliment: 'Love me, sage, for I love you.' But he was hardly gone
before I began to examine my books attentively, as well as
their boxes, that is to say their covers, which seemed to me
admirable in their richness. One was carved out of a single
diamond, which was more brilliant beyond compare than any
of ours. The second appeared to be nothing but a monstrous
pearl split in two. My demon had translated the books into
the language of that world, but since I have none of their
print I am simply going to explain what these two volumes
were like.

On opening a box, I discovered in it a metal object, not
unlike one of our clocks, which was filled with all manner of
tiny springs and mysterious machines. It was a book indeed,
but a miraculous book, with neither pages nor letters: it was,
in short, a book where the eyes were useless for reading and
for which only the ears were needed. When someone desires to
'read,' he winds up this machine with a great quantity of little

threads of all kinds, then he turns the needle to the chapter he wishes to hear and at once there issue from it, as from the mouth of a man or from a musical instrument, all the distinct and different sounds which the great lunarians employ for the expression of their language.

When I have later reflected upon this miraculous invention for making books, I am no longer astonished to see how the young men in that country possessed more understanding at sixteen or eighteen than the greybeards do in ours, since, knowing how to read as soon as they can talk, they are never without reading matter. In their room, on a walk, in town, or on a journey they can carry some thirty of these books in their pockets or slung from their belts. They have only to wind up a spring in order to hear a single chapter, or several, indeed, if they are in a mood to listen to a whole book. Thus you can have all the great men, both dead and alive, perpetually about you, to address you *viva voce*.

This gift occupied me more than an hour. Finally, having attached them to myself in the form of ear pendants, I went out for a walk, but as soon as I had reached the end of the road, I met quite a large company of sorrowful people. Four of them were carrying a kind of coffin on their shoulders, draped in black. I enquired from a bystander the significance of this procession, so like the funeral ceremonies of my own country. He replied that the wicked ▬▬▬▬ , whose name in the common people's jargon was a fillip of the finger on the right knee, who had been convicted of envy and ingratitude, had deceased the day before and that Parliament had condemned him more than twenty years previously to die a natural death in his bed and then be buried after death.

I began to laugh at this reply and when he asked me why, I said: 'You astonish me by saying that what are marks of blessedness in our world, such as a long life, a peaceful death and an honourable burial, should serve in this one as an exemplary punishment.'

'What! You take burial for a mark of blessedness!' this man retorted. 'By your faith, can you conceive of anything more frightful than a corpse brim-full of crawling worms, at the mercy of the toads which gnaw at its cheeks—in short, the plague clothed in the body of a man? Good God! The very idea, even in death, of having one's face smothered with a cloth and a clod of earth upon one's mouth almost chokes my breath! This wretched man you see being carried has, in addition to the disgrace of being thrown into a ditch, been condemned to be accompanied in procession by a hundred and fifty of his friends. As a punishment for having loved an envious and ungrateful man, they are commanded to appear at his funeral with sad faces, and if the judges had not had pity on him, imputing his crimes partly to his meagre intelligence, they would have ordered that there should be weeping!

'Apart from criminals, everyone here is burnt and it is a very decent and reasonable custom, for we believe that when the fire has separated the purities from the impurities, the heat draws together, by sympathetic attraction, all the natural warmth which made up the soul and gives it sufficient strength to rise steadily. When it has ascended as high as a star (which is in fact the earth of some peoples more immaterial and more intellectual than us, since their temperament must correspond and contribute to the purity of the globe they inhabit), the original flame is further refined by the subtlety of this world's elements and it comes to form one of the citizens of this fiery country.

'But this is still not our most beautiful method of sepulture. When one of our philosophers reaches an age at which he feels his mind growing weak and the ice of his years freezing the passions of his soul, he summons his friends to a sumptuous banquet. When he has explained his reasons for resolving to take leave of nature and the small hope there is of his adding anything more to his fine actions, he is either given grace, that is to say he is ordered to die, or else he is given a severe commandment to live. When his life's breath has been put into his own hands by a majority vote, he informs his dearest friends of the time and place appointed. They purge themselves and fast for twenty-four hours and when they have arrived at the sage's house and sacrificed to the sun, they enter the chamber where the noble man awaits them on a cere-monial bed. Each man wishes to embrace him and when it is the turn of the one he loves the best and he has kissed him tenderly, he supports him on his stomach, joins his mouth with the other man's and with his right hand plunges a dagger into his own heart. The loved one does not remove his lips from those of his beloved until he feels him expire, and then he withdraws the steel from his breast and, closing the wound with his mouth, he drinks his blood, which he continues sucking until a second takes his place, then a third, a fourth and finally the whole company: and four or five hours after-wards a girl of sixteen or seventeen is brought to each of them and during the three or four days which they spend in tasting the pleasures of love, they are only nourished from the flesh of the dead man, which they are made to eat quite raw. Thus if anything may be born of a hundred embraces, they are assured that it is their friend who lives again.'

I interrupted this discourse by telling the speaker that these customs had much in common with those of a people in our world and continued my walk, which was so long that when I returned, dinner had been ready for two hours. I was asked why I had arrived so late.

'It was not my fault,' I replied to the cook, who was grum-bling about it. 'I frequently asked people the time in the streets but they only replied by opening their mouths, clench-ing their teeth and turning their faces askew.'

'What!' exclaimed all the company, 'do you not know that in this way they are telling you the time?'

'By my faith,' I retorted, 'what was the good of them ex-posing their great noses to the sun for me to find out?'

'It is a device,' they told me, 'which enables them to do without a clock; for with their teeth they make a sundial so precise, that when they want to tell anyone the time they open their lips and the shadow of this nose falling upon their teeth indicates what the questioner is anxious to know, just like a sundial. Now, in case you want to know why everyone in this country has a large nose, learn that as soon as a woman is brought to bed, the midwife takes the child to the Prior of the Seminary and if at the end of the year when the experts are assembled, its nose is found shorter than a certain measure kept by the Syndic, it is declared snub-nosed and handed over to people who castrate it. You will ask me the cause of this barbarousness and how it can be that we, among whom virginity is a crime, should establish continence by force. But learn that we do it after having observed for thirty centuries that a large nose is the mark of a witty, courteous, affable, generous, and liberal man and that a small one is a mark of the opposite. That is why we make eunuchs of our snub-nosed babies, because the Republic would rather have no children, than any more like these.'

He was still speaking when I saw a completely naked man coming in. I sat down at once and put my hat on, for these are the marks of the greatest respect one can show anyone in that country.

'The Realm,' he said, 'desires that before returning to your world, you should notify the Magistrates, because a mathematician has just promised the Council that, provided when you return home you are willing to construct a certain machine according to his instructions, he will attract your globe and join it to this one.'

I promised not to fail in this.

'Now tell me, pray,' I said to my young host when the other man had gone, 'why that ambassador carries *pudenda* made of bronze at his belt.' Indeed I had observed this a number of times when I was in my cage, without daring to ask about it, since I was always surrounded by the Queen's ladies-in-waiting, whom I feared to offend if I had turned the conversation to so coarse a topic in their presence.

In reply to me he said: 'The females here are not, any more than the males, so ungrateful as to blush at the sight of that which forged them, and virgins are not ashamed to admire upon us in memory of their mother, nature, the only thing which bears her name. Know then that the sash with which this man is honoured and from which the image of a virile phallus hangs as a medal, is the symbol of the gentleman and the mark which distinguishes the nobleman from the commoner.'

This paradox seemed to me so extravagant that I could not keep myself from laughing. 'It seems a most extraordinary custom to me,' I retorted, 'for in our world the mark of nobility is to carry a sword.'

But without losing his composure my host cried out: 'Oh, indeed, my little man! So the great ones in your world are frantic to parade an instrument which designates the executioner and is only forged to destroy us—in short, the sworn enemy of all living things, and on the contrary to hide an organ without which we should be among the ranks of the non-existent, the Prometheus of every animal and the tireless repairer of the weaknesses of nature! Unhappy country where the symbols of generation are ignominious and those of destruction are honourable! Yet you call that organ your *pudenda*, as if there could be anything more glorious than giving life and anything more shameful than taking it.'

During all this discourse we continued dining, and as soon as we had risen from the table we went into the garden to take the air.

9

The fate of an unbeliever

For a while the events of our walk and the beauty of the place occupied all our attention but, as I itched more than anything with a most noble longing to convert to our religion a soul so highly elevated above the common herd, I exhorted him a thousand times over not to sully with material considerations the fine genius which heaven had bestowed on him, and to rescue from the throng of the animals a spirit capable of the vision of God. Lastly I urged him seriously to consider the prospect of one day seeing his immortality spent in a state of bliss rather than one of pain.

'What!' he answered with a shout of laughter, 'do you hold your soul to be immortal to the exclusion of the beasts? To be frank with you, my dear friend, you have a most insolent pride. From whence, pray, do you deduce this immortality at the expense of the beasts? Might it be because we are gifted with reason and they are not? In the first place I deny this and I will prove to you, any time you please, that they can think just like us. But even if it were true and reason had been handed out to us as a prerogative, a privilege reserved solely for our species, would this mean that God must enrich man with immortality because He had already lavished reason upon him? Then, by that reckoning, I must give this pauper a pistole today because I gave him a crown yesterday? You can see for yourself the fallacy in this logic and that, on the contrary, if I am just, instead of giving this man a pistole, I should give the next man a crown, because he has had nothing from me. And from that one must conclude, O my dear companion, that God, being yet a thousand times more just than us, would not have given everything to some and left nothing for the others. You may cite the example of the elder sons in your world who carry off almost all the goods in the house as their patrimony. This, however, is a weakness on the part of their fathers, who want to perpetuate their name and are afraid of it being ruined or lost through poverty. But God, who is incapable of errors, would certainly take good care not to commit such a great one, and besides, since there is neither a before nor an after in God's eternity, in His sight juniors are no younger than seniors.'

I will not conceal the fact that these arguments shook me.

'If you will allow me,' I said, 'I will drop this subject, because I do not feel confident enough to answer you. I am going to our common mentor to seek the solution to the difficulty.'

Without waiting for his reply, I went up at once to the ingenious demon's room and, dispensing with all preliminaries, I put before him the objection that had just been made to me concerning the immortality of our souls and here is how he answered me:

'Well, my son, so this young hothead is eager to convince you that man's soul is not likely to be immortal, since God, who calls Himself the common father of all beings, would not be so unjust as to have given one species all the advantages while generally abandoning the others to oblivion or unhappiness. These arguments, it is true, have a certain superficial brilliance. I could, of course, ask him how he knows that what is just for us, should also be just for God; how he knows that God measures Himself by our yardstick; how he knows that our laws and customs, which were instituted merely to remedy our own disorders, are also used to apportion God's omnipotence. But I will pass over all these things, together with all that the Fathers of your Church have so divinely replied upon this matter and uncover a mystery which has hitherto never been revealed.

'You know, O my son, how earth turns into a tree, the tree into a pig, the pig into a man. Can we not believe that, since all things in nature tend towards perfection, they all aspire to become men, this state being the achievement of the finest and best conceived compound in the world, because it is the only one which links the life of the brutes with that of the angels? Only a pedant will deny that these metamorphoses take place. We can see how the plum tree sucks up, as if with a mouth, and digests the surrounding turf by means of its inner heat. A pig devours the fruit and turns it into a part of itself and a man, by eating the pig, resuscitates this dead flesh, joins it to himself, and makes the animal live again, as a more noble species. Thus the great pontiff you see with a mitre on his head was perhaps sixty years ago a tuft of grass in my garden. If God is the common father of all His creatures, loving them all equally, is it not highly likely that when—by means of this metempsychosis, more logical than the Pythagorean—all sentient and vegetative beings and, in short, all matter has passed through man, then will come the great Day of Judgement, which the prophets make the culmination of all the secrets of their philosophy.'

I went down to the garden very satisfied and I was beginning to recite to my companion what our master had taught me, when the physiognomist arrived to conduct us to the dining room and the dormitory.

As soon as I was awake the following day, I went off to rouse my antagonist. 'It is as great a miracle,' I greeted him, 'to find a powerful mind like yours entombed in sleep, as to see a flame standing still.' This doubtful compliment caused him some discomfort.

'But will you never,' he cried in a rage, passionate with affection for me, 'rid your lips and your brain of these mythical expressions like "miracle"? You should know that such names disgrace the name of philosopher and that as the wise man sees nothing in the world which he does not comprehend or judge capable of comprehension, he must abhor all such terms as "miracles", "prodigies", and "unnatural events", which stupid people have invented to excuse the feebleness of their own intellects.'

I then thought myself obliged in conscience to speak and undeceive him. 'Even though you do not believe in miracles,' I replied, 'they happen just the same, many of them. I have seen them with my own eyes. I have known more than twenty sick men miraculously cured.'

'You say,' he interrupted, 'that these people were cured by a miracle, but you do not realize that the power of the imagination is capable of all the cures which you attribute to supernatural causes, on account of a certain natural balm, which is distributed throughout our bodies, containing antidotes to each of the illnesses which attacks us. This happens when our imagination, alerted by the pain, seeks out and selects the specific remedy and brings it to the poison. That is why, in our world, a good doctor will advise a sick man to go to an ignorant doctor, who is reputed to be clever, rather than to an able one with a reputation for ignorance. For he will be of the opinion that if our imagination works for our health, it is capable of curing us, providing it is aided by remedies, whereas the most powerful of these are too weak if the imagination does not come to their assistance.

'Are you surprised that the first men in your world lived for so many centuries without any knowledge of medicine? No. And what do you think the reason could be, if it was not the original resilience of their constitutions and the universal balm—that your doctor's drugs, which are now using you up, have still not succeeded in dissipating? In order to achieve convalescence in those days, they had only to desire it strongly and imagine themselves to be cured. Their vigorous imagination would plunge into this vital oil and draw forth the elixir, and by applying an active remedy to the passive disease, they found themselves as healthy as before, almost in the twinkling of an eye. Despite the corruption of nature, this still continues to happen today—although rather rarely, in fact—and the populace attribute it to a miracle. But for my part, I do not believe that at all, basing my opinion on the fact that it is easier for all the doctors to be mistaken than for this not to be so.

'For I say to them: during the course of his illness it seems likely that this man, who has just recovered from a fever, very much desired to be cured and even made vows to this end. Now he was absolutely bound either to die, or to remain sick, or to get well. If he had died it would have been said that God wanted to recompense him for his suffering (or one might even indulge in malicious irony and say that He had indeed heard the sick man's prayers and cured him of all his ills!). If he had remained unwell it would have been said that he had no faith. But since he is cured it is "quite evidently" a miracle! Yet is it not much more probable that his imagination, excited by his violent desire for health, has done its work? In this example I let the man be cured, but why cry "miracle", since we can see so many people who have also made vows, perishing miserably, along with their vows?'

'But at the very least,' I retorted, 'if what you say about this balm is true, it indicates that our souls are endowed with reason. For without employing the instruments of our reason, without relying upon the co-operation of our will, they act independently, as if they were outside us, in applying active to passive. Now if they are both detached from us and reasonable, they must of necessity be spiritual: and if you admit that they are spiritual, then I must conclude that they are immortal—since death in animals only takes place through a transformation of forms which matter alone can adopt.'

The young man then sat up on his bed, made me sit down, and held forth more or less as follows: 'As for the souls of beasts, which are corporeal, I am not surprised that they should die, seeing that they are conceivably no more than a harmony of the four qualities, a strength of the blood and a proportion of organs well attuned to one another. But I am very surprised that ours, if they are intellectual, disembodied, and immortal, should be forced to leave us by the same causes which make an ox die. Has your soul made a pact with your body, that when the latter receives a sword thrust through the heart, a ball of lead through the brain or a hail of musket shot through the torso, it will abandon its riddled house at once? If so, it must often break its contract—for some men die of a wound from which others will recover—or else each soul must have struck a special bargain with its own body. To be frank with you, if it has as much wit as we are led to believe, it is quite mad to leave its lodging at all, when it sees that on its departure from there it will be allotted to an apartment in hell!

'And if this soul were as clever and as independently reasonable as they say, and as capable of intelligence, when it is separate from our bodies, as when it is clothed in them, why cannot people born blind, with all the marvellous advantages of this intellectual soul, imagine what it is like to see? Why cannot the deaf hear? Is it perhaps because they have not yet been deprived by death of all the rest of their senses? So I suppose I cannot use my right hand because I still have a left one? They claim to prove that it could not function without the senses even if it were spiritual, by taking the example of a painter, who cannot paint a picture if he has no brushes. Yes, but that is not to say that if this painter, who cannot work without brushes, had lost, as well as his brushes, his colours, his chalks, his canvases, and his palettes, he could then work better. Quite the contrary! The more obstacles there are standing in the way of his work, the more impossible it will be for him to paint. And yet they would have it that this soul, which can only function imperfectly during the course of life on account of the loss of one of its tools, can none the less operate to perfection when it has lost them all after death. But if they come harping to me on the theme that it does not need these instruments to perform its functions, I shall harp to them on the theme that the inmates of the Quinze Vingts Hospital for the Blind must be whipped for pretending not to see a thing.'

'But,' I said to him, 'if our souls were to die, as I see you wish to conclude, the Resurrection to which we look forward would be nothing but an illusion, for God would have to create them all over again—and that would not be resurrection.'

He interrupted me with a toss of his head. 'Eh? What's all this, in heaven's name?' he cried. 'Who has been putting you to sleep with that fairy story? What! You? What! Me? What! My chambermaid? Brought to life?'

'It is not,' I replied, 'a story made up for amusement: it is an indubitable truth, which I will prove to you.'

'And I,' he said, 'will prove the contrary to you.

'Let us begin by supposing that you eat a Mohammedan. Consequently you convert him into your substance! For is it not true that this Mohammedan, when digested, is transformed partly into flesh, partly into blood, and partly into sperm? You then lie with your wife and cast a handsome little Christian into the matrix with seed entirely drawn from the Mohammedan corpse. My question is: will the Mohammedan ultimately get his body back? If the earth gives it back to him, the little Christian will not get his, since he is, in his entirety, nothing but a part of the Mohammedan's. But if you tell me that the little Christian will have his, that means that God will be taking away from the Mohammedan what the little Christian had only received from him. Thus one or other of them is bound to lack a body!

'Now you may reply that God will produce more matter to provide for the one who has not enough. Yes, but then another obstacle holds us up, which is that when the damned Mohammedan is resuscitated and God provides him with a completely new body (on account of his old one being stolen from him by the Christian), since the body alone does not make the man, any more than the soul (each being as much an integral part of the man as the other), if God models a fresh body for this Mohammedan, he is no longer the same individual. So God damns a different man from the one who deserves hell. This body has fornicated, this body has criminally abused all its senses—and in order to punish it, God throws a different one into the flames, one which is virgin, which is pure, which has never lent its organs to the commission of the smallest crime! And what is even more ridiculous is that this body deserves hell and paradise at the same time, for, as a Mohammedan it must be damned and as a Christian it must be saved. God cannot send it to paradise without being unjust and rewarding it with glory in place of the damnation it earned as a Mohammedan. He cannot hurl it into hell without being equally unjust, rewarding it with eternal death, instead of the blessedness it had earned as a Christian. If He wishes to be fair, He must both damn and save this man eternally.'

I then spoke in my turn. 'I have nothing to reply,' I retorted, 'to your sophistical arguments against the Resurrection, for God has told us and God cannot lie.'

'Not so fast,' he replied. 'You have already got as far as: "God has told us." But you must first prove that there *is* a God, for personally I flatly deny it.'

'I will not amuse myself,' I said to him, 'by reciting to you the clear proofs, by means of which the philosophers have established this, for I should have to repeat all that reasonable men have ever written. I will only ask you what inconvenience you find in believing it, and I am certain you cannot offer me a single pretext. Since it is impossible to derive anything but benefit from the belief, why do you not convince yourself? For if there is a God, apart from the fact that in not believing this you will be wrong, you will have disobeyed the precept which commands us to believe in Him. While now, even if there is none, you are still no better off than us.'

'Indeed I am better off than you,' he replied, 'for if there is none, you and I are evenly matched: but if on the contrary there is one, it will be impossible for me to have offended something which I did not believe existed at all, since in order to sin, one must either know it or wish it. Do you not see that a man, however lacking in wisdom, is not going to be offended by a mere street-porter insulting him, if the porter did not intend to, if he mistook him for someone else, or if it was the drink inside him making him talk? How much less should God, in His omnipotence, be angry with us for not acknowledging Him, since it is He who has denied us the means to know Him.

'But by your faith, my little animal, if a belief in God were so necessary to us, in short, if eternity were at stake, would not God himself have flooded this truth with light, making it as clear to us as the sun, which hides from no one? For to pretend that He wanted to play hide-and-seek with men, as children do, saying: "Peep-bo, here I am!", now masking and now unmasking Himself, disguising Himself from some, only to manifest Himself to others, is to create for oneself a god who is either stupid or malicious. For if the force of my genius makes me recognize Him, the credit is all His, since he could easily have given me the soul and faculties of an imbecile, which would have kept me from knowing Him. And if, on the contrary, He had given me a mind incapable of understanding Him, that would not have been my fault either, but His, since He could quite well have given me one lively enough for me to understand Him.'

These ridiculous and diabolical opinions gave me a fit of shuddering which went right through my body. Then I began to study this man with a little more attention and I was quite aghast to observe that there was something terrible about his face which I had not noticed before. His eyes were small and deep set, his complexion dark, his mouth large, his chin hairy, his nails black. 'Oh God!' I said to myself at once. 'This wretch is damned, once his life comes to an end. He may even be the Antichrist they talk about so much in our world.'

I did not wish to reveal my thoughts to him, however, on account of the respect I had for his intelligence, and indeed the favourable aspects with which nature had looked upon his cradle had made me conceive some friendship for him. But I could not contain myself sufficiently not to let fly some imprecations, threatening him with a bad end.

Outbidding my wrath, he shouted: 'Yes, by the death . . .'

I do not know what he contemplated saying to me, for at this moment there was a knock at our chamber door and I saw a great black man coming in, hairy all over. He came up to us, seized the blasphemer by bodily force, and carried him off up the chimney.

The compassion I felt for the fate of this unfortunate man made me fling my arms about him, in order to tear him from the claws of the Ethiopian, but he was so powerful that he carried both of us away and in a moment we were both in the clouds. It was no longer love for my neighbour that obliged me to cling to him tightly, but fear of falling. After plunging through the heavens for more days than I can tell, without knowing what would become of me, I perceived that I was drawing near to our world. I could already distinguish Asia from Europe and Europe from Africa. Then, as I came lower, and I could not even see beyond Italy, I knew in my heart that this devil was doubtless taking my host to hell, body and soul, and bringing him by way of our earth for the reason that hell lies at its centre. However, this consideration, together with all that had befallen me since the devil had become our chariot, was driven right out of my mind by the terror now inspired in me by the sight of a mountain in flames, almost near enough to touch. The spectacle of this fiery object made me cry out: 'Jesu Maria!'

Hardly had I uttered the last syllable, when I found myself stretched out on the heather at the top of a small hill, with two or three shepherds round me, reciting litanies and addressing me in Italian.

'Oh!' I cried. 'God be praised! At last I have found Christians in the world of the moon. Pray tell me, my friends, what province of your world am I in now?'

'In Italy,' they replied.

'How?' I broke in. 'Is there also an Italy in the world of the moon?' For I had as yet given the incident so little thought that I had not noticed that they were speaking to me in Italian and I was answering them in the same language.

When, accordingly, I was completely disabused and nothing else stood in the way of my realizing that I had returned to this world, I allowed myself to be led where the peasants chose to take me. But before I had got as far as the gates of ——, all the dogs in the town came and flung themselves upon me and if fear had not driven me into a house, where I put up a barricade between myself and them, I would undoubtedly have been devoured.

Within a quarter of an hour, as I rested in this dwelling, there was such a sabbath to be heard all round that I believe all the dogs in the kingdom had joined in. From mastiff to lap-dog, one could see them there, howling with a fury so appalling that they might have been celebrating the memory of their first Adam.

This occurrence caused all the people who saw it no little amazement, but as soon as I had roused myself to reflect on the subject, I at once concluded that these animals were raging at me on account of the world I had come from. 'For,' I said to myself, 'that as they are in the habit of barking at the moon because of the pain it causes them from afar, doubtless they want to hurl themselves at me because I smell of the moon, whose odour annoys them.'

To purge myself of this bad air, I exposed myself stark naked to the sun upon a terrace. I tanned myself there for four or five hours, at the end of which time I came down and the dogs, no longer smelling the influence which had made me their enemy, left the place and went back to their own homes.

I inquired at the port when a vessel would be leaving for France, and, once I was on board, my mind could do nothing but ruminate on the marvels of my recent voyage. A thousand times over I admired the providence of God, who had banished those men that are naturally impious to a place where they could not corrupt His loved ones and had punished their pride by abandoning them to their own devices. Moreover, I do not doubt that He had hitherto postponed sending anyone to preach the Gospel to them, because He knew that they would abuse it and that this stubbornness would only serve to win them a more severe punishment in the other world.

THE STATES AND EMPIRES
OF THE SUN

10

The traveller's return

At last our ship sailed into the port of Toulon. After first giving thanks to the winds and the stars for a happy voyage, we all embraced one another in the harbour and exchanged farewells. As for myself, since I had just come from the world of the moon, where the currency consists of entertaining stories, I had, as it were, lost all recollection of the stuff. In exchange for payment of my passage, the master therefore contented himself with the honour of having carried a man fallen from heaven on board his ship. There was now nothing to stop us going on to the house of one of my friends near Toulouse. Hoping to delight him with the recital of my adventures, I was afire with impatience to see him. I will not bore you by recounting all that befell me on the way: I grew tired; I rested; I was thirsty; I was hungry; I drank; I ate.

Although I was in a very poor state, thin and roasted with sunburn, he did not fail to recognize me in the midst of the twenty or thirty dogs which made up his pack. Overcome with joy, he fell upon my neck and embraced me a hundred times and more. Then, still shaking with emotion, he took me into his castle. As soon as he had dried his tears and found his tongue, he cried out: 'At last! We are alive and we shall live despite all the accidents with which fortune buffets our existence! But, great heavens! So it was not true, then, the rumour that went round about you having been burnt in Canada in that great firework you invented? And yet among those who brought me the sad news there were two or three reliable witnesses who swore to me that they had seen and touched the wooden bird in which you were carried away. They told me how you had unfortunately climbed into it, just at the moment when it was set on fire, and the speed of the rockets going off all around you lifted you up so high that the bystanders lost sight of you. And you were, they protested, so completely consumed by the fire, that when the machine fell back to earth they found very little of your ashes.'

'Then these ashes, sir,' I replied, 'were those of the contrivance itself, for the fire only damaged me indifferently. The contrivance was attached on the outside and consequently its heat could not cause me any discomfort.

'You must know that as soon as the saltpetre was used up, the machine was no longer sustained by the hurtling ascent of the rockets and it fell back to earth. I saw it fall and, just when I thought I was going to tumble with it, I was greatly astonished to feel myself rising towards the moon. But I must explain to you the cause of this phenomenon, which you might otherwise take for a miracle.

'On the day this occurred I had rubbed the whole of my body with marrow on account of some bruises I had sustained. But because we were in the last quarter, during which the moon attracts marrow, it exerted such a strong pull on what had soaked into my flesh—especially when my box had arrived above the middle region of the air, where there are no intervening clouds to weaken its influence—that my body followed this attraction. And I protest to you that it went on sucking me up for so long, that in the end I landed in that world, which is here called the moon.'

I then recounted all the details of my voyage to him at great length and Monsieur de Colignac, delighted to hear such extraordinary things, begged me to set them down in writing. Being a lover of peace and quiet, I resisted for a long time, on account of the visitors which such a publication was likely to attract to me. But I was shamed by his reproach that I did not have enough regard for his entreaties, and at length I resolved to satisfy him. I therefore took up my pen and, as fast as I finished a notebook, he would go to Toulouse, itching with far more impatience for my renown than for his own, to extol it in the finest assemblies. As he was reputed to be one of the greatest geniuses of his age, my praises, of which he seemed to be the tireless echo, made me known to everyone. Already the print-makers had engraved my portrait—without having seen me—and every cross-roads in the town rang with the hoarse cries of the pedlars shouting at the tops of their voices: 'Get your portrait of the author of *The States and Empires of the Moon!*'

Among those who read my book there were many ignorant people who merely skimmed through it. In imitation of the wits of the top flight, they applauded with the rest, even to the point of clapping their hands at every word—for fear of making a mistake—and exclaiming joyfully, 'How good it is!' at places which they did not understand at all. But then, in the guise of remorse, superstition, which bites with very sharp teeth beneath the shirt of a fool, was soon gnawing at their hearts so much, that they preferred to renounce their reputations as philosophers (an ill-fitting suit for them in any case) rather than have to answer for them on the Day of Judgement.

And thus behold the medal reversed and see how they vie with one another in recanting! The work they had previously made so much of is now nothing but a hotch-potch of ridiculous stories, a heap of disjointed fragments, a collection of bedtime fairy tales for children; and men who cannot even understand the book's syntax begin telling the author to go and light a candle to Saint Mathurin.[1]

This contrast between the opinions of wise men and fools increased its reputation. Quite soon copies in manuscript were being sold clandestinely. The whole of society as well as what is outside society (all, that is, from the gentleman to the monk) bought the work. Even women took sides. Every family was divided and interests in the dispute went so far that the town was split into two factions, the lunar and the anti-lunar.

The battle had come to skirmishes, when one morning I beheld the entry into Colignac's room of nine or ten beards with long robes, whose first words to him were these: 'Sir, you know that there is not one of us in this company who is not your ally, your relative, or your friend, and that, in conse-

---

[1] The patron saint of fools.

quence, nothing shameful can happen to you, which does not bring shame on to our own heads. Nevertheless, we are informed upon good authority that you are harbouring a sorcerer in your castle.'

'A sorcerer!' cried Colignac. 'Ye gods! Tell me his name and I will deliver him into your hands. But take care that this is not a calumny.'

'How's that, sir,' interrupted one of the most venerable of them, 'is there any parliament more expert in detecting sorcerers than ours? In short, my dear nephew, to keep you in suspense no longer, the sorcerer we denounce is the author of *The States and Empires of the Moon*. After what he has admitted himself, he could not deny that he is the greatest magician in Europe. How! to have gone up to the moon? Can such a thing be possible without the intervention of— I would not dare to name the beast. For tell me, when all's said and done, what business had he on the moon?'

'You may well ask!' interrupted another. 'He went to attend the sabbath which was no doubt being held there that day: and he says, in fact, that he was acquainted with the *Demon* of Socrates. Are you surprised, after that, that he should, as he says, have been brought back to this world by the devil? But be that as it may, don't you see, all these *moons*, all these *chimneys*, all these *journeys through the air* are neither here nor there, neither here nor there, I say. For between you and me'—at these words he brought his mouth close to Colignac's ear—'I have never seen a sorcerer who did *not* have commerce with the moon.'

After voicing these sound opinions they fell silent, and Colignac was left so dumbfounded at their general extravagance that he could not utter a single word. Seeing this, a venerable booby, who had so far not spoken at all, said: 'Look here, cousin, we know where the shoe pinches. This magician is a particular friend of yours. But have no fear. Out of consideration for you, the matter will be dealt with discreetly. You have only to hand him over to us and, out of love for you, we give you our word of honour to have him burnt without any scandal.'

At these words Colignac, although he was pressing his fists into his sides, could not contain himself. He was seized by a spasm of laughter which offended the gentlemen, his relatives, not a little, so that he was unable to reply to any of the points in their harangue except by a repeated: *ha ha ha ha!* or *ho ho ho ho!* Thereupon our gentlemen departed, highly scandalized, and I would say that they had received short shrift—had it not been such a very long way back to Toulouse.

When they had gone, I drew Colignac into his study and, as soon as I had closed the door behind us, I said to him: 'Count, these ambassadors with long hair seem like bearded comets to me. I am afraid that the sound and fury of their outburst may be the rumble of a shaking thunderbolt which is about to fall. Although their accusation may be ridiculous and may well be caused by their stupidity, I should not be any the less dead if a dozen intelligent people, who had seen me roasted, afterwards declared my judges to be fools. All their proofs of my innocence would not bring me to life again and my ashes would stay as cold in a tomb as in the common sewer. That is why, unless you can give me better advice, I should gladly yield to the temptation which bids me leave them nothing of me in this province but my portrait. For I should be doubly vexed to die for something I can scarcely believe myself.'

Colignac had barely the patience to wait for me to finish before replying. At first he teased me, however, but then he saw that I was taking it seriously. 'Ha! By God,' he exclaimed with a look of alarm. 'They shall not touch the hem of your cloak without myself, my friends, my vassals, and all those who respect me perishing first. My house is such that it cannot be stormed without cannon. It is very advantageously situated and well protected on the flank. But I am insane to be taking precautions against mere parchment storms.'

'They are sometimes more to be feared,' I answered, 'than those from the middle region of the air.'

From that time hence we spoke of nothing but our pleasure. One day we would hunt, another we would ride, another we would receive visitors, sometimes we went visiting; but at length we would always leave off each pastime before we had begun to grow weary of it.

The Marquis of Cussan, a neighbour of Colignac's and a man with an excellent taste for the good things of life, was generally of our company and we of his. In order to make our sojourns still more agreeable by varying the scene, we would go from Colignac to Cussan and return from Cussan to Colignac. As for our pleasures, the innocent ones of which the body is capable only made up the lesser portion of them. We forewent none of those such as the mind can take, in study and conversation: our libraries, combined like our minds, summoned all learned men to our company. We mixed reading with conversation, conversation with good fare and this with excursions to fish and hunt. In a word, we enjoyed both ourselves, so to speak, and all the most delightful things nature has provided for our use, allowing reason alone to limit our desires.

To the detriment of my peace of mind, however, my reputation spread through all the neighbouring villages and even the towns of the province. Attracted by this rumour, everybody found a pretext for coming to see the squire in order to have a look at the sorcerer. When I came out from the castle, not merely the children and women but even the men stared at me as if I were the Beast, and chief among them was the Curé of Colignac, who, from ignorance or malice, was secretly my greatest enemy. Though apparently a simple man, whose lowly and ingenuous spirit was infinitely charming in its ingenuousness, he was in fact extremely mischievous. He was vindictive to the point of madness, more backbiting than a Norman and such a trickster that a love of chicanery was his ruling passion. He had a lawsuit of long standing with his squire, whom he hated all the more because he had found him firm in resisting his attacks. He feared his resentment and at one time he had wanted to change his benefice in order to escape it. But he now gave out to the contrary, having either really altered his intention or else simply put it off in order to take revenge upon Colignac, in my person, while he remained on his lands. His frequent journeys to Toulouse gave some ground for suspicion that the latter was the case.

There he told a thousand ridiculous tales of my enchantments and the voice of this malicious man combined with those of simple and ignorant people there to bring my name into execration. No one there spoke of me as anything but a new Agrippa de Nettesheim and we learned that someone had informed against me, at the instigation of the Curé, who had been the tutor of his children. We had notice of this through several people who were allies of Colignac and the Marquis, and although it caused us some astonishment and mirth to see a whole district in such an ugly mood, I was nevertheless secretly frightened when I considered more closely what the troublesome consequences of this folly might be. It was doubtless my Good Genius that inspired this terror in me, illuminating my reason with all these lights, so that I might see the precipice over which I was to fall, and, not content with advising me thus tacitly, he also sought to express himself for my own good more explicitly.

One of the most delightful days we had had at Colignac was followed by one of the most unpleasant nights that ever was and I got up at dawn. In order to dissipate the anxieties and clouds which still fogged my mind I had gone into the garden where the greenery, the flowers and fruits, and the works of art and of nature were enchanting to both eye and soul. I at once perceived the Marquis there, pacing alone down a broad walk, which divided the flower garden in two. His step was slow and his face pensive. I was very surprised to see him up so early against his custom and this made me hasten up to him and ask him the reason. He replied that he had been disturbed by several troublesome dreams which had driven him out into the daylight earlier than usual, in order to cure a malady which had been caused by the darkness. I confessed to him that a similar distress had kept me from sleeping and I was going to tell him about it in detail. But I was just opening my mouth when, round the corner of a hedge which ran to meet our path, we caught sight of Colignac, walking along with great strides.

As soon as he saw us he called out from where he was: 'You see a man who has just escaped from the most terrible visions —a spectacle enough to turn my wits! I scarcely gave myself time to put on my doublet before coming down to tell you about it, but you were neither of you in your rooms any more. That is why I ran into the garden, suspecting that you must be out here.'

The unfortunate gentleman was, in fact, almost completely out of breath. As soon as he had recovered, we urged him to unburden himself. For such things, though they may often be extremely trivial, can nevertheless be very oppressive.

'That is my intention,' he replied. 'But first let us be seated.'

An arbour of jasmine conveniently offered us seats in the cool. We withdrew there and when we had each made ourselves comfortable, Colignac continued thus: 'You must know that I dozed off two or three times during the night and each time found myself in a considerable predicament. Then, in the nap I took during the twilight before dawn, I dreamed that my dear guest here was between the Marquis and myself and that we were holding him in a tight embrace, when a great black monster, consisting of nothing but heads, suddenly came and snatched him away. I think it was even going to throw him into a lighted bonfire near by, for it was already holding him over the flames, but a girl resembling the muse known as Euterpe threw herself at the knees of a lady, begging her to save him (this lady had the bearing and characteristics which our painters employ to represent nature). Hardly had she heard the prayers of her handmaiden when she cried out in amazement: "Alas! he is one of my friends!"

'At once she put a kind of blow-pipe to her lips and blew through the tube so hard under my dear guest's feet that she made him rise up to heaven and saved him from the savagery of the monster with a hundred heads. I seem to have called after him for a very long time, begging him not depart without me, until an infinite number of little round angels, who said they were children of the Dawn, carried me off to the same country towards which he appeared to be flying. There they showed me things which I will not relate to you because I hold them to be too ridiculous.'

We begged him not to refrain from telling us.

'I imagined,' he continued, 'that I was in the sun and that the sun was a world. And I would still not be disabused, had it not been for the neighing of my barbary horse, which woke me up and made me perceive that I was in bed.'

When the Marquis saw that Colignac had finished, he said:

'And you, Monsieur Dyrcona, what was yours?'

'As for mine,' I replied, 'although it was out of the ordinary, I consider it of no account. I am bilious and melancholic by temperament: that is why I have always dreamed of caverns and fire since the day I was born. In the prime of my youth I used to dream that I had become weightless and was flying off into the clouds to escape a band of assassins that was after me. But when I had made long and strenuous efforts, there would always be some wall, after I had flown over many others, at the foot of which, exhausted by my exertions, I would invariably be caught. Or else, if I imagined I was flying straight upwards, I would spend a very long time swimming with my arms in the sky, but I would still find myself close to the ground and, contrary to all reason, without my seeming to become either tired or heavy, my enemies had only to reach out a hand in order to grasp me by the foot and drag me down to them.

'I have had scarcely any dreams but ones like that, ever since I have been acquainted with myself, except that last night, after having flown for a long time as usual and having several times given my persecutors the slip, it seemed to me that I finally lost them from view. With my body relieved of all its heaviness, I continued my voyage through a clear and brilliantly illuminated sky as far as a palace where heat and light are produced. I would doubtless have observed many other things there, but with my flying I had been tossing about, which brought me so near to the edge of the bed that I fell on to the floor beside it, with my belly completely bare on the plaster and my eyes wide open.

'That, gentlemen, is the whole extent of my dream, which I consider to be nothing more than a pure effect of those two qualities which predominate in my temperament. For although this one differs a little from those which I always have, in that I flew up into the heavens without falling back, I attribute this change to my blood, which has circulated more generously than usual, thanks to my enjoyment of yesterday's pleasures, and penetrated the melancholy, buoying it up and relieving it of that heaviness which used to make me fall back to earth. But the science of dreams is, after all, one which depends largely on guesswork.'

'In faith,' Cussan took up, 'you are right. They are a hotch-potch of everything we have been thinking about when we were awake, a monstrous chimera, an assembly of confused elements, which our fancy—no longer guided by our reason when we are asleep—presents to us in complete disorder. Yet, none the less, we believe that, by twisting them about, we can squeeze the true sense out of them and extract knowledge of the future from dreams, as we can from oracles. For my part, I have never found any other similarity between the two, unless it be that dreams and oracles are both incomprehensible.

'At any rate you can judge the value of all the others from mine, which was in no way extraordinary. I dreamed that I was very sad and that I kept meeting Dyrcona everywhere calling out to us. But without further racking my brains to find an explanation of the dark enigmas, I will discover their mystical import to you in a couple of words. And this, by God, is that at Colignac we have very bad dreams, and if you agree with me we will go and try to have better ones at Cussan.'

'Very well, let us go there,' the Count said to me, 'since this spoil-sport is so keen to do so.'

We agreed to leave the same day. I begged them to go

ahead, as I should be very glad (seeing I would be staying a month there, as they had just agreed) to arrange for a number of books to be brought over. They fell in with this and immediately after breakfast they put their arses into the saddle. Meanwhile I, heaven help me, made a parcel of the volumes, which I believed would not be in the library at Cussan, and loaded it on to a mule. I set out at about three o'clock, mounted on a good fast horse. I only went at walking pace, however, in order to accompany my little library and to feast my soul at greater leisure upon the delights of the scene. But now I will tell you of an adventure which will surprise you.

After travelling more than four leagues, I found myself in a country which I was convinced I had seen somewhere before. Indeed I taxed my brain, wondering how I came to know this landscape, until the objects in front of me prompted my memory and I recalled that it was the very place I had seen in my dream the previous night. This bizarre occurrence would have occupied my attention for longer than it did, had it not been for a strange apparition, which brought me back to my senses.

A spectre (at least I took it for such) presented itself to me in the middle of the road and seized the bridle of my horse. This phantom was of enormous stature and, to judge by the little that could be seen of its eyes, it had an expression both fierce and mournful. I could not, however, say if it was handsome or ugly, for it was covered from top to toe by a long robe, which had been sewn together from the pages of a book of plain-song, and its face was hidden by a card, on which the *In principio* had been written.

The phantom then delivered his first words: '*Satanus Diabolas!*' he cried out in terror, 'I conjure you by the *Great Living God....*' At these words he faltered and continued to repeat the *Great Living God*, while searching with a frightened expression for his priest to prompt him with the rest. When he saw that, whichever way he looked, his priest was nowhere to be seen, he was seized by such a dreadful trembling that his teeth chattered until half of them fell out, and two-thirds of the musical scales which covered him came off in shreds. He turned back towards me, however, and with a look which was neither mild nor fierce, but in which I could see his spirit wavering and trying to resolve whether it was more appropriate to grow angry or to soften, he said: 'So ho, *Satanus Diabolas!* God's blood! I conjure you, in the name of God and of my Lord St. John, to let me get on with it. For if you budge nor foot nor paw, the devil take it, I'll rip your guts out!'

I tried to jerk the bridle of my horse free from his grip, but I was choking with fits of laughter, which took away all my strength. Added to that, some fifty villagers came out from behind a hedge, crawling on their knees and making themselves hoarse with singing the *Kyrie Eleison.* When they were quite near, four of the most robust of them grasped me by the collar, after first dipping their hands in a basin of holy water, which the servant from the presbytery was holding for that purpose. As soon as I had been seized, Master Jean appeared, devoutly removed his stole and garrotted me with it. Next a mob of women and children arrived and, despite all my struggles, they stitched me into a sheet. I was, indeed, so well wrapped up in it that only my head could be seen, and in this outfit they took me off to Toulouse, as if they were carrying me to the family vault.

One man would shout that if they had not done this there would have been a famine, because when they met me I was going out to cast a spell on the crops as sure as anything. Then I would hear another moaning that the sheep-pox had only broken out in his flock after I had struck him on the shoulder one Sunday, coming out of Vespers. But what made me feel some inclination to laugh, despite all the mishaps that had befallen me, was a young peasant girl calling in terror after her betrothed, alias the phantom, who had taken my horse from me (for you must know that the clown had mounted astride it and was already spurring it on in good earnest, as if it were his own).

'You wretch!' screeched his beloved. 'Have you only one

eye in your head? Can't you see that the magician's horse is blacker than coal and it is Satan himself, carrying you off to the Sabbath?'

Our rustic tumbled off over the croup in alarm and so my horse was given the freedom of the fields.

They next discussed whether to lay hands on the mule and decided that they would. They ripped open the package, but when they came upon the *Physics* of Monsieur Descartes in the first volume they looked into and perceived all the circles, which this philosopher employs to show the movement of each planet, they all howled with one voice that these were the rings I drew to call up Beelzebub. The one who was holding it dropped it in apprehension and unfortunately it fell open at a page where the properties of the loadstone are explained. I say unfortunately, because at the place of which I am speaking there is a picture of this metallic stone in which the little bodies that stand out from its mass to catch hold of the iron are represented like arms. Hardly had one of the rogues perceived it, when I heard him bawling that this was the toad which had been found in the trough in his cousin Fiacre's stable when his horses died. At these words the ones who had seemed the most valiant hid their hands in their breasts or plunged them into their pockets. Master Jean, for his part, shouted at the top of his voice that they must beware of touching anything, that all the books were nothing but black magic and the mule was a devil. The mob, thus frightened, allowed the mule to depart in peace, but I saw Mathurine, the parish priest's servant girl, driving it towards the presbytery stable, for fear that it might go into the churchyard and pollute the grass of the departed.

It was at least seven o'clock in the evening when we arrived at a small town, where, in order to refresh me, they dragged me to the gaol. The reader would not believe me if I said that they buried me in a hole, but this account is as near as any could be to the truth, for with a single pirouette I could make a tour of the entire premises. In short, nobody who saw me in that place could fail to take me for a lighted candle under a cupping glass. When my gaoler first threw me into this cave, I said to him: 'If you are giving me this stone garment for a suit, it is too big, but if it is for a tomb, it is too tight. One can only count the days here by nights and out of my five senses, I am left with the use of but two, those of smell and touch: the one to make me aware of the stenches of my prison and the other to render it palpable to me. Indeed I confess I should believe I were damned, if I did not know that no innocent people enter hell.'

At the word 'innocent', my gaoler burst out laughing. 'Why, upon my soul,' he said, 'then you are truly one of our people? For I have never kept any but them under lock and key!'

After other compliments of this nature, the good fellow took the trouble to search me. I do not know what his intention was, but from the diligence which he employed I conjecture that it was for my own good. His researches were fruitless, since I had slipped my gold into my hose during the battle of *Diabolas*, and when, at the conclusion of a most exact anatomy, he found himself as empty-handed as before, I nearly died of fear, for he came near to dying of grief.

'Ho! Damn it!' he roared, foaming at the mouth, 'I knew he was a sorcerer the moment I set eyes on him! He is as skint as the devil! Go to, go to, my friend,' he continued. 'Look to your conscience in good time!'

He had hardly finished these words when I heard the jingling of a bunch of keys, from which he was selecting the key to my cell. He had his back turned, which is why I drew three pistoles dexterously from their hiding place, fearing that he might take some revenge for the unhappiness of his visit, and said to him: 'Monsieur le Concierge, here is a pistole. I beg you to have a morsel brought to me; I have not eaten since eleven o'clock.'

He took it most graciously and protested to me that my misfortune touched him. When I perceived that his heart was softened, I continued: 'Here is another, in acknowledgement of the trouble which I am ashamed to give you.'

He opened his ear, his heart, and his hand and I added, counting out three of them instead of two, that, with the third one, I begged him to set one of his fellows beside me to keep me company because the unhappy must fear solitude.

Ravished by my prodigality, he promised me all things, embracing my knees, declaimed against justice, told me he saw clearly that I had enemies but that I should come out of it with my honour untarnished, that I must have a good courage and that, besides all this, he undertook to have my cuffs laundered within three days. I thanked him very solemnly for his courtesy and after a thousand embraces, with which he came near to strangling me, this dear friend bolted and barred the door.

11

In and out of prison

I WAS left all alone and very melancholy, my body doubled up on a pile of powdered straw, which was not so fine, however, that over fifty rats were not grinding it up still smaller. The roof, the walls, and the floor were composed of six tomb-stones, so that, having death above, below, and all about me, I was left in no doubt as to my burial. The cold slime of the slugs and the sticky venom of the toads trickled on to my face. The lice there had teeth longer than their bodies. Thus I found the complaint I suffered from was a stone, which harmed me none the less for being external to my body. Briefly, I think all I needed to be the complete Job was a wife and a potsherd.

I had survived the ordeal of two very painful hours there, however, when the sound of a whole gross of keys, added to that of the bolts on my door, aroused me from the contempla-tion of my misfortunes. Following this clatter I perceived, by the light of a lamp, a hulking great oaf. He dumped a basin between my legs and said: 'There, there, don't you fret yourself. There's some cabbage soup as ever was. And 'tis all proper soup made by our mistress, and so, by my troth, as the saying goes, there's not a drop of the grease has been took out of it.'

So saying, he plunged his five fingers right in to the bottom of the dish by way of invitation to me to do the same. I modelled myself on the original, for fear of discouraging him, and a light of joy came into his eye.

'Dang it!' he cried. 'You are a good brother! They say there's some of 'em don't like you, Lord bless us. But I say they're all traitors, yes, Lord help us, all traitors! Well, let them just come here and see for theirselves! Ah! Well enough. As long as there's something, you've done your best and no one can do better than that!'

Two or three times I felt I was about to guffaw at his simplicity, but I was lucky enough to stop myself. I saw that fortune seemed to have offered me in this rogue a chance to regain my liberty. For this reason it was very important for me to cherish his good graces, for, as to my escaping by any other routes, the architect who built my prison had made several entrances to it, but he had forgotten to make a way out.

It was with all these considerations in mind that I addressed him as follows, in order to sound him out: 'Is it not true, my big friend, that you are poor?'

'Alas, sir,' replied the clown, 'if you had come from the fortune-teller itself, you could not have hit upon it better.'

'Here, then,' I went on, 'take this pistole.'

I found his hand shaking so much when I put the coin into it that he could hardly close it. This beginning seemed to me a bad omen. However, I soon discovered from the fervour of his thanks that he had only been trembling with joy, which was my reason for continuing: 'But if you should be the man to want to help me in the fulfilment of a vow that I have made, twenty pistoles (in addition to the salvation of your soul) would be just as much your own as your hat. For you must know that not a good quarter of an hour—in short, but a moment—before your arrival, an angel appeared to me and promised me to make the justice of my cause known, provided I go and have a mass said to Our Lady of this town at the High Altar tomorrow. I tried to excuse myself on the ground that I was too closely locked up, but he replied that a man would come, sent by the gaoler to keep me company, whom I would simply have to instruct in his part of leading me to the church and bringing me back to prison. I should recommend him to secrecy and unquestioning obedience on pain of dying within the space of one year, and if he should doubt my word I should tell him as a sign that he is a Brother of the Scapular Confraternity.' (For the reader must know that beforehand I had glimpsed a scapular through a slit in his shirt which suggested the whole invention of this apparition to me.)

'Why, yes, to be sure, my good lord,' he said, 'I will do what the angel has commanded us. But it must be at nine o'clock then, because at that time our master will be in Toulouse for the betrothal of his son to the daughter of the public executioner. Lord save us, a hangman has just as good a name as a sheep tick! They say she will have as many crowns from her father when she marries as you need for a king's ransom. As you see, she is rich and pretty, but such things take care not to happen to a poor fellow. Alas! my good sir, you see . . .' At this point I interrupted hastily, for, from the beginning of his digression, I anticipated a long string of red herrings.

After we had well and truly digested our plot, the oaf took leave of me. The next day he did not fail to come and exhume me, sharp on the promised hour. I left my clothes at the prison and fitted myself out with some rags, as we had agreed I should the night before, in order to avoid being recognized. As soon as we were in the open I did not forget to count him out his twenty pistoles. He looked at them hard, with very wide eyes.

'They are gold and fully up to weight,' I told him, 'I give you my word.'

'Hey, no sir,' he replied to me, 'I'm not thinking of that.

I'm thinking that Big Macé's house is up for sale with its garden and its vine. I could get it easily for two hundred francs, but it will take a week to strike a bargain and I should like to beg you, my good sir, if it was your pleasure, not to let your pistoles turn into oak leaves until Big Macé has them well and truly counted and in his chest.'

The simplicity of the villain made me laugh. However, we continued to walk towards the church until we reached it. Some time later they began high mass there, but as soon as I saw my guard getting up to take communion in his turn, I measured the length of the nave in three strides and in as many again I had swiftly lost myself in a deserted side-street. Of all the various ideas racing through my mind at that moment, the one I followed up was that of getting to Toulouse, which was only half a league distant from that town, intending to take the post-chaise from there.

I reached the suburbs in quite good time but I found myself so ashamed to see everyone looking at me that it quite put me out of countenance. Their astonishment proceeded from my outfit, for as I was a complete novice in matters of beggary, I had arranged the rags upon me in such a bizarre fashion that, what with this and a gait which in no way suited my garb, I appeared more like a man in fancy dress than a pauper. In the end, reflecting that such universal attention threatened me with dangerous consequences, I swallowed my shame. As soon as I saw someone looking at me, I held out my hand to him. I even begged charity of those who were not looking at me at all. But you may marvel now at how, very often, by seeking to be too ingenious in schemes where fortune wishes to play some part, we ruin them by irritating this proud lady! I make this reflection as a result of my own experience, for, seeing a man with his back to me, dressed as a common citizen, I dragged at his cloak and said to him: 'Sir, if pity can touch . . .'

Before I could begin the next word the man had turned his head. O gods! What an effect this had on him! But, O gods! What an effect it had on myself! This man was my gaoler! We were both astonished and aghast at seeing one another where we did. He could not take his eyes off me, while my gaze was riveted to him. At length our respective interests, although differing, summoned us both out of the trance in which we had been lost.

'Ha! wretch that I am,' cried the gaoler, 'must I be caught?' These ambiguous words at once gave me the idea for the stratagem, about which you shall now hear.

'Hey! Help me gentlemen! Stop thief!' I cried, as loud as I could bawl. 'This thief has stolen the Countess of Mousseux' jewels: I have been looking for him for a year. Gentlemen,' I continued, gasping for breath, 'a hundred pistoles to the man who arrests him!'

I had hardly uttered these words when a mob of roughs knocked the poor, startled man down. The amazement into which my extraordinary impudence had plunged him, joined to his fancy that unless I had walked through the walls of my cell without breaking them, I could not have escaped, petrified him so much that for a long time he was quite beside himself. He came to in the end, however, and the first words he spoke to undeceive the rabble were that they should take care not to be mistaken, for he was truly a man of honour. Doubtless he was going on to unravel the whole mystery, but a dozen fruit-women, lackeys, and chairmen, anxious to serve me for my money, closed his mouth with fisticuffs and each one of them was the more eager to punish him with hand or foot because they imagined their reward would be in proportion to the number of insulting outrages they had committed against the poor dupe when he was down.

'Look at the man of honour,' jeered the riff-raff. 'But as soon as he recognized the gentleman, he couldn't stop himself saying he was caught.'

The cream of the jest was that my gaoler, being in his best clothes, was ashamed to admit that he was the hangman's partner and was even afraid that, if he made himself known, he might be beaten still worse.

As for myself, I took flight during the heat of the brawl. I entrusted my safety to my legs and they would soon have carried me to freedom. But unfortunately for me, the looks that all the people were beginning to cast my way aroused my original anxieties once more. If the sight of a hundred tatters fluttering about me, like so many little ragamuffins dancing a jig, attracted the stares of some idler, I became afraid that he could read on my brow that I was an escaped prisoner. If a passer-by brought his hand out from under his cloak, I imagined him to be a sergeant reaching out his hand to arrest me. If I noticed another striding along the pavement without looking my way, I would persuade myself that he was pretending not to have seen me, in order to seize me from behind. If I noticed a merchant going into his shop, I would say: 'He is going to take down his halberd!' If I came across a district more crowded with people than usual, I would think: 'So many people cannot be assembled here without some plan.' If another was deserted: 'Here, they are ready to ambush me.' If congested traffic impeded my flight: 'They have barricaded the streets to shut me in.'

At length my fear undermined my reason. Every man seemed to be a constable; every word, 'Halt!' and every sound the intolerable creaking of the bolts of my late prison. Agitated as I was by this panic terror, I resolved to start begging again, so as to cross the rest of the town as far as the Post without arousing suspicion. But for fear of being detected by my voice, I supplemented the activities of a mendicant with the subterfuge of counterfeiting dumbness. Now if I notice people looking at me I go up to them. I point with my finger under my chin and then at my mouth, and I open it wide with an inarticulate cry, in order to convey, by my grimacing, that a poor, dumb man is asking for alms. Sometimes, out of pure charity, I would be donated a shrug of sympathy. Sometimes I heard women murmuring that I might well have been martyred like this in Turkey, for the Faith. In short, I learned that beggary is a vast book, which can teach us about the manners of peoples much more cheaply than all those great voyages of Columbus and Magellan.

This stratagem, however, still failed to exhaust the stubbornness of my fate, and win over its malevolence. But to what other invention could I have had recourse? For in crossing a great town like Toulouse, where prints of me had made me known even to the fishwives, clad in an assortment of rags as motley as a harlequin's, was it not likely that I should be noticed and recognized immediately and that the only counter-charm was the character of a beggar, a role which may be played with all kinds of faces? And then if I had not planned this ruse and all the precautions that went with it, I should have had to be very strong-minded not to be driven mad in the midst of such an unhappy predicament.

I was therefore proceeding on my way, when all of a sudden I felt compelled to retrace my steps, for my revered gaoler and some dozen constables of his acquaintance, who had delivered him from the hands of the riff-raff, after giving chase and patrolling all the town in search of me, had unfortunately appeared in my path. As soon as they caught sight of me with their lynx eyes, it was but the work of a moment for them to begin to fly with all their strength and for me to take flight with all mine. I was so hotly pursued that sometimes my liberty felt upon the back of its neck the breath of the tyrants who sought to oppress it. But it seemed that the air they were driving along, as they ran behind me, drove me along in front of them. Finally either heaven or fear gave me a lead of four or five side streets. It was then that my hunters missed the scent and the spoor and I the sight and the din of this alarming chase.

I am sure that anyone who has not been through such agonies, for I speak as one who has, would find it hard to get the measure of the joy which left me trembling all over, when I saw that I had escaped. However, because my safety demanded the whole of my attention, I resolved to be very thrifty in making use of the time they took to catch up with me. I dirtied my face, rubbed dust into my hair, stripped off my doublet, lowered my breeches and threw my hat in at a cellar window. Then I spread out my handkerchief on the pavement and placed four little stones at the corners, as men do who are stricken with the plague. I lay down beside it, my belly against the earth and set up a melancholy whining in a piteous voice. I had hardly taken up my station, when I began to hear the mob shouting itself hoarse, long before I heard the sound of their feet. I had still enough presence of mind, however, to stay in the same position, in the hope of not being recognized by them at all—and I was not disappointed. They all took me for a victim of the plague and passed very quickly, stopping their noses, and most of them threw a coin on to my handkerchief.

The storm thus dissipated, I ducked into an alley, put my clothes on again and abandoned myself once more to fortune, but I had apparently run so far that she was tired of following me. One is compelled to believe that this was so, for after a good deal of traversing squares, running the length of streets, and cutting across them, this haughty goddess, unaccustomed to travelling at such speed and the better to have done with my wanderings, allowed me to fall blindly into the hands of the constables who were pursuing me. On meeting me they gave throat to a thunderous cry so enraged that it left me completely deaf. Thinking they had not enough arms to arrest me with, they used their teeth as well. One dragged me by the hair, another by the collar, while the more dispassionate of them were searching me. This search was better fated than the one in prison: they found the rest of my gold.

While these charitable doctors were engaged in curing the dropsy of my purse, a great uproar arose. The whole square resounded with the words: 'Kill! kill!' and at the same time I saw the flashing of swords. The gentlemen who were dragging me along shouted that it was the Grand Provost's constables trying to rob them of their capture. 'But beware of falling into their hands,' they said to me, pulling at me harder than ever, 'for you will be condemned within twenty-four hours, and the King will not save you.'

In the end, however, alarmed by the scuffle in which they

were beginning to be involved, they abandoned me so completely that I was left all alone in the middle of the street, while the aggressors were carrying out a butchery of all they encountered. I will leave you to imagine whether I took flight, having equal reason to fear both parties. In a little while I got away from the brawl and I was already asking the way to the Post, when a torrent of people in flight from the fray disgorged into my street. Not being able to resist the crowd, I went with it and, growing weary after running for such a long time, in the end I reached a very dark little door, through which I threw myself pell-mell with the other fugitives. We barred it behind ourselves and then, when everybody had got their breath back, one of the troop said: 'Comrades, if you will take my advice, let us pass through the two grilles and hold fast in the courtyard.'

These fearful words struck my ears with such a distressing shock that I thought I should fall dead upon the spot. Alas, all at once—but too late—I perceived that instead of escaping to a place of safety, as I had believed, I had come and thrown myself into prison, so impossible is it to escape the vigilance of one's star. I looked at this man more closely and recognized him as one of the constables who had run after me for so long. A cold sweat rose to my brow at this; I paled and began to feel faint. The people who saw me so weak were moved with compassion and called for water. Everyone crowded round to help me and by ill chance this accursed constable was one of the first. As soon as he clapped eyes on me, he recognized me at once. He made a sign to his companions and all together they greeted me with one great: *I arrest you in the King's name!* Nothing further was needed to put me in prison.

I remained in the reception cell until the evening when, one after the other, every turnkey came to trace my picture on the canvas of his memory by making an exact dissection of the parts of my face.

On the stroke of seven the sound of a bunch of keys gave the signal for the retreat. I was asked if I desired to be conducted to the one-pistole chamber and I replied with a nod.

'Where's your money then?' my guide answered me.

I was well aware that I was in a place where I should have a lot more of this kind of thing to swallow and so I begged him —if his courtesy could not bring itself to give me credit until the following day—to tell the gaoler on my behalf to return the money he had taken from me.

'Ho! by my troth,' replied the ruffian, 'our kind-hearted master gives nothing back. Is it for the sake of your pretty nose then? ... All right, come along! It's the black cells for you!'

As he finished these words he showed me the way by giving me a great blow from his key ring, the weight of which made me stagger and go hurtling down from top to bottom of a dark slope until I was halted by the foot of a door. I would not even have known it was there but for the violent crash with which I struck it, for I no longer had the use of my eyes. I had left them behind at the top of the staircase in the light of the candle, which my executioner of a guide was holding, eighty steps above me. Finally this human tiger padded down the stairs, undid thirty great locks, lifted off as many bars, half opened the cell door, and plunged me, with a thrust of his knees, into a pit, the full horror of which I did not have time to observe, so quickly did he close the door behind him. I was left up to my knees in filth. If I tried to reach the edge, I was engulfed up to the waist. The terrible croaking of the toads which paddled about in the slime made me wish I was deaf. I felt lizards crawling up the length of my thighs and serpents entwining themselves about my neck. I glimpsed one of these by the sombre glow of its own glittering eyeballs, darting a triple-forked tongue from a mouth all black with venom, and, what with the fire from its eyes, its rapid flickering resembled a thunderbolt.

So far as the rest is concerned, I cannot describe it. It surpasses all belief. Besides, I dare not try to remind myself of it, so great is my fear that my present conviction that I have broken out of my prison may turn out to be a dream, from which I shall wake.

12

Into space again

THE hand on the dial of the great tower had reached ten o'clock before anyone knocked on my tomb. But about that time, when the pain of a bitter sorrow was beginning to constrict my heart and upset the balanced harmony that makes for life, I heard a voice recommending me to grasp the pole which was being offered to me. After feeling for it in the darkness above me for quite a long time, I found one end of it. In great excitement I took hold of it and, by drawing up the other end to himself, my gaoler fished me out of the midst of this morass. I suspected that my affairs had taken on a new aspect, for he used me with profound civility. He only spoke to me bare-headed and told me that five or six persons of quality were waiting in the courtyard to see me. Even the savage beast who had locked me up in the cellar, which I have described to you, had the impudence to address me. He went down on one knee, kissed my hands, and with one of his paws he removed a quantity of slugs, which were stuck to my hair, while with the other he brushed off a great pile of leeches, which masked my face.

After this admirable piece of courtesy, he said to me: 'At least, my good lord, you will remember the trouble and care big Nicholas took of you. 'Fore God, I tell you, 'twould be the same for the King! You are not to be blamed for it, swelp me!'

Incensed with the effrontery of the ruffian, I made him a sign that I should remember. After a thousand frightful detours, I finally arrived in the light and then in the courtyard. As soon as I appeared there I was seized by two men whom I did not recognize at first, because they flung themselves upon me at the same time, and each held me with his face pressed against mine. It was a long time before I guessed their identity, but when the transports of their affection had abated a little, I recognized my dear Colignac and the brave Marquis. Colignac had his arm in a sling and Cussan was the first to come to his senses.

'Alas!' he said. 'We should never have suspected that such a disaster had befallen you, had it not been for your horse and the mule arriving at the gates of my castle that night. Their breast straps, saddle girths, and cruppers were all broken and that gave us some intimation of your misfortune. We mounted at once and had not ridden two or three leagues towards Colignac before the whole country, which was buzzing with the incident, gave us the particular circumstances. We at once galloped as far as the town, where you were in prison, but learning there of your escape, from the current rumour that you had made off in the direction of Toulouse, we came on here at full speed with those of our people we had with us.

'The first person we asked for news of you said that you had been recaptured. On the instant we spurred our horses towards this prison, but some other people assured us that you had vanished from the hands of the sergeants. And as we continued in our way, citizens were telling one another that you had become invisible. At length, after making good use of our tongues, we learned that having captured, lost, and recaptured you heaven knows how many times, they were taking you to the prison in the great tower. We cut off your constables' road, met them head on, attacked them, fought them, and put them to flight with an advantage to ourselves more apparent than actual. But as for what became of you, we were unable to learn, even from the wounded men we took prisoner, until this morning someone came and told us that, in trying to escape, you had blindly come to the gaol yourself.

'Colignac was wounded in several places but only very lightly. For the rest, we have come to make an application for you to be housed in the best chamber here. As you love the open air, we have had a small single apartment furnished for you right at the top of the great tower, whose battlements will serve you as a balcony. Your eyes, at least, will be free to wander, though your body holds them fast!'

'Ah! my dear Dyrcona,' cried the Count, taking up the thread. 'How unlucky we were not to have taken you with us when we left Colignac! My heart gave me a presentiment of something fearful by means of a blind feeling of grief, whose cause was unknown to me. But no matter. I have friends. You are innocent, and in any case I know very well how to die honourably. A single thing dismays me. The ruffian on whom I wanted to try the first blows of my revenge (you can easily guess that I refer to my village priest) is no longer in a state to feel them: the wretch has given up the ghost. I will tell you the manner in which he died. He was running along with his servant, trying to drive your mount into his stable, when the horse, whose native sense was perhaps reinforced by faithfulness to its master, began to rear wildly, with such fury and to such good effect that under three kicks this fool's head caved in and he vacated his benefice.

'You probably do not understand the causes of this madman's hatred, but I will acquaint you with them. You must know, to tell you the whole story, that this holy man, a Norman by race and a confidence trickster by profession, who used to officiate at an abandoned chapel which was kept up by money from the pilgrims, had designs upon the benefice of Colignac. Despite all my efforts to maintain the possessor in his rights, this droll fellow blarneyed his judges so successfully that he ended up as our priest.

'A year later he took me to court as well, on the grounds that I should pay him a tithe. In vain it was demonstrated to him that my land had been free from time immemorial: he would not abandon his lawsuit, which he lost. But in the course of the proceedings, he started so many side issues that more than twenty fresh cases were spawned by the original one, which will now remain on the shelf, thanks to your horse's hoof turning out to be tougher than Master Jean's brain.

'This is all I can conjecture about our pastor's caprices. But you may marvel at the prudence with which he pursued his madness! I have just been assured that, having got the unhappy scheme for your imprisonment into his head, he had secretly exchanged the benefice of Colignac for another in his own country, to which he intended to retire as soon as you were captured. His servant has even said that he had heard him muttering, on seeing your horse near his stable, that there was something to take him to a place where he would be out of reach.'

After telling me this, Colignac warned me to be wary of any offers or visits which a very powerful person, whom he named, might make me, for it was through this man's credit that Master Jean had won his case over the claim. This person of quality had intervened in the affair on his behalf, in return for services rendered to his son at college by the good priest who was at that time a sizar.

'And since it is very hard,' Colignac continued, 'to be involved in litigation without bitterness, and without retaining in one's soul a trace of enmity which is never effaced, although we have been reconciled, he has always secretly sought occasions to cross me. But it does not matter: I have more connections than him in the courts and I have many friends, or in the last resort we can arrange for the intervention of the royal authority.'

After Colignac had said this, they both tried to console me, but these evidences of such a solicitous grief only served to increase my own.

Meanwhile my gaoler had returned to find us and tell us that the room was ready. 'Let us go and see it,' replied Cussan, starting off, and we followed him.

I found it very well furnished. 'I lack nothing,' I told them, 'but books.' Colignac promised to send me all those I listed for him the following day.

When we had taken a good look and had fully appreciated from the height of my tower the moats with sheer sides, which surrounded it, and from all the arrangements of my apartment, that to escape would be an enterprise beyond the power of man, my friends looked at one another and then turned their eyes towards me and began to weep. But, as if our grief had all at once softened the wrath of heaven, a sudden joy took possession of my soul, the joy attracted hope and the hope, a secret enlightenment, which so dazzled my brain that with an irrational exultation which seemed ridiculous even to myself, I said to them: 'Go! Go and wait for me at Colignac. I shall be there in three days. And send me all the mathematical instruments I generally use for my work. Apart from these, you will find a large box containing a number of crystals cut in various fashions: do not forget these—but the quickest way will be to specify the things I need in a memorandum.'

They took charge of the note I gave them, without being able to fathom what my intention was, after which I sent them away.

From the moment of their departure I did nothing but reflect upon the execution of the things which I had planned, and I was still reflecting upon them the following day when everything I had listed in my catalogue was brought to me from them. One of Colignac's servants told me that his master had not been seen since the previous day and that no one knew what had become of him. I was not disturbed by this news, because it occurred to me that he might possibly have gone to court to solicit for my release. I therefore set to work without anxiety. For eight days I hewed, I planed, I glued, and by the end of it I had constructed the machine which I shall now describe to you.

It was a large, very light box, which closed very tightly. It was six feet high or thereabouts and three feet square. There was a hole in the bottom of the box; on the top of the roof, which also had one in it, I placed a vessel of crystal, which was similarly pierced. This was made in the form of a very capacious globe, with a neck which was finished off evenly and fitted into the aperture I had fashioned in the top of the box.

This vessel was deliberately constructed with a number of surfaces, however, in the form of an icosahedron, and as each facet was both convex and concave, my ball produced the effect of a dazzling mirror.

Neither the gaoler nor his turnkeys ever came up to my room, without finding me busy at this task, but they were not surprised at this, on account of the variety of ingenious pieces of machinery which they saw about the place, and of which I told them I was the inventor. Among other things there were a wind clock, an artificial eye, with which one can see at night, and a sphere on which the stars move as they do in the sky. All this led them to believe that the machine on which I was working was a similar curiosity—and then the money with which Colignac greased their palms helped them to tread softly along many difficult paths.

It was nine o'clock one morning, my gaoler had gone down, and the sky was overcast, when I brought this machine out on to the summit of my tower, that is to say on to the most exposed part of my terrace. It could be sealed so tightly that not a single particle of air could squeeze inside, except through the two apertures. Inside it I had fitted a small, very light plank, which served me as a seat.

Everything being arranged in this way, I shut myself inside it and remained there for nearly an hour, awaiting the dictates of fortune.

When the clouds cleared from the sun and it began to shine upon my machine, the transparent icosahedron caught the solar riches upon its facets and transmitted their light into my cell through the medium of the glass jar. As this splendour was enfeebled, because the rays could not bend without being split up many times, so the powerful light was refracted and converted my chamber into a miniature heaven of gilded purple.

In the midst of my raptures over the beauty of this rainbow of colours, I suddenly feel my stomach quivering, like that of a man being lifted up by a block and tackle.

I was going to open my hatch in order to learn the cause of

this feeling, but as I was stretching out my hand, I noticed through the hole in the floor of my box that my tower was already far away beneath me, and my little castle in the air, thrusting upwards under my feet, gave me a momentary view of Toulouse plunging downwards into the earth. This marvel did not surprise me because of the suddenness of my flight, but simply because of the frightening leap taken by the human brain towards the achievement of a scheme, which had alarmed me merely to imagine it. Nothing else astonished me, for I had clearly foreseen that the vacuum created in the icosahedron, when the rays of the sun were brought together by the concave glasses, would attract a furious rush of air in order to fill it, which would raise my box. Moreover, as I went up, the fearful wind streaming through the hole could not reach the roof without driving the machine upwards as it forced its way violently through.

Although my plans had been considered with much care, however, one circumstance did take me by surprise, because I had not had sufficient faith in the effectiveness of my mirrors. I had fixed a small sail outside my box, which could easily be controlled by means of a string passing through the bowl of the vessel, of which I held the other end. I had imagined that in this way, when I was in the air, I could take as much wind as I needed to reach Colignac. But in a twinkling the sun which was beating both directly and obliquely upon the shining mirrors of the icosahedron, had hoisted me so high that I lost Toulouse from view. This made me abandon my string, and a very short time later, through one of the four windows which I had set in the sides of the machine, I saw my little sail being snatched away and flying off at the mercy of a whirlwind which had sucked it in.

I recall that in less than an hour I found myself above the middle region of the air. I soon noticed this because I could see it hailing and raining below me. I may perhaps be asked, where this wind came from (without which my box could not mount), at a level in the heavens which is exempt from meteors. But provided you listen to me, I will answer this objection. I have told you that with the sun beating hard upon my concave mirrors, which focused all its rays together in the middle of the vessel, the air which filled it was driven by the heat through the pipe in the top and that thus a vacuum was left in the vessel. Nature, which abhors this, made it suck in more air through the lower opening, in order to refill itself. If it lost a lot of air, it recovered as much. So you ought not to be amazed that I should have continued to soar in a region above the middle one, where the winds are, because the upper air was turned into a wind by the furious speed at which it rushed in to prevent the vacuum forming and was consequently forced to drive my machine upwards without stopping.

I was scarcely troubled by hunger at all, except when I was crossing the middle region, for actually the coldness of the climate did give me a distant glimpse of it. I say 'distant' because the bottle of cordial essence which I always carried and from which I took several draughts, helped me to keep it at bay.

During the whole of the rest of my journey I felt no pangs at all. On the contrary, the more progress I made towards this blazing world, the more robust I felt. I felt my face grow a little warm and brighter than usual. My hands appeared tinged with an agreeable ruddiness and an indefinable joy flowed in my very blood, which made me feel quite elated.

I remember that once when I was pondering about this phenomenon I reasoned in this way: 'Doubtless, hunger could not assail me, because this pain is but an instinct of nature, which she uses to induce animals to replace with food what they have lost from their substance. But today she senses that the pure, uninterrupted, and proximate radiation from the sun is making me supplement my bodily heat faster than I am losing it and so she no longer gives me this appetite, which would be useless to me.'

To this argument, however, I found the objection that, since the constitution which makes life is composed not only of natural heat, but also of radical moisture—to which this heat must be *attached*, as the flame is to the oil of a lamp—the rays from this furnace of life could not by themselves nourish the soul, unless they encountered some oily matter to hold them fast.

I immediately overcame this difficulty, however, when I noted that the radical moisture and the natural heat of our bodies are one and the same thing. For what is called 'moisture', whether in animals or in the sun—that great animus of the universe—is nothing but a flow of bodies more continuous on account of their mobility; and what is called 'heat' is a light drizzle of atoms of fire, which appear rarefied on account of their interruption. But even if radical moisture and heat were two distinct things, it is still true that moisture would not be necessary for life so close to the sun, since the only function of this moisture in living creatures is to hold the heat, which would otherwise be spent too quickly and not replaced in time, and I was in no danger of running short of natural warmth in a region, where more of the little bodies of flame, which make life, were joining my being than leaving it.

Another thing which may cause surprise is why my approach to this flaming globe did not burn me up, since I had almost come within range of the full activity of its sphere; but here is the reason for it. It is not, strictly speaking, fire itself which burns, but a grosser matter, which fire drives here and there by the thrusts of its volatile nature. The powder of fine sparks, which I call 'fire', has its own motion, but very likely depends for all its effects on the roundness of the other atoms. For they tickle, warm, or burn according to the shape of the bodies with which they combine. So straw does not produce as fierce a flame as wood, and wood burns less violently than iron. This is due to the fact that fire in iron, wood, and straw, although it is itself the same substance, acts differently according to the diversity of the bodies which it activates. That is why in straw, fire (this almost spiritual dust), being only combined with a soft material, is less destructive. In wood, whose substance is more compact, it does more damage. And when it penetrates iron, whose mass is almost completely solid and bound together by angular particles, it consumes what is thrown on to it in an instant. All these observations are so familiar that it will come as no surprise that I should draw near to the sun without being burnt. For what burns is not fire, but the matter to which it is attached, and the fire of the sun cannot be combined with any other matter.

After all, do we not experience how joy (which is a fire that merely causes the circulation of an airy mixture of blood, whose greatly rarefied particles brush softly against the membranes of our flesh) titillates and arouses an indefinable blind voluptuousness? This pleasure, or let me rather call it this first step on the way to pain, does not go as far as to threaten the body with death but only to make us feel a desire which causes our spirit an emotion, which we call 'joy'. That is not to say that fever, although it has quite contrary effects, is not a fire just as much as joy. But it is a fire combined with a substance, whose particles have horns. Such is the black bile or melancholy, which goes thrusting its crooked points wherever its mobile nature sends it, piercing, cutting, and lashing, and by means of this agitation produces what is called 'fever heat'.

But this string of proofs is quite unnecessary. The most everyday experiences are quite sufficient to convince the obdurate, and I have no time to lose. I must think of myself. I am still following Phaeton's example, in the midst of a chariot race which I cannot abandon and in which, if I make one false move, all nature together cannot save me.

I was able to recognize very distinctly that, as I had previously suspected, on my way up to the moon, it is indeed the earth which revolves about the sun from east to west and not the other way round. For after France I saw the foot of the boot of Italy, then the Mediterranean Sea, then Greece, then the Bosphorus, the Black Sea, Persia, the Indies, China, and finally Japan, passing opposite the hole in my box, one after the other: and some hours after my take-off, the whole of the

Pacific Ocean had spun by and the continent of America had taken its place.

I could make out these revolutions quite clearly and I remember that a good deal later I even saw Europe reappearing on the scene, although I could no longer tell the separate countries apart, since my altitude had become too great. As I journeyed on, I passed several earths like ours, now to the left and now to the right of my route and if I came into their spheres of influence, albeit but slightly, I would feel myself wavering. But the vigorous speed of my flight overcame the force of these attractions.

I skirted the moon, which was at that time situated between the sun and the earth, and left Venus to my right. With regard to this star, the astronomy of the ancients has been so insistent in preaching that the planets are heavenly bodies which revolve about the earth, that we moderns dare not doubt it. And yet I remarked that during the whole of the time in which Venus appeared beyond the sun, about which she revolves, I saw her always as a crescent. But when she had completed her revolution, I observed that as she passed from behind it, her horns drew close to one another and her black belly grew gold again. Now this variation of light and shadow shows quite clearly that the planets are, like the moon and the earth, globes without their own brilliance, only capable of reflecting what they borrow.

In fact, as I rose higher, I made exactly the same observation of Mercury. I also noticed that all these worlds have other small worlds travelling round them. Reflecting later upon the reasons for the design of this great universe, I decided that when chaos was being ordered, after God had created matter, similar bodies must have been joined together in obedience to that unknown principle of affinity, according to which we experience that like things are attracted to one another. Particles shaped in one way congregated to make air. Others, whose shapes may have given them a spinning motion, came together to compose the globes which are called heavenly bodies. This inclination to pirouette upon their poles, which their shape forces on them, must not only have made them mass themselves into the spherical shape we observe, it must also have caused the lesser orbs which are to be found in their sphere of activity to turn, as they evaporated off the main body and adopted a similar motion in their flight. That is why Mercury, Venus, the Earth, Mars, Jupiter, and Saturn were all compelled to pirouette and roll round the sun together. Not that one cannot imagine all these other globes to have once been suns—since despite its present extinction, the earth still retains enough warmth to make the moon revolve round it with the circular motion of a body which has broken free from its mass, and Jupiter retains enough to make four revolve. But in the course of time these suns have suffered such a considerable loss of light and fire, through continually giving off those small bodies which produce heat and illumination, that they are now left as cold, shadowy, and also impotent husks.

We can even observe how the spots on the sun, which the ancients never noticed, are growing from day to day. Who knows, then, if this is not a crust forming upon its surface — its fire gradually going out as it gives off more and more light? Or if, when all these mobile bodies have abandoned it, it will not become an opaque globe, like the earth? There are very distant ages before which no vestige of the human race appears. Perhaps the earth was once a sun, peopled with creatures suited to the climate which produced them, and perhaps these animals were the demons of which antiquity records so many instances. Why not? Could not these creatures still have lived here for some time after the extinction of the earth and before the changes in their globe had completely destroyed all their race? It is a fact that, according to the evidence of Plutarch, they continued to exist until the time of Augustus.

Even the prophetic and sacred Testament of our first patriarchs would seem to take us by the hand and lead us to the same truth: for there one reads about the revolt of the angels before there is any talk of man. Is not this time sequence, which the Scriptures observe, virtually a proof that the angels inhabited the earth before us? And that these proud ones, who had dwelt on our world at that time when it was a sun, very likely scorning to continue their residence there as soon as it became extinct and knowing that God had placed his throne in the sun, dared to try and usurp it? But to punish their impudence, God banished them even from the earth and created man, less perfect, but in consequence less proud, to take their place there.

13

A small world and the end of a hazardous journey

AFTER travelling for some four months—at least as far as one could calculate, with no nights intervening to mark off the days—I landed on one of the little earths which hover about round the sun (known to the mathematicians as *sunspots*). Some clouds had got in the way, so that my mirrors attracted less heat and the wind began to propel my cabin with less vigour. The remaining current of air was only capable of breaking my fall and lowering me on to the tip of a very high mountain, where I landed gently.

I will leave you to imagine the joy I experienced at finding my feet on solid ground after having played the part of a bird for so long. In fact words are powerless to express the surge of emotion I felt on emerging and finally seeing my head bathed in the brilliance of the heavens. This rapture did not transport me so completely, however, that I omitted, on leaving it, to cover the top of my box with my shirt before I moved off; because I was afraid that if the air cleared and the sun once more heated up my mirrors, as was likely, I should never find my house again.

Through gorges which bore traces of having been carved

out by water, I climbed down on to the plain, where I could hardly walk on account of the thick mud, which enriched the soil. However, after going for some distance I arrived at a quagmire, where I came upon a little man, stark naked, sitting resting on a stone. I do not remember if I spoke to him first or if it was he who questioned me, but I have a recollection quite as fresh as if I were still listening to him, of how he addressed me for three solid hours in a language, which I am perfectly sure I had never heard before and which had no connexion with any in this world, but which, none the less, I understood more readily and more clearly than my mother tongue. He explained, when I asked him about this marvel, that in the sciences there is a truth, outside of which nothing is easy. The more a language departs from this truth, the more it falls short of the concepts it seeks to express and the harder it is to understand.

'Similarly,' he continued, 'in music one never encounters this truth, without the soul being at once exalted and blindly attracted to it. We cannot see it, but we sense that nature sees it, and, without our knowing how, we are absorbed by it. It never fails to ravish our souls, even though hidden from our eyes. It is exactly the same with language. A man who discovers this truth in letters, words, and their sequence can never fall short of his original conception in expressing himself: his speech is always equal to his thought. It is ignorance of this perfect idiom that makes you falter, knowing neither the order nor the words to explain what you have in mind.'

I remarked that the first man in our world had doubtless made use of this original language, because the name he had given to each thing proclaimed its essence.

He interrupted me and continued: "It is not merely that it is necessary to the expression of all that the spirit conceives: without it one cannot be universally understood. As this idiom is the instinct or voice of nature, it is perforce intelligible to all that lives under nature's control. That is why, if you had command of it, you could communicate your ideas and hold forth upon them to the beasts and they could tell you theirs, because it is nature's own medium of communication with all the animals.

'You should no longer be surprised at the ease with which you can grasp the sense of a tongue that has never sounded in your ears before. When I speak, your soul recognizes in each one of my words that truth for which it blindly gropes, and though your reason does not understand it, you have natural instincts which cannot fail to do so.'

'Aha! Then it is, without a doubt,' I exclaimed, 'the energetic idiom by means of which our first father once conversed with and was understood by the animals. He was given dominion over all species and they obeyed him, because he commanded them in a language they knew. This is also why (the original language being lost) they do not now come when we call them, as they used to, because they no longer understand us.'

The little man did not appear to wish to answer me and, taking up the thread of his own discourse once more, he would have continued—if I had not once more interrupted him. I asked him what world it was whose air we were breathing, if it was greatly populated, and what kind of government kept order there.

'I am going,' he replied, 'to unfold secrets to you, which are quite unknown in the clime you come from.

'Take a good look at the earth we are walking on. Until a short while ago it was an undigested and formless mass, a chaos of confused matter, a sticky black impurity expelled by the sun. After the vigour of the sun's rays beating down upon it had blended, compressed, and made compact the clouds of countless atoms, when, I say, the most dissimilar bodies in this globe had been separated and the most similar united, in the course of a long and powerful coction, its overheated body sweated so much that it caused a flood, which covered it for more than forty days. For the great quantity of water required all this space of time to run away down the slopes to the lowest regions of our globe.

'From these amalgamated torrents of moisture was formed

the sea, whose salt still bears witness to the fact that it must be a collection of sweat, for all sweat is salty.

'After the waters had subsided, the earth was left covered with rich, fertile mud. When the sun shone on this, a kind of blister arose, containing a seed which could not germinate on account of the cold. It then received another coction, which improved and perfected the mixture more precisely and produced an embryo which was not only able to vegetate but also capable of feeling. But because the waters (which had stagnated for so long on top of the slime) had chilled it too much, this pimple did not burst. So the sun baked it once more, and after a third coction this womb was heated up so much that the cold no longer impeded its delivery. It opened and gave birth to a man, who retained in his liver (which is the seat of the vegetative soul and the place of the first coction) the power of growth; in his heart (which is the seat of action and the place of the second coction) the power of movement; and in the brain (which is the seat of the intellect and the place of the third coction) the power to think. Otherwise why should we be longer in our mothers' bellies than all the rest of the animals, if not because our embryo needs three separate coctions to form the three separate faculties of our soul and those of the beasts only two to form their two powers?

'I am well aware that the horse is only completed within ten, twelve, or fourteen months in the belly of the mare. But it has a constitution so opposed to that which makes us men that it never begins its life (note this!) except in the months which are quite antipathetic to our own, when we remain in the womb—defying the natural course of things. Thus it is no wonder that the period of time nature needs to deliver a mare should be different from one taken to bring a woman to bed with child.

' "Yes, but all the same," I can hear someone saying, "the horse remains in its mother's belly longer than us and consequently it receives there more perfect or more numerous coctions!"

'I reply that this does not follow. I do not seek support from the observations made by many learned men on the energy numbers, from which they prove that, since all matter is in motion, certain creatures are completed in a certain number of days, which are destroyed in another. I do not fortify myself with the proofs they adduce, having explained the cause of all these motions, to the effect that the number nine is the most perfect of all. I simply content myself with replying that the seed of a man is hotter, so that the sun, working on it, brings to perfection more organs in nine months than it sketches in a year in that of the foal. For it cannot be doubted that a horse is much colder than a man, since this beast only dies of the swelling of the spleen and other diseases which proceed from melancholy.

' "None the less," you will say to me, "in our world one does not see anyone hatched out of mud and produced in this fashion."

'I can well believe it; your world is too hot nowadays. When the sun draws up a germ from the earth, it does not have to overcome that cold humidity, or rather that fixed period for a completed stage which forces it to go through several coctions. It produces a plant straight away. Or, if there are two coctions, since there will not be time for the second to be perfectly completed, it only engenders an insect. I have also noticed that the apes, which resemble us in carrying their young for almost nine months, tend to be so like us that many naturalists have not distinguished between our two species and the reason is that their seed, being of a more or less similar constitution to ours, has almost time during this period to complete all three coctions.

'You will certainly ask me from whom I have the story I have given you. You will say that I could not have learned it from people who were not there. Well, it is true that I am the only one who was there and that even I could not bear witness to it, for the reason that it had occurred before I was born. That is also true. But then you must learn that in a region near to the sun, like this one, our minds, being full of fire, are more lucid, more subtle, and more penetrating than those of the other creatures in more distant spheres. And since even in your world there used to be prophets, whose spirits, heated by a strong passion, had presentiments about the future, so in this one, which is much nearer the sun, and in consequence more luminous than yours, it is not impossible for some odour of the past to reach a powerful genius and for his mobile mind to travel backwards as well as forwards and be capable of arriving at the cause via the effects, seeing that it can deduce the effects from the cause.'

He completed his recital in this manner, but after a still more detailed lecture, in which he revealed to me some deeply hidden mysteries, some of which I wish to keep secret and the rest of which have escaped my memory, he told me that it was less than three weeks since a mound of earth, made pregnant by the sun, had given birth to him.

'Take a look at this tumour!' He drew my attention to a mysterious swelling in the mud, like a molehill. 'It is,' he said, 'a pimple, or let me rather call it a womb, in which the embryo of one of my brothers has been hidden for nine months. I am waiting here with the intention of offering him my services as a midwife.'

He would have continued, had he not noticed the earth quivering at the edge of this lump of clay. From this and the bigness of the bubo, he judged that the earth was already in labour and that the palpitation was caused by the strain of the birth pangs. He left me at once to run over to it, while I went off to retrieve my cabin.

I climbed back up the mountain down which I had come and reached the summit in a state of considerable weariness. You can imagine how distressed I was to find that my machine was no longer where I had left it. I had begun to lament its loss when I perceived it flitting along, a great distance away. I ran to it as fast as my legs could carry me, making myself quite out of breath. It was certainly a comical sport for anyone to contemplate, this new style of hunting, for sometimes when I almost had my hand upon it, the bowl of glass would undergo a slight rise in temperature. This would draw up the air with more force: the current became stronger and lifted my box above me, making me leap after it, like a cat after a hare it sees hanging from a butcher's hook. Had my shirt not remained on top of it, to counter the effect of the mirrors, it would have made the journey alone.

But what is the good of refreshing my memory about an adventure I cannot recall without suffering the same anguish as I felt at the time? It is enough for you to know that it bounded, ran, and flew, and that I walked and strode until eventually I saw it fall at the foot of a very high mountain. It could well have led me still further if the shadows of this haughty protuberance of the earth, which blotted out the heavens far in front of itself on the plain, had not spread darkness for half a league all round. For when my cabin entered these shades, its glass had no sooner felt the coolness of them than the vacuum ceased to be produced by it. No more wind blew through the hole and there was consequently no more upthrust to sustain it, so that it fell and would have smashed itself into a thousand smithereens if by lucky chance it had not fallen into a pool, which yielded beneath its weight. I recovered it from the water and put back into shape what was damaged. I then put my arms about it and held it as tightly as I could, while I carried it to the summit of a hill which was situated quite close by. There I unwrapped my shirt from round the vessel, but I could not put it on because my mirrors were beginning to work and I could see my cabin was already frisking to take off. All I had time to do was to climb swiftly into it and shut myself up as before.

The sphere of our world no longer looked to me like anything more than a heavenly body about the size the moon seems to us. As I rose, it shrank even more, becoming first a star, then a speck of light, and finally nothing at all, inasmuch as it was a luminous point as fine as the one which marks the ultimate range of my vision. So in the end it appeared to me to emerge into the general colour of the heavens.

Someone will perhaps express surprise at the fact that sleep should not have overcome me during such a long journey.

But as the only cause of sleep is the mild exhalation given off by food rising from the stomach to the brain, or a need which nature feels, to mend our souls and repair while we are at rest, such of their spirits as have been consumed by work, I had not the least inclination to sleep, since I was not eating and the radiant heat of the sun was restoring my supply of energy much faster than I used it up.

Meanwhile my ascent continued, and as it brought me closer to this fiery world I felt a certain joy flowing in my blood, which purified it and penetrated into my very soul. From time to time I looked up to admire the brilliance of the tints shining into my little crystal dome and I still have a vivid memory of how, at a moment when I am directing my gaze up into the globe of my vessel, with a sudden start I can feel something heavy flying away from every part of my body. An eddy of smoke, very thick and almost palpable, plunged my glass into darkness, and when I sought to stand up and study this night, which had blinded me, I could now see neither the vessel nor the mirrors, nor the glass, nor the lid of my cabin. I therefore lowered my eyes, hoping to discover what had made my masterpiece collapse thus in ruins, but where it should have been, with the four walls and the floor, I could find nothing but the sky, completely surrounding me. What alarmed me still more was to feel some invisible obstacle repulsing my arms, when I thought to extend them, just as if the fluidity of the air had become petrified. The notion came to me that, as a result of rising so high, I must have reached the firmament, which certain philosophers and some astronomers have alleged to be solid. I was already beginning to be afraid that I should be left encrusted in it forever, but the shock caused me by this bizarre occurrence was greatly increased by those that followed, for my gaze, in wandering here and there, having chanced to fall upon my chest, instead of stopping at the surface of my body, passed right through it! Then a moment later I became aware that I could see directly behind myself. As if my body had no longer been anything but an organ of sight, I felt my flesh, purged of its opacity, transmitting straight through itself, objects to my eyes and my vision to objects. Finally, after bumping against the roof, the floor, and the walls of my chair a thousand times without seeing them, I discovered that, through some secret law governing the light near its source, we had become transparent, my cabin and I.

If it had merely become diaphanous, I should still have been able to see it, since one can quite easily make out glass, crystal, and diamonds which are the same. But I deduce that in a region so near to it, the sun must purge bodies of their opacity much more perfectly, aligning the imperceptible openings in matter straighter than in our world, where its strength is almost used up by the long distance it has to travel, so that it is only just capable of infusing its brilliance into precious stones. At all events, on account of the internal evenness of their surfaces, the sun makes them pour out through their glass (as if through little eyes) either the green of emeralds, the scarlet of rubies, or the violet of amethysts—according as the different pores in the stones are straighter or more tortuous and as the varying quantities of reflections either extinguish or rekindle this enfeebled light.

One difficulty may be troubling the reader, namely to know how I could see myself yet not see my box, since I had become transparent just as much as it had. My answer to this is that doubtless the sun affects living bodies and inanimate ones differently, since no part of my flesh, bones, or bowels, although transparent, had lost its natural colour. On the contrary, my lungs still kept their soft delicacy beneath a tinge of pinkish red; my heart, ever vermilion, see-sawed easily between systole and diastole; my liver seemed to burn in a purple fire, heating the air which I breathed and maintaining the circulation of the blood; in a word, I could see and feel myself to be just the same—even if in fact I was not.

While I was considering this metamorphosis, my journey was growing ever shorter, but then my pace was much slower on account of the stillness of the upper air, which grew more rarefied as I drew nearer to the source of the daylight. For as matter at this level is very dilute, on account of the great amount of vacuum it contains, which, being inactive makes it very lazy, this air could not produce more than a gentle breeze as it passed through the hole in my box, which was scarcely capable of sustaining it.

I never reflect upon the malicious caprices of fortune, who continually opposed herself so obstinately to the success of my enterprise, without being astonished at how I did not take leave of my senses. But hearken to a miracle, which future centuries will find difficult to believe.

Enclosed in a translucent box, which I had just lost from view, with my impetus so reduced that I was lucky to keep from falling—in short, in a predicament where the whole system of the cosmos was powerless to save me—I found myself stranded in a state of extreme distress. However, just as when we are dying we are internally impelled to want to embrace those to whom we owe our existence, so I raised my eyes to the sun, our common father. This upsurge of my will not only sustained my body, but projected it on towards the thing it aspired to embrace. My body pushed my box and in this fashion I continued my journey. As soon as I noticed this, I stiffened all the faculties of my soul with more concentration than ever, in order to fasten them, in imagination, to what attracted me. But the burden of my cabin on the top of my head (for I was pressed against the ceiling in spite of myself by the effects of my will) incommoded me to such an extent that I was eventually constrained by its weight to feel for the place where the invisible door was. Happily I found it, opened it and flung myself out; but the natural fear of falling, which all animals have when they are caught in mid-air, made me stretch out my arms briskly to catch hold of something. I was only guided by an unthinking instinct of nature, however, and that is why fortune, her enemy, maliciously thrust my hand against the crystal top.

Alas! How the sound of the icosahedron smashing to pieces rang in my ears like a thunderclap! Such an accident, such a misfortune, and such terror are beyond all description. The mirrors attracted no more air, for there was no longer any vacuum being created. The air no longer became a wind rushing in to fill it. The wind ceased to propel my box upwards. In short, immediately after this wreck, I saw it falling for a very long time through the vast zones of the universe. It recovered its shadowy opacity in the region where it had breathed it out. The energetic virtue of the light ceases to take effect in that locality and so my box avidly resumed its obscure density, which seemed as if it was essential to it, just as spirits have been seen coming in search of their bodies and wandering round their tombs for a hundred years, trying to rejoin them. I suppose that this is how it lost its diaphanousness, for I have since seen it in Poland in the same state as it was in when I climbed into it for the first time. I later discovered that it fell below the equinoctial line in the kingdom of Borneo. A Portuguese merchant bought it from the Islander who found it and it passed from hand to hand until it came into the possession of the Polish engineer who now uses it for flying.

Suspended thus in the wastes of the heavens and already thrown into consternation by the prospect of falling to my death, I lifted up my eyes sadly towards the sun, as I have told you. My vision carried my thoughts there and my gaze, firmly fixed on its globe, marked out a path, whose traces my will could follow in order to carry my body up to it.

This vigorous upsurge of my soul will not be incomprehensible to anyone who considers the most simple effects of our will power. It is common knowledge that when I wish to jump in the air, my will, aroused by my imagination, stirs up the whole microcosm of my body and strives to carry it up towards the goal it has set itself. If it does not always reach it, this is because the principles in nature which are universal prevail over those which are restricted. Since the power of the will is confined to sentient beings, while the impulse to fall towards the earth's centre is distributed throughout all matter, my leap is halted just as I am drawing near to my goal, when my mass has overcome the insolence of my will, which had taken it by surprise.

I will pass over what followed during the rest of my journey, for fear of taking as long to relate it as I did to make it. It suffices to say that at the end of twenty-two months I finally made a happy landing upon the broad plains of the daylight.

14

The little people of the sun and the love-sick nightingale

THIS land is so luminous that it resembles snowflakes on fire. There is, however, one rather incredible thing, which I have never been able to make out and that is whether, once my box had fallen, I was mounting or descending towards the sun. All I can remember is that when I had arrived there, I walked lightly upon it. I only touched the ground at a single point and often rolled like a ball, finding it no more inconvenient to travel upon my head than on my feet. Although I sometimes had my legs pointing towards the sky and my shoulders against the ground, it felt as natural to be placed in this position as if I had my feet on the ground and my shoulders towards the sky. Whichever part of my body I rested on, whether on my belly, my back, an elbow, or an ear, I felt as if I were standing upright. From this I learned that the sun is a world which has no centre, and that, as I was very far from the sphere of influence of our own, and of all those I had encountered, it was consequently impossible for me to continue to have any weight, since weight is simply the attraction exercised by a centre within its sphere of influence.

The awe I felt in printing my steps upon that luminous countryside gave pause for a while to my burning eagerness to continue my journey. I felt quite ashamed to be walking upon the daylight. My very body was bewildered and sought the support of my eyes. But since this transparent land, through which their vision penetrated, could offer them nothing to rest upon, my instinct got the better of my mind and drove it on and on, in spite of myself, seeking out the depths of a light which was bottomless. However, my reason gradually regained control of my instinct. I planted firm and untrembling footsteps upon the plain and measured my paces so proudly that if men could have seen me from their world, they would have taken me for the great god, who walks upon the clouds.

After travelling, as I believe, for fifteen days, I came to a country of the sun less dazzling than that which I had left. I felt greatly overjoyed and I imagined that this joy must proceed from a secret sympathy which my body still felt for its opacity. However, my awareness of this did not make me desist from the course I was pursuing. For at this time I was like those slumbering old men, who know that sleep is harmful to them and have ordered their servants to wake them from it, but still become very angry when they are aroused. Now, as I gradually reached the darker provinces, my body became opaque and once more contracted the weaknesses which matter—that infirmity—brings with it; I became tired and sleep took hold of me. Yet so much pleasure flowed into my senses from the exquisite laziness with which sleep flatters us, as it approaches, that they succumbed to its delights and obliged my soul to be grateful to the very tyrant which chained up its servants. For sleep, which has for so long been the tyrant that rules half of our days, cannot bear the light, on account of his great age, nor look upon it without fainting, and had been constrained to abandon me on my entry to the more brilliant climes of the sun. He had gone to wait for me on the frontiers of the darker region of which I am speaking, where he caught up with me once more, took me prisoner and closed my eyes, his declared enemies, beneath the dark roof of my eyelids. And fearing lest my other senses, cheating him, even as they had betrayed me, should interfere with his peaceful occupation of the conquered territory, he pinioned each one of them to its bed. All of which is to say, in a couple of words, that I lay down upon the sand in a deep stupor.

It was a bare country, so open that there was not a single bush as far as the eye could see, and yet, upon my awakening, I found myself beneath a tree by comparison with which the tallest cedars would seem like so many blades of grass. Its trunk was of solid gold, its branches of silver, and its leaves were emeralds, in which were mirrored beneath the brilliant green of their precious surface the images of the fruit which hung about the tree. But judge whether the fruit owed anything to the leaves. Half of each of them was made up of the blazing scarlet of a fat carbuncle and the other would be composed either of a chrysolite or a piece of gilded amber. The flowers in bloom were very broad roses of diamond and the buds were great pear-shaped pearls.

A nightingale, most excellently beautiful with its smooth plumage, perched on the topmost twig, and with its song it seemed to be trying to make one's eyes admit to one's ears that it was not unworthy of the throne on which it sat.

For a long time I was left dumbfounded by this splendid spectacle and could not gaze at it enough. But while my whole mind was taken up with the contemplation of an extraordinarily beautiful pomegranate, among the other fruits, the flesh of which was formed by a cluster of several large rubies fused together, I perceived the little crown, which took the place of its head, moving and stretching itself sufficiently to form a neck. Then I saw something white seething on top, which thickened, swelled, advanced, and withdrew its substance in certain places until it finally appeared to be a face on top of a small bust of flesh. This little bust terminated in a sphere, round about the waist; that is to say, it still kept its apple shape down below. However, it stretched itself little by little and when its stalk had turned into two legs, each of its feet divided into five toes.

Thus humanized, the pomegranate detached itself from its stem and fell right at my feet with a gentle bump. I freely admit that when I saw this reasonable fruit walking proudly in front of me—this little bit of a dwarf no bigger than my thumb and yet powerful enough to have created itself—I was awestruck.

'Human animal,' he said to me (in that original language of which I have spoken to you already), 'after observing you for some time from up on the branch where I hung, I thought I could read in your face that you were not a native of this world. It is because of this that I have come down to be enlightened as to the truth of the matter.'

When I had satisfied his curiosity about all the subjects on which he questioned me, I said to him: 'But as for yourself, reveal to me who you are. For what I have just witnessed is so very astounding, that if you do not teach me I must despair of ever knowing the cause of it. What do I see? An entire tree of pure gold, whose leaves are emeralds, whose flowers are diamonds, whose buds are pearls and, amidst all this, fruits which turn into men in the twinkling of an eye! I must confess that to understand such a miracle is quite beyond my power.'

After this outburst I waited for his reply. 'You can have no objection,' he said, 'since I am the King of the whole nation which makes up this tree, to my summoning it to follow my example.'

When he had spoken these words I observed him withdraw into himself. I do not know if, by winding up the internal mechanism of his will, he set off some movement outside himself which caused what you are about to hear of to happen: but at all events, immediately afterwards all the fruits, all the flowers, all the leaves, all the branches and finally the whole tree disintegrated into little men that saw, felt, and walked and, as if to celebrate their birthday at the very moment of their birth, began to dance all round me.

Only the nightingale, amid all the rest of them, retained its shape and was in no way transformed. It came and perched on the shoulder of our little monarch, where it sang an air so melancholy and so love-sick that the whole assembly, including the prince himself, was moved by the sweet langours and dying falls of its voice, and wept several tears over it. I was then overcome with a curiosity to learn where this bird came from, that gave me such an extraordinary itching of the tongue that I could no longer contain it.

'Sire,' I said, addressing the King, 'if I were not afraid to trouble your Majesty I should ask you why, among so many metamorphoses, the nightingale alone has retained its shape.'

The little prince heard me with a condescension which gave good proof of his natural bounty and, acknowledging my curiosity, he replied to me: 'The nightingale has not changed its shape, as we have, because it could not: it is a true bird, which is no more than what it appears to you to be. But let us walk towards the opaque regions. I will tell you, as we go along, who I am, and give you the story of the nightingale.'

I had hardly expressed the satisfaction his offer had given me, when he jumped lightly on to one of my shoulders. He raised himself on his little toes to reach my ear with his mouth. One moment he was swinging on my hair and the next he was tormenting himself with the strappado from it.

'Upon my soul!' he said to me. 'You really must excuse a body who feels out of breath already. Being in a tiny frame, my lungs are constricted, and my voice is so faint, in consequence, that I am obliged to strain myself a good deal in order to be heard. The nightingale himself will see fit to tell you about himself. Let it sing then, if it wishes! At least we shall have the pleasure of hearing its story in music.'

I replied that I had not yet sufficient familiarity with the bird language. It was true that a certain philosopher, whom I had met on my way up to the sun, had indeed given me several general principles for understanding that of the brutes, but these were not sufficient for me to understand the complete vocabulary, nor for me to be touched by all the subtleties, which are to be found in an adventure such as this must be.

'Very well,' he said. 'Since you wish it, your ears will be deprived not merely of the nightingale's beautiful songs, but of almost all its history, for I can only tell you the part of it which has come to my knowledge. However you will have to be content with this sample, since even if I knew the whole of it, the brevity of our journey into its country, whither I am returning it, would not allow me to pursue my story any further.'

Having spoken thus, he leapt off my shoulder on to the ground. He then joined hands with all his little people and began to dance with them in a kind of figure, which I cannot describe, for nothing comparable has ever been seen. But hearken, peoples of the earth, to something I would not oblige you to believe, since even in the world where what you would call 'miracles' are but natural phenomena, what follows passes for a miracle! As soon as these little men had set themselves a-dancing, I seemed to feel their movements in myself and mine in theirs. I could not watch this dance without being perceptibly drawn from where I stood as if by a vortex which was spinning with its own momentum. All the parts of my body were agitated by the various movements of each of theirs and I would feel the same joy spreading across my face, which a similar action had caused to spread across theirs.

As the dance became more intense, the dancers were merged together with a stamping which grew much swifter and more imperceptible. It seemed that the aim of the ballet was to imitate an enormous giant, for as they drew nearer together and redoubled the speed of their movements, they blended so closely that all I could make out was a great luminous and half-transparent colossus, although my eyes could still see them entering into one another.

It was at that time that I began to be unable to distinguish one spinning creature from another on account of their rapid rotations, and also because these rotations were continually contracting as they approached the centre, and each vortex finally occupied so little space that it escaped my sight. However, I assume that the parts continued to draw closer, since this human mass, which had formerly been huge, gradually shrank to form a young man of medium stature, whose every limb was shaped with a symmetry, to which the greatest ideal of perfection has never attained. He was beautiful beyond all the loftiest dreams of the painters, but what I found quite marvellous was that the joining of all the component parts of this perfect microcosm took place in the twinkling of an eye. Some of the most agile of our little dancers had leaped up to the height and into the posture essential to the formation of the head; some, warmer and less refined, formed the heart; and some, much heavier, only went into the making of the bones, the flesh, and the fat.

When this tall, handsome young man was quite completed, although the swiftness of his construction had hardly left me any time to notice the stages in his progress, I saw the King of all those peoples, of whom he was a hotch-potch, entering through his mouth. It seems to me, furthermore, that he was inhaled into the body by its own respiration. All this mass of little men had not previously given any sign of life, but as soon as it had swallowed its little King, it no longer felt like anything but one being. He considered me for some time and having apparently collected himself as he looked at me, he drew near to me, caressed me, and gave me his hand.

'And now, without injuring the delicacy of my lungs, I can tell you about the things you were so anxious to know,' he said. 'But it is reasonable enough, first of all, to reveal the hidden secrets of our origin. Know then that we are creatures native to the brightest regions of the sun. The most usual of our occupations and the most profitable is to travel through the vast countries of this great world. We observe with curiosity the customs of the nations, the character of the climates and the nature of anything which deserves our attention. Thus we are able to establish a certain science of what is.

'You must know that my vassals used to travel under my leadership and that in order to have the leisure to scrutinize things more searchingly, we did not retain that conformation peculiar to our bodies, which cannot be perceived by your senses and the subtlety of which would have made us travel too fast, but turned ourselves into birds. At my command all my subjects had become eagles, and as for myself, for fear that they might grow weary, I transformed myself into a nightingale, in order to sweeten their task with the charms of music. I accompanied the rapid flight of my people without flying myself, for I was perched upon the head of one of my vassals, and we were continuing on our way as usual when a nightingale, which lived in a province of the opaque country which we were then crossing, astonished to see me in the power of an eagle (for it could not do otherwise than take us for our outward shapes), began to lament my misfortune. I called my people to a halt and we flew down to the tops of several trees, where this charitable bird was sighing.

'I took so much pleasure in the sweetness of its sad songs, that in order to have more time and leisure to enjoy them, I had no desire to undeceive it. I invented a story on the spot, in which I related the imaginary misfortunes which had made me fall into the hands of this eagle. I brought in such amazing adventures, summoning up my passions so adroitly and choosing each note of my song so well, that the nightingale was beside itself.

'We serenaded one another by turns with the musical stories of our mutual loves. In my airs I sang that I was not only comforted but that I even rejoiced at my disaster since it had won me the honour of being lamented in such beautiful songs. And the inconsolable little bird replied to me in its own that it would have accepted with joy all the esteem in which I held it, if it could have had the knowledge that this might make it worthy of the honour of dying in my place. But since fortune had not reserved so much honour for a wretch like itself, it would only accept as much of my esteem as was needed to save me from blushing to be its friend.

'I replied in my turn with all the raptures, all the tenderness, and all the subtleties of a passion so moving that two or three times I saw it on the branch ready to die of love. In truth, I mixed so much skill with the sweetness of my voice and surprised its ear with touches so cunning and ways so little frequented by its own species, that I had its fair soul at the mercy of all the passions to which I wished to subject it.

'This exercise took up the space of twenty-four hours and I think we should have never tired of making love if our throats had not prevented us going on. For, feeling that the effort was beginning to rend my throat and that I could not continue any longer without falling into a faint, I signed to it to come close to me.

'Its belief that I was in danger amidst the host of eagles convinced it that I was calling it to my aid. It flew to help me at once and, wishing to give me a glorious proof that it knew how to brave death, even on his very throne, for the sake of a friend, came and sat proudly upon the great hooked beak of the eagle where I was perched. Such great courage in so tiny an animal certainly inspired me with some reverence. For even if I had been calling for it, as it imagined, and although there is a law between animals of the same species that they must help one of their number in distress, none the less the instinct of its timid nature should have made it hesitate—and yet it did not hesitate for one instant. On the contrary it moved so swiftly that I cannot tell which flashed sooner, the sign I made or the nightingale. Proud to see the head of the tyrant beneath its feet, and ravished to think that for love of me it was going to be sacrificed almost between my wings, and that perhaps a few happy drops of its blood would spurt on to my feathers, it turned its eyes tenderly towards me and after apparently bidding me adieu with a look, in which it seemed to be asking me permission to die, it plunged its little beak so smartly into the eyes of the eagle that they appeared to be burst rather than pierced.

'When my bird felt himself blinded he at once gave himself completely new eyesight. I softly reprimanded the nightingale for its over-hasty action, and judging that it would be dangerous to conceal our true nature any longer, I revealed myself to it and told it who we were. But the poor little thing, persuaded that these monsters, whose prisoner I was, were forcing me to invent this fable, gave no credence to anything I told it. When I realized that all the arguments by which I tried to convince it were lost on the winds, I gave some orders in a low voice to ten or twelve thousand of my subjects and immediately the nightingale saw a river flowing at its feet, beneath a boat, which floated on the water. This was no larger than was needed to accommodate me twice over. At the first signal I gave them, my eagles took to the air and tossed me into the skiff and I called out to the nightingale from there that if it still could not bring itself to abandon me straight away, it should embark with me. As soon as it came on board, I commanded the river to take its course towards the region whither my people were flying. But the fluidity of the waters being less than that of the air, the speed of their flight was consequently greater than that of our navigation and we were somewhat left behind.

'Throughout the whole journey I attempted to disabuse my little guest. I pointed out once more that it could expect no fruit from its passion, since we were not of the same species, that it must surely have recognized this when the eagle, whose eyes it had burst, visibly forged itself new ones, or when twelve thousand of my vassals had transformed themselves at my command into this river and this boat in which we were travelling. My remonstrances met with no success. It replied that as for the eagle, which I wished to make it believe had forged eyes for itself, this bird had had no need to do this, since it had not applied its beak firmly enough to its eyeballs, and as for the river and the boat, which I said had only been engendered by a metamorphosis of my people, they had been in the wood since the creation of the world, but had not been noticed.

'Seeing the nightingale so very ingenious at deceiving itself, I agreed with it that my vassals and I would change ourselves before its eyes into whatever it wanted, on condition that after that it would return to its homeland. First it asked us to become a tree; next it would have us become a flower, then a fruit, then stone. Finally, in order to satisfy all its desires simultaneously, when we had met up with my court at the place where I had commanded them to wait for me, we turned ourselves before the nightingale's eyes into the precious tree which you encountered on your road and whose shape we have just abandoned. For the rest, now that I see this little bird resolved to return to its country, we are going, my subjects and I, to resume both our shape and the direction of our journey.

'But it is reasonable to reveal to you first who we are, namely animals born and bred in the brilliant part of the sun—for there is an extremely marked difference between the peoples which the luminous region produces and the peoples of the opaque country. It is us whom you in the world of the earth call "spirits," and your presumptuous stupidity has given us this name, because, not being able to imagine animals more perfect than man and seeing certain beings which do things beyond human power, you have presumed these animals to be spirits. You are nevertheless mistaken: we are animals like you. For although, when we choose, we can give our substance the essential appearance and shape of anything we want to turn into, as you have just seen, this does not prove that we are spirits.

'But listen, and I will explain how all these metamorphoses, which seem to you to be so many miracles, are nothing but simple natural phenomena. You must know that being inhabitants of the pellucid part of this great world, where the principle of matter is to be in action, we are bound to have much more active imaginations than those of the opaque regions, and bodies composed of a much more fluid substance.

'Once one supposes this, it inevitably follows that our imagination, encountering no resistance in the matter of which we are composed, can arrange it at will, and, having become the complete master of our bodies, manœuvres them, by moving all their particles, into the arrangements necessary to constitute the objects it has pictured in miniature. Thus each one of us imagined the place and the part of this precious tree into which he would change. By this effort of imagination, we excited in our substance the movements necessary to produce them and so changed ourselves into them. Thus my eagle, when his eyes were blinded, had only to imagine himself to be an eagle with good sight in order to restore them; for all our transformations come from movement.

'That is why, when we were transmuted from leaves, flowers, and fruits into men, you saw us dancing for some time afterwards, because we had not yet recovered from the momentum which we had to give our matter, to turn ourselves into men. In this we are like bells, which, though they have stopped ringing, still murmur for some time afterwards, softly repeating the sound produced by the clapper when it strikes them. It is also why you saw us dancing before making this great man, because, in order to produce him, we had to give ourselves all the general and specific movements necessary for his construction. Thus, as this motion gradually drew our bodies together and absorbed them into one another, each one of us, in each part of the whole, provided with his own individual movement the particular movement it ought to have. You men cannot do such things on account of the heaviness of your substance and the frigidity of your imagination.'

He continued his exposition and supported it with examples so familiar and so concrete, that I was eventually disabused of a great number of the ill-proven opinions with which our stubborn doctors of science blinker the feebleminded. I then began to understand how, in fact, the imagination of these solar peoples, being warmer, perforce, on account of the climate, their bodies being lighter for the same reason, and their personalities more volatile (since their world exerts no central pull, as ours does, to wrench their bodies away from the movements inspired by their imagination), I conceived, I say, how this imagination, without the aid of any miracle, could bring about all the 'miracles' it had just performed.

I was ultimately convinced by a thousand examples of almost comparable events, to which the peoples of our globe give credence. Cippus, King of Italy, watched bulls fighting. He had horns on the brain all night and next found his forehead had sprouted a pair. Gallus Vitius taxed his mind and strove so hard to grasp the essence of madness, that the effort of his imagination gave his body the actions which constitute madness and he became mad. King Codrus was consumptive but concentrated his eyes and thoughts upon the freshness of a young face. The bloom of youth which radiated from the young lad induced in him the action of imagining he had the health of a young man and he began to mend. And finally, many pregnant women have been brought to bed of monsters after having children already formed in their wombs. The fancies that come to them were not powerful enough to give them the shape of monsters themselves, but they were enough to mould the substance of the foetus, which was much more hot and malleable than their own, into the pattern necessary for the production of such monsters. I was even persuaded that if, when the famous hypochondriac of antiquity imagined himself to be a pitcher, his substance (which was too compact and heavy) could have followed the flight of his fancy, his body would have become a perfect pitcher; and everyone would have seen that he really was a pitcher, the way he saw himself.

A host of other examples satisfied and convinced me and I no longer doubted any of the marvels which the spirit-man had recounted to me. He asked me if I did not desire anything more of him but I thanked him with all my heart. And in conclusion he had the further goodness to advise me that, since I was an inhabitant of the earth, I should follow the nightingale to the opaque regions of the sun, because they conformed more to the pleasures for which human nature has an appetite.

He had hardly finished this speech when his mouth opened very wide and I saw the king of these little animals emerging from the depths of his gullet in the form of a nightingale. The great man collapsed at once and at the same time all his limbs flew off bit by bit in the shape of eagles. The self-created nightingale perched upon the head of the most handsome of them and from there he sang an admirable tune, with which I take it he was bidding me good-bye.

The true nightingale also took flight, but not in their direction. Nor did it soar so high, so that I did not lose sight of it. We travelled at about the same speed, for as I had no plan to visit one country rather than another, I was glad enough to go with it; all the more because, the opaque regions of the birds being in conformity with my constitution, I hoped to find adventures there which would likewise suit my temperament. I travelled in this hope for at least three weeks, with every kind of delight, as far as my ears were concerned, for the nightingale did not leave me in want of music. When it was tired it came and rested on my shoulder, and when I stopped it waited for me. In the end I arrived in the country of the kingdom of this little minstrel, which then took no further trouble to accompany me.

Having lost it from view, I looked for it and called to it, but at length I grew so weary from my vain pursuit of it that I resolved to take a rest. For this purpose I stretched myself out upon a lawn of soft grass which carpeted the roots of a lofty crag. This rock was covered with many young trees, green and leafy, whose shade charmed my exhausted senses in the most agreeable way in the world and obliged me to abandon them to sleep, in order to restore my strength in the shelter of this cool and tranquil place.

15

The story of the birds

I WAS beginning to fall asleep when I perceived a marvellous bird hovering in the air above my head. It kept aloft with a movement so slight and imperceptible that I several times wondered if it was not another little world, balanced by its own centre. However, it gradually descended and finally came so close to me that my uplifted eyes were quite filled with its image. Its tail appeared green, its belly a glossy blue, its wings crimson; and the movement of its purple head produced the glinting of a golden crown, whose rays sprang from its eyes.

For a long time it flew about in the sky and I kept my gaze glued to all its movements, with my whole being so completely screwed up and concentrated on the single operation of looking that it was hardly capable of listening at all to what the bird was saying as it sang.

As I gradually unwound from my ecstasy, I began to distinguish the syllables, words, and sentences that it uttered.

Here, as well as I can remember them, are the terms in which it presented the tissue of its song.

'You are a stranger,' the bird trilled most pleasantly, 'and you were born in the world of which I am a native. That secret inclination which draws us to our compatriots is the instinct which makes me want to impart to you the history of my life.

'I can see you are racking your brains to understand how it is possible for me to explain myself to you in coherent speech, since although birds imitate your talk, they do not understand it. But then equally, when you imitate the barking of a dog or the song of a nightingale, you do not understand what the dog or the nightingale were saying. You may therefore deduce that this does not make either birds or men any less intelligent.

'However, just as some of your number have been so enlightened that they understood and spoke our language—like Apollonius Tianeus, Anaximander, Aesop, and many whose names I will not repeat to you, because they have never come to your knowledge—so among us there are some who understand and speak your language. Many of these, it is true, only know the language of one nation, but just as there are birds that say nothing, some that merely warble, and others that can speak, so there are some even more gifted ones that have a command of all kinds of idioms. For myself, I have the honour to be among that small number.

'Furthermore, you must know that nature has implanted a

secret desire in birds, whichever world they are in, to fly to this one. Perhaps this yearning impulse is what makes us sprout wings, just as pregnant women produce in their children the image of things they longed for; or rather as people who long to know how to swim have been seen to plunge into rivers while fast asleep and to negotiate more skilfully than an experienced swimmer hazards they would not even have dared to look at when awake; or like that son of King Croesus, to whom a violent desire to speak in order to save his father suddenly gave the power of language; or, in short, like that old man who was cornered by his enemy and surprised without weapons and felt the horns of a bull growing on his forehead as the result of the desire inspired in him by a fury which resembled that of this animal.

'When birds arrive at the sun, they make their way to the republic of their species—but I can see you are bursting to learn who I am. Where you come from they call me the phoenix. There is only one at a time in each world and it lives there for the space of a hundred years. At the end of a century, when it has delivered itself of a great egg upon some Arabian mountain amidst the cinders of its pyre (which is built of aloe branches, cinnamon, and incense), it takes flight and sets course towards the sun, the homeland to which its heart has long aspired. Indeed we make every effort to accomplish this journey sooner, but the weight of our eggs, whose shells are so thick that it takes a century for them to hatch, always retards the enterprise.

'I do not doubt that you would find this miraculous form of reproduction difficult to understand. I will therefore explain it to you. The phoenix is a hermaphrodite, but even among hermaphrodites it is still as rare as a phoenix, for . . .'

It stopped speaking for ten minutes and then added: 'I can see that you suspect that what I have just told you is false; but if I am not speaking the truth, may I never land upon your globe without an eagle pouncing upon me.'

It remained hovering in the sky for some time more and then flew off.

The amazement its story had caused me made me curious to follow it, and as it cut through the vastness of the heavens with an unhurried flight, my eyes and my feet could keep pace with it quite easily.

After about fifty leagues I found myself in a country so full of birds that their number almost equalled that of the leaves on the trees which held them. What surprised me even more was that these birds, instead of being alarmed at my approach, fluttered all round me. One twittered in my ear, another strutted about on my head and, to be brief, after their little antics had occupied my attention for a considerable time, I suddenly felt my arms burdened with more than a million of all kinds of species, which weighed so heavily upon me that I could not move them.

They held me in this state until I saw four large eagles arriving. Two of these gripped my legs with their talons and the other two my arms and thus they lifted me high into the air.

Among the crowd I noticed a magpie flying up and down and hither and thither in great haste, and I heard it calling out to me that I should not try to defend myself at all, since its companions were already contemplating poking my eyes out. This warning prevented any resistance I might have made, and so these eagles carried me more than a thousand leagues from there to a great wood, which was (so the magpie told me) the town where their king had his residence.

The first thing they did was to throw me into prison in the hollow trunk of a great oak tree, and a number of the sturdiest of them perched upon the branches, where they exercised the functions of a company of armed soldiers.

At the end of about twenty-four hours others came on guard to relieve them. While I awaited whatever disasters fortune was pleased to ordain for me in a state of deep melancholy, my charitable magpie kept me informed about everything that was going on.

Among other things, I remember it warned me that the populace of the birds had protested loudly against my being kept for such a long time without being devoured, complaining that I was growing so thin that there would be nothing left of me but bones to gnaw.

The tumult threatened to erupt into sedition, for when my magpie took the liberty of arguing that it was a barbarous proceeding, thus to take the life of an animal which in some measure approached their own intellectual level, without a fair hearing, they nearly tore it to pieces, asserting that it would be ridiculous in the extreme to believe that a wholly naked animal, which even its mother, nature, had not bothered to furnish with the essentials for survival, should be capable of thinking like them.

'Possibly,' they added, 'if it were an animal which came a little closer to our own shape . . . but it is the most completely unlike us and the most hideous. Briefly, it is a bald beast, a plucked bird, a chimera compounded of all kinds of creatures and which brings terror to all; man, I say, so stupid and so vain that he is convinced we were only made to serve him; man, whose mind is so perceptive, but who cannot tell sugar from arsenic, and will swallow hemlock, which his fine judgement tells him is parsley; man, who maintains that reasoning can only be based on the evidence of the senses, but who has the feeblest, dullest, and most faulty senses of all the creatures; man, in short, whom nature created out of pieces of everything, like a freak, but whom she inspired with the ambition to rule all other animals and to exterminate them.'

That is what the wisest among them said: as for the common mob, they cried out that it was horrible to believe that a beast without a face like theirs should be possessed of reason.

'What?' they murmured to one another. 'It has neither beak, nor feathers, nor claws—and yet its soul is supposed to be spiritual! O gods! What impertinence!'

The pity which the more magnanimous of them felt for me in no way prevented criminal proceedings being instituted against me. All the documents for this were drawn up upon the bark of a cypress and then at the end of several days I was taken before the Tribunal of the Birds. The only lawyers, counsellors, and judges at this session were magpies, jays, and starlings; furthermore they had only selected those that understood my language.

Instead of putting me in the dock for interrogation, they set me astride a stump of rotten wood. After clacking with his beak two or three times and shaking his feathers majestically, the one presiding over the hearing asked me where I came from, my nation, and my species. My charitable magpie had given me some instructions beforehand, which were very salutary to me—among them, that I should be careful to refrain from admitting that I was a man. I therefore replied that I came from that small world known as the earth, about which they might have heard from the phoenix and several others, whom I saw in the assembly. The climate that had witnessed my birth was situated below the temperate zone of the northern hemisphere in an extremity of Europe called France. As for my species, I was not a man at all, as they imagined, but an ape. Some men had stolen me from my cradle when I was very young and brought me up among themselves. The bad education they gave me had made my skin delicate and they had made me forget my native language and taught me theirs. In order to please these wild animals, I had become accustomed to walking on two legs only and finally, as it is easier to be degraded in species than to rise, the opinions, customs, and food of these horrible beasts had gained such a hold over me that my family, who were apes of the best class, would scarcely recognize me themselves. In justification of myself I added that they should have me examined by experts, and that in the event of my being found to be a man, I would submit to being annihilated as a monster.

'Gentlemen,' cried a swallow from the assembly, as soon as I had finished speaking, 'you will not have forgotten that it has just said that the country which witnessed its birth was France. But you know that apes do not breed in France. Judge now whether it is what it pretends to be!'

I replied to my accuser that I had been ravished from the bosom of my family and taken to France so young, that I could fairly call my 'native country' the one of which I had my earliest memories.

This argument was, in fact, specious and inadequate, but the majority of them, delighted to hear that I was not a man, were only too glad to accept it, for those that had never seen one could not believe that a man was not far more horrible than I appeared to them, while the wisest added that man was something so abominable, that it was useful for them to believe it to be a purely imaginary being.

So all the audience clapped their wings in rapture and I was immediately handed over to the Syndics for an examination. They were charged to bring me back the following day and report on their findings to the company when the courts opened. They undertook this charge and took me to a secluded grove. While they held me there they did nothing but perform a hundred kinds of somersaults all round me and make processions, carrying nutshells on their heads. Now they clapped their feet together, now they dug little ditches —only to fill them in again—and in the end I was astonished to see that they had all disappeared.

The day and night were spent on these trifles until the following day, when the appointed hour arrived, they took me back to appear before my judges once more. My Syndics were called upon to speak the truth and replied that in order to satisfy their consciences they felt obliged to advise the Court that I was certainly not an ape, as I claimed to be.

'We have vainly pranced, marched, pirouetted and invented a hundred antics in front of it,' they said, 'hoping to encourage it to do the same, as apes generally do. For even if it had been reared among men, once an ape, always an ape, and we contend that it would not have been in its power to abstain from imitating our monkey tricks. These, my lords, are our findings.'

The judges then came together in order to reach an

opinion, but it was seen that the sky was clouding over and looked heavy. This caused the assembly to rise.

I was left under the impression that the threat of bad weather had provoked this, until the Attorney General came and told me, by order of the Court, that I should not be judged all that day. A criminal case was never settled when the sky was not serene, because they were afraid that the bad atmospheric conditions might have some effect upon the sound constitution of the judges' minds and that the mood of depression which overcomes birds when it rains might influence the course of the trial, indeed, that the Court might vent its ill humour upon the accused. That is why the judgement of my case was put off until the weather improved. I was therefore taken back to prison and I remember that my charitable magpie hardly deserted me all the way. It flew at my side continually and I believe it would not have left me at all, if its companions had not approached us.

At last I arrived at my prison, where I was fed during my captivity on nothing but 'the King's bread,' this being their name for some four dozen worms and as many maggots, which they brought for me to eat every seven hours.

I was expecting to appear in court again on the following day and everybody thought the same, but after five or six days one of my guards told me that all this time had been taken to dispense justice to a community of goldfinches who had implored it against one of their companions. I asked this guard what crime the wretch was accused of.

'Of the crime,' replied the guard, 'of the most terrible crime with which a bird's name can be sullied. He is accused —would you ever believe it? He is accused—But, Gods! the very thought of it makes the feathers on my head stand on end. In short, he is accused of not having deserved a friend for the past six years! That is why he has been condemned to be a King—and the King of a different species from his own.

'If his subjects had been of his own kind, he could at least have feasted his eyes and his longing upon their pleasures: but as the delights of one species have no connection with those of another, he must endure all the weariness and drink all the bitterness of kingship, without being able to enjoy any of its sweetness.

'He was sent off this morning, surrounded by a great many doctors, to watch that he does not take poison on the way.'

Although my guard was a great chatterbox by nature, it did not dare to talk to me alone for any longer, for fear of being suspected of intelligence.

Towards the end of the week I was brought before my judges again.

They perched me upon the fork of a little tree without any leaves. The birds of the long robe, advocates, counsellors, and magistrates alike, roosted in tiers, each according to its status, in the upper part of a great cedar tree. As for the rest, who were only present at the assembly out of curiosity, they sat here, there, and everywhere, until all the seats were taken, or rather until all the branches of the cedar were covered with feet.

The magpie, which I had always observed to be full of compassion for me, came to perch on my tree, where it pretended to be amusing itself pecking at the moss and said to me: 'You have really no idea how much I feel for your misfortune, for although I am not unaware that, of all living creatures, a man is a pest of which every well-policed state should be rid, yet when I remember how I was raised among them from the cradle, how I learned their language so perfectly that I have almost forgotten my own, and how I ate from their hands soft cheeses, so excellent that I cannot think of them without my eyes and my mouth watering, I feel a sympathy for you which prevents me from siding with the party which is in the right.'

It was just finishing these words when we were interrupted by the arrival of an eagle, which came and sat among the branches of a tree quite close to mine. I would have got up in order to kneel in front of it, believing it to be the King, if my magpie had not kept me in my place with its claw.

'Did you think, then,' it said, 'that that great eagle was our sovereign? That is a notion invented by you men, who, because you allow yourselves to be commanded by the biggest, strongest and cruellest of your fellows, have got the stupid idea (judging all things by yourselves) that the eagle must be our leader.

'But our policy is quite different, for we choose none but the weakest, the most gentle and the most pacific to be our King and, in addition, we change him once every six months. We choose him weak, so that the least one of us who might be wronged by him could take his revenge. We choose him gentle, so that he should not hate nor be hated by anybody, and we desire him to be of a peaceful disposition, in order to avoid war, the source of all injustice.

'Each week he holds the States General, where everyone with a complaint against him is received. If but three birds are found dissatisfied with his rule, he is dispossessed and a fresh election is held.

'Throughout the day of the States General our King is placed on the summit of a great yew tree at the edge of a lake, with his feet and wings bound. All the birds pass in front of him, one after another, and if one of them knows him guilty of a capital crime, he can throw him into the water. But he must at once justify his action, otherwise he is condemned to the sad death.'

I could not help interrupting to ask it what it meant by this 'sad death' and it explained this to me as follows:

'When a felon's crime is judged so monstrous that mere death is insufficient to expiate it, we try to find one which encompasses the agony of several and we go about it in this manner.

'Those of us with the most melancholy and funereal voices are sent to the guilty party, who is laid on a bier of sad cypress. There these mournful musicians gather round and through his ears they fill his soul with songs so lugubrious and tragic that the bitterness of his grief upsets the functioning of his organs and oppresses his heart. He pines away visibly and dies, choked with sadness.

'But such a spectacle rarely occurs, for as our kings are very good-natured, they never drive anyone to run the risk of so cruel a death, in order to take revenge.

'The reigning one at present is a dove, who is so peaceable by nature that the other day, when two sparrows had to be reconciled, we had all the trouble in the world to make him understand what enmity was.'

My magpie could not carry on a conversation for so long without some of those present taking note of it and, as it was already suspected of some intelligence, the principals of the assembly gave the order for it to be put under arrest by an eagle of the guard, which secured its person. Meanwhile King Dove arrived. Everyone fell silent and the first thing which broke the silence was the accusation made by the Birds' Public Prosecutor against the magpie.

When the King was fully informed of the scandal it had caused, he asked its name and how it knew me. 'Sire,' it replied, greatly surprised, 'I am called Margot. There are many birds of quality here who will answer for me. One day in the world of the earth, of which I am a native, I learned from Chirp the Snuffler here (who heard me crying in a cage and came to visit me at the window where I was hanging) that my father was Shorttail and my mother Crunchnut. But for him I should never have known, for I had been stolen from under my parents' wing in my nest at a very early age. My mother died of grief a short time afterwards and my father, who was then past an age to beget more children, despaired at seeing himself without heirs and went off to the Wars of the Jays, where he was killed by a peck in the brains.

'Those who carried me off were certain wild animals known as swineherds, which took me to be sold at a castle, where I saw this man who you are now trying. I do not know if he conceived some affection for me, but he took the trouble to instruct the servants to chop up my food and sometimes had the goodness to prepare it for me himself. If I was chilled in winter, he would take me near the fire, wrap up my cage or tell the gardener to warm me in his shirt. In his presence the servants did not dare to tease me and I remember the day when he rescued me from the jaws of a cat, when my lady's little lackey had delivered me into its clutches.

'But it will not be beside the point to tell you the cause of this barbarous deed. To please Shrimp (which was the little lackey's name), I was one day repeating the trifles he had taught me. Now unfortunately it occurred that, although I always recited my phrases together, one after the other, just when he had come in and given a false message I happened to say in order: "Hold your tongue, you son of a whore! You lie!" The accused here, who knew the dishonest nature of the rogue, imagined that I might well have spoken prophetically and sent round to the place to see if Shrimp had been there. Shrimp was convicted of deception; Shrimp was whipped and, but for him, Shrimp would have made pussy eat me.'

The King nodded, to indicate that he was pleased with the pity it had taken on my disaster, but he forbade it to talk to me in secret any more. He then asked the counsel for the prosecution if he was ready to open his case. The latter signified with its claw that it was about to speak and here, as far as I can recall, are the main points it made against me.

16

Indictment of an animal accused of being a man, delivered before the assembled chambers of the Parliament of the Birds

'My lords, the injured party in the case against this criminal is Guillemette the Plump, partridge by extraction, recently arrived from the world of the earth with a gaping wound in her breast from a lead pellet fired at her by men, plaintiff against the human race and, in consequence, against an animal which is, I maintain, a member of that great tribe. It would not be difficult for us to prevent any outrages it might commit by simply putting it to death. Nevertheless, since our

Republic of the living is concerned with the preservation or destruction of all living things, it seems to me that we should deserve to have been born men—that is to say deprived of the reason and immortality which make us their superiors—if we imitated a single one of their acts of injustice.

'Let us therefore, my lords, submit the difficulties of this case to the keenest scrutiny of which our divine spirits are capable.

'The case turns on whether this animal is a man and, in the event of our determining that it is, whether, for this, it deserves to die.

'For myself, I find no difficulty whatever in concluding that it is one, firstly from the feeling of horror which overwhelms us all at the sight of it, without our being able to give the reason; secondly, because it laughs like a fool; thirdly, because it weeps like an idiot; fourthly, because it wipes its nose like a knave; fifthly, because its plumage is mangy; sixthly, because it wears its tail in front; seventhly, because it always has a quantity of little square stones in its mouth, which it has not the wit either to spit out or swallow; eighthly, and in conclusion, because every morning it lifts up its eyes and its great beak, sticks its open hands flat against one another with the points towards heaven and makes of them a single captive one—as if it were tired of having two free hands—and breaks its legs in half so that it falls upon its hams: then, as a result of the magic words it mutters, I have observed that its broken legs are mended and it gets up afterwards as cheerful as before. Now you know, gentlemen, that of all the animals, only man has a soul black enough to give himself up to magic: consequently this is a man. We must now examine if, for being a man, it deserves to die.

'I think, my lords, that it has never been called into doubt that all creatures are produced by our common mother to live in society. Now if I prove that man seems to be born only to disrupt society, will I not prove that, by opposing the very purpose of his own creation, he deserves that nature should repent of her handiwork?

'The first and most fundamental law for the administration of a republic is equality, but man would never be able to endure this for long. He pursues us in order to devour us. He convinces himself that we were only made for him, and advances, in justification of his claim to superiority, the barbarous fashion in which he massacres us and the small resistance he encounters in overcoming our weakness—yet he will not admit as his masters the eagles, the condors, and the griffins, who can conquer the most robust of his kind.

'But why should size and the arrangement of limbs indicate a qualitative difference, since among themselves there are both dwarfs and giants to be found?

'Furthermore, their much vaunted mastery is an imaginary privilege. On the contrary, they are so disposed to servility that for fear of having no one to serve, they sell their liberty to one another. Thus, the young are the slaves of the old, the poor of the rich, the peasants of the gentry, the princes of the monarchs, and even the monarchs are the slaves of the laws they establish. But for all that, these poor serfs are so afraid of lacking masters that, as though to guard against being surprised by liberty from some unexpected quarter, they fabricate gods for themselves all over the place: in the water, in the air, in fire, and under the ground. They will make them out of wood rather than not have any, and I believe they even delude themselves with false hopes of immortality, less because of their horror of ceasing to exist than from their dread of having no one to order them about when they are dead.

'Such are the fine effects of this "sovereignty" of this "natural mastery" of man over the animals—and over ourselves, for his insolence goes as far as that! And as a consequence of this preposterous "dominion", he quite gaily arrogates to himself the rights of life and death over us. He sets traps for us. He chains us up. He throws us into prison. He slits our throats. He devours us. And he makes the right to kill those of us left at liberty a privilege of the nobility. He believes that the sun was lit to provide him with illumination for making war on us; that nature allows us to venture across the sky merely so that he can draw good or bad omens from our flight; and that when God put entrails in our bodies, His only intention was to provide a great book in which man could study the science of the future.

'Well now! Is not such pride quite intolerable? Does anyone with such notions deserve a lesser punishment than to be born a man? None the less, those are not the grounds on which I urge you to condemn this one. Since the wretched beast has not the use of reason, like us, I excuse those errors which result from its lack of intelligence. But, for those which are nothing but the fruits of its will, I demand justice. Namely for the fact that it kills us without being attacked by us; for the fact that it eats us, though it could satisfy its hunger with more seemly food; for the fact that it debauches the good nature of some of our people, like the hawks, the falcons, and the vultures, and teaches them to massacre their own kind, to spill the blood of their fellows and deliver us into its hands.

'This consideration is by itself so grave that I ask the Court for its extermination by means of the sad death.'

17

Verdict and sentence

THE whole Bench shuddered in horror at the mention of so harsh a punishment and in order to have grounds for mitigating it, the King signalled to my counsel to reply.

This was a starling, a great master of jurisprudence, which struck its foot three times on the branch on which it stood and addressed the assembly as follows: 'It is true, my lords, that moved by pity, I had accepted a brief for this unfortunate beast. But now I am on the point of pleading, my conscience is overcome with remorse, as if a secret voice had forbidden me to perform so detestable an action. And so, my lords, I declare before you and all the court, that, for the sake of my soul's salvation, I do not wish to contribute in any way to the continued existence of such a monster as man.'

All the crowd clicked their beaks as a token of delight and approval at the sincerity of so good a bird.

My magpie presented itself to plead in its place but was ordered to be silent, for the reason that, as it had been reared among men and perhaps infected by their morals, it was to be feared that it might not bring an open mind to my case. The Court of the Birds will not allow an advocate who sympathizes more with one party than the other to be heard, unless he can show that this bias proceeds from the justice of their case.

Seeing that no one came forward to defend me, my judges stretched their wings and flew at once to confer upon the judgement.

The majority of them, as I afterwards learned, strongly favoured my extermination by means of the sad death, but when it was perceived that the King was inclined towards clemency, everyone came round to his opinion. Thus moderated, my judges spared me the sad death and instead deemed it appropriate—in order to make my punishment fit at least one of my crimes and to annihilate me with a penalty which would serve to undeceive me, by flouting man's pretended mastery over the birds—that I should be abandoned to the wrath of the weakest of them: that is to say, they condemned me to be eaten by the flies.

The assembly rose at once and I heard it murmured that they had refrained from going into more detail over the circumstances of my fate on account of the accident which had befallen a bird in the crowd that had just collapsed in a faint as it was about to speak to the King. It was thought that this was caused by the horror it experienced from staring at a man too intently. This is why the order was given for me to be taken away.

Before this my sentence was announced, and as soon as the osprey, which acted as Clerk of the Court, had finished reading it to me, I saw that the sky round about me was black with flies, bumble bees, bees, wasps, and fleas, all buzzing with impatience.

I was expecting my eagles to carry me off once more in the usual manner, but in their place I saw a great black ostrich that set me ignominiously astride its own back (for among them this position is the most humiliating one a criminal can be put into and no bird, whatever offence it has committed, can ever be subjected to it).

The constables that led me out to my punishment were four dozen condors and as many griffins, which went in front, and behind these flew a solemn procession of crows, croaking out something lugubrious; and in the distance I thought I heard owls replying to them.

As we left the place where judgement had been passed on me, two birds of paradise, which had been given the task of assisting me to make a good end, came and sat upon my shoulders.

Although my mind was greatly disturbed at the time with horror at the step I was about to take, I have nevertheless remembered most of the arguments with which they tried to console me.

'Death,' they told me (putting their beaks into my ear), 'is doubtless no great misfortune, since nature, our good mother, subjects all her children to it; and it cannot be an event of much significance, since it can come at any moment and from such trivial causes. For if life were as excellent as all that, we should not have the power to withhold it; and if death brought in its wake consequences of the importance you imagine, we should not have the power to inflict it. On the contrary, it seems very likely that since animals begin their lives at play, they end them in a similar manner.

'I am speaking to you thus because your soul is not immortal, like ours, and you may fairly consider that when you die, everything dies with you. But you should not be distressed to be doing sooner what some of your fellow creatures will be doing later. They are in a worse position than you, for if death is a misfortune, it is only one to those who have it to look forward to. Unlike yourself, who have no more than an hour to wait, they will have to endure fifty or sixty years in a state of being able to die. Besides, tell me: the unborn are not unhappy, are they? Well, you are going to be like someone who has not been born. In the twinkling of an eye after the end of your life you will be what you were a twinkling of an eye before it began, and once this twinkling of an eye is past, you will be as long dead as someone who died a thousand centuries ago.

'But in any case, supposing that life is a blessing, cannot the same conjunction amidst the infinity of time, which caused you to be, some day cause you to be once again? Cannot the matter, which, by dint of mixing itself up, finally arrived at the quantity, state, and arrangement necessary to the construction of your being, mix itself up once again and arrive at a disposition such that you feel yourself to exist once more?

' "Yes, but ——" you will say to me, "I should not remember having existed before." But, my dear brother, what does that matter, provided you can feel that you exist now? For have you not a good chance of thinking of the same arguments again, to console yourself for the loss of your life, as I am now putting before you?

'These are considerations powerful enough to make you drink this cup of bitterness patiently, but I still have others, even more weighty, which will actually induce you to crave it. You must, my dear brother, accept the fact that as you and the other brutes are material, and as death, rather than destroying matter, does no more than rearrange its economy, you may be quite sure that when you cease to be what you are, you will begin to be something else. And even if you then become nothing more than a clod of earth or a stone, you will still be something less wicked than a man. But I have a secret to reveal to you, that I would not want any of my fellows to hear me utter: this is that in being eaten, as you will be, by our little birds, you will pass into their substance. Yes, you will have the honour of contributing, however blindly, to the intellectual operations of our flies and—though you cannot think for yourself—you will at least share in the glory of helping them to think!'

At about this stage in the homily we arrived at the place appointed for my punishment.

There were four trees of the same height very close together and almost equidistant, and on top of each of them a tall heron was perched. I was brought down from my seat on the black ostrich and a number of cormorants lifted me up to where the four herons were waiting for me. These birds, facing one another, each one firmly supported by its tree, wound their necks (which were of a prodigious length) about me like ropes, two round my arms and two round my legs. They bound me so tightly that although each of my limbs was only held fast by a single one of their necks, I was quite powerless to move a muscle.

They were due to remain in this position for a long time, for I heard the cormorants which had lifted me being ordered to go and catch some fish to stuff into the herons' beaks.

We were still waiting for the flies, because they had not cleft the air with a flight as powerful as ours. But it was not long before we heard them.

The first thing they did was to divide up my body between them, and this distribution was so cunningly arranged that my eyes were allotted to the bees, so that they should sting them as they ate them; my ears to the bumble bees, so that they should deafen and devour them at the same time; my shoulders to the fleas, so that they should nibble into them with bites that would make me itch; and so on with the rest. It was as if all the atoms of which the air is composed had turned into flies, for I was barely touched by two or three rays of light—which would seem to have donned a disguise in order to make their way through to me—so tightly packed and close to my flesh were these battalions.

But just as each one of them was already choosing the spot it fancied to bite, I suddenly saw them fall back abruptly and amidst the confusion of countless thunderclaps, which resounded to the heavens, I several times made out the word: 'Reprieve! Reprieve! Reprieve!'

Two turtle doves flew up to me. On their arrival all the grim apparatus of my death was dismantled. I felt my herons relaxing the coils of their long necks, which entwined me, and my spreadeagled body hurtling down from the top of the four trees to the roots at their base.

I expected nothing more from my fall than to smash to the ground against some rock; but when I got to the bottom of my fear I was thoroughly astonished to find myself sitting upon a white ostrich, which set off at a gallop as soon as it felt me upon its back.

They took me on a different road from the one by which I came, for I remember that I went through a great forest of myrtles and another of turpentine trees, ending in a vast grove, where King Dove awaited me in the midst of all his court.

As soon as he saw me he made a sign for me to be helped down. At once the two eagles of the guard offered me their feet and carried me to their prince.

I wished to embrace and kiss His Majesty's little claws out of respect, but he drew back. Before doing so, however, he said to me: 'And now let me ask you, do you know this bird?'

At these words they showed me a parrot, which began to flutter and flap its wings when it saw me looking at it.

'Yes,' I cried to the King, 'it does seem to me that I have seen him somewhere, but fear and joy have so confused my senses that I cannot yet recall clearly where it was.'

At these words the parrot came and embraced my face with its two wings and said to me: 'What? Have you forgotten your cousin's parrot, Caesar, in respect of whom you have so often maintained that birds can think? I was the one just now at your trial who wished to declare my obligation to you after the hearing, but my grief at seeing you in so great a peril made me fall into a faint.'

Its words opened my eyes. Recognizing it, I embraced and kissed it and it embraced and kissed me.

'So,' I said to it, 'is it you, my poor Caesar, whose cage I opened to give you back the liberty of which the tyrannous custom of our world had robbed you?'

The King interrupted our caresses and spoke to me thus: 'Man, among us a good action is never forgotten; that is why, although, being a man, merely because you have been born you deserve to die, the Senate grants you your life. It is fitting thus to acknowledge the lights with which nature illumined your instinct, when she gave you a presentiment of that faculty of reason in *us*, which you were not capable of knowing *yourself*. Go, then, in peace, and live happily!'

He gave some orders in a low voice and my white ostrich, led by the two turtle doves, carried me from the assembly.

After galloping with me for about half a day, it left me near a forest, into which I plunged as soon as it had gone. There I began to taste the delights of liberty and of eating the honey that trickled down the bark of the trees.

18

The trees

I THINK I should never have stopped walking—for such was the agreeable diversity of the place that I was continually discovering something more beautiful—if my body could have withstood the effort. But as I finally found I was quite weak from exhaustion, I let myself slip on to the grass.

Stretched out thus in the shadow of these trees, I was just feeling the sweet coolness and the still solitude inviting me to sleep, when a faint sound of confused voices, which I seemed to hear hovering about me, aroused me with a start.

The terrain appeared very flat and was quite clear of undergrowth which might have blocked the view, so I could see for a long way between the forest trees. Yet the murmuring which reached my ears was certainly coming from very close to me. When I listened even more attentively, I quite distinctly heard a succession of words in Greek and from among a number of people conversing I could make out one who was expressing himself as follows:

'Doctor, one of my relatives, the three-headed elm has just sent me a chaffinch to inform me that he is sick of a withering fever and a bad attack of moss, which has covered him from head to foot. In the name of the friendship that you bear me, I beg you to prescribe something for him.'

I waited for a short time without hearing anything, but after a little while, someone seemed to reply thus: 'Even if the three-headed elm were no relative of yours and if, instead of you, who are my friend, one of our species who was a complete stranger were to make this request to me, my profession obliges me to help everybody. So send word to the three-headed elm, that to cure his sickness he needs to absorb as much moisture and as little dry matter as he can; that to this end he should direct the little hairs on his roots into the dampest part of his bed, that he should converse only upon cheerful topics and have himself supplied with music every day by several excellent nightingales. Afterwards he should let you know how he fares with this regimen and then, according to the course his sickness takes, when we have prepared his humours, I will arrange for a stork I know to give him an injection, which will set him fully on the road to recovery.'

After these words I heard not the slightest sound more until a quarter of an hour later a voice came to my ears which I did not seem to have noticed before, and this is how it spoke: 'Hullo there, Fork-stump! Are you asleep?'

Then I heard another voice, which replied: 'No, Green Bark, why?'

'Well,' continued the one that had first broken the silence, 'I have the feeling we used to experience when those animals which are called men approached us, and I should like to ask you if you feel the same.'

Some time elapsed before the other replied, as if it had wanted to test this discovery with its most secret senses. Then it cried out: 'By God! You are right! I swear I find my organs so full of the traces of a man that unless I am utterly deceived there is one very close by.'

Then several voices joined in, saying that they definitely sensed the presence of a man.

I vainly cast my eyes all about me. I could not discover where these words might be coming from. Finally, after I had somewhat recovered from the horror first inspired by this circumstance, I replied to the voice I thought I heard asking if there was a man there, that there was. 'But I entreat you,' I went on at once, 'whoever you are, speaking to me, tell me where you are.'

A moment later I heard these words: 'We are in your presence. You are looking at us with your eyes—and yet you do not see us! Consider the oak trees, on which you can feel your gaze resting: it is we who are speaking to you. You may be surprised that we should speak a language used in the world from which you have come, but you must know that our forefathers were natives of it. They dwelt in Epirus, in the Forest of Dodona, where their natural benevolence led them to speak oracles to people in distress who consulted them. For this purpose they had learned Greek, the most universal language there was in those days, so that they might be understood; and because we are descended from them, the gift of prophecy has been handed down from father to son, until it has passed to us.

'Now you must know that one day a great eagle, to whom our fathers in Dodona were giving shelter, was feeding upon the acorns which their branches offered it, because it had broken one of its claws and could not go hunting. Tired of living in a world where it had suffered so much, it took flight to the sun and made such a successful trip that it finally reached this luminous globe, where we are now. But on its arrival, the heat of the climate made it vomit and it brought up a number of still undigested acorns. These acorns germinated and from them there grew the oak trees which were our ancestors.

'That is how we came to change our abode. Although you heard us talking in a human language, that does not mean to say that other trees express themselves in the same way. There are none, apart from us oaks descended from the Forest of Dodona, who speak like you. Other plants express themselves in the following manner: you must have noticed the soft and subtle breezes which are always rustling at the edge of woods; these are the breath of their speech and this low murmuring or delicate sound with which they break the sacred silence of their solitude is, to be precise, their language. But although the sounds of different forests may always seem identical, they are nevertheless so various that each species of plant has its own particular one. Thus the birch does not speak like the maple, nor the beech like the cherry.

'If the stupid people of your world heard me talking as I am now, they would believe that there was a devil imprisoned under my bark. For, far from supposing that we can think, they do not even imagine we have any feelings. Yet every day they can observe how, at the first blow with which a wood-cutter assaults a tree, the axe goes four times deeper into his flesh than at the second. They ought to deduce from this that the first blow must have surprised him and caught him off his guard, since as soon as he was alerted by the pain, he roused himself and summoned his forces to do battle and seemed to turn himself to stone in order to resist the hardness of his enemy's weapons.

'But I have no intention to try and make the blind see the light. One individual is the same to me as the whole species and the whole species is to me no more than one individual, provided that individual is not contaminated with the errors of the species. Therefore take heed, for, in speaking to you, I consider I am speaking to the whole human race.

'In the first place you must know that almost all the music in the concerts given by the birds is composed in praise of trees. But equally, in return for their diligence in celebrating our fine actions, we take upon ourselves that of concealing their love affairs. For do not imagine, when you have so much difficulty in discovering one of their nests, that this is the result of their prudence in hiding them. It is the tree that has himself folded his branches all round the nest, in order to protect his guest's family against the barbarism of man. For you have only to consider the nests of the ones that are born to the destruction of their fellow birds, such as those of sparrow hawks, hobby hawks, kites, falcons, etc.; or those that only make trouble when they speak, like jays and magpies; or those that delight in frightening us, like wood owls and screech owls. You will notice that the eyrie of one of these birds is always exposed for all to see, because the tree has withdrawn his branches from it, in order to make it an easy prey.

'But there is no need to go into so many details to prove that trees, whether in body or soul, fulfil all the same functions as you yourselves. There cannot be one among you who has not noticed how in the spring, when the sun titillates our bark with fertile sap, our branches grow longer and we stretch them, laden with fruit, over the bosom of the earth, our beloved. The earth, for her part, cracks open a little, heated by a similar ardour, and as if each one of our branches were a ——, she draws near to it, in order to consummate her union with it and our branches, transported with pleasure, discharge into her womb the seed which she burns to conceive. She takes nine months to form this embryo, however, before bringing it to the light of day: but the tree, her husband, fearing lest the cold of winter should harm her in her pregnancy, sheds his green robe to cover her, contenting himself, to hide his nakedness a little, with an old cloak of dead leaves.

'Ah well, you men, you are constantly looking upon such things and yet you never think about them. Far more convincing things have happened before your very eyes without even shaking your obstinacy.'

My attention was firmly concentrated on the words which this arboreal voice addressed to me and I was awaiting the sequel, when suddenly it broke off with a sound like someone too out of breath to speak.

As it seemed quite obstinate in its silence, I conjured it, by all the things I believed might move it most, that it should deign to enlighten someone who had only risked the perils of so great a journey in order to learn.

Then I heard two or three voices making the same entreaties for love of me, and I distinguished one of them saying to it, as if in anger: 'Very well, since you are having such trouble with your lungs, take a rest. I will tell him the story of the affectionate trees.'

'Oh! whoever you may be,' I cried, throwing myself down on my knees, 'the wisest of all the oaks of Dodona, that deigns to instruct me, know that you will not be giving your lesson to an ingrate. For I vow that if ever I return to my native globe I shall publish all the marvels which you honour me in permitting me to witness.'

As I was finishing this protestation I heard the same voice continuing as follows:

'Look, little man, twelve or fifteen paces to your right and you will see two twin trees of medium size whose roots and branches are interlaced, as they attempt in a thousand ways to become a single tree.'

I directed my gaze towards these amorous plants and observed how the leaves on both of them were faintly trembling with an agitation which seemed as if controlled by their own volition and which gave rise to a murmuring so soft that it hardly impinged on one's ear. And yet with it one would have said that they were trying to exchange question and answer.

After about enough time had passed for me to observe this double plant, my good friend, the oak, resumed the thread of its speech as follows:

'You can hardly have lived for so long without the famous friendship between Pylades and Orestes having come to your knowledge.

'I should depict to you all the joys of their sweet passion and I should tell you all the miracles with which these friends astonished their age if I did not fear that so much enlightenment might dazzle the eyes of your reason. I will therefore only describe these two young suns in their eclipse.

'So it will be enough for you to know that one day the noble Orestes, engaged in battle, was seeking out his dear friend Pylades in order to enjoy the pleasure of either conquering or dying at his side. Seeing him surrounded by a hundred arms of steel which were raised against his head, alas, what did he do? He hurled himself in desperation through a forest of pikes, he shouted, he roared, he foamed at the mouth—but how badly I express the horror of that inconsolable man's agitation! He pulled out his hair, he bit his hands, he tore at his own wounds. But even now, at the end of this description, I am forced to say that his way of expressing his grief died with him. Then, when he thought to make a road with his sword to go and help Pylades, a mountain of men stood in his path. Nevertheless he cut through them and after treading under foot for a long time the bloody trophies of his victory, he gradually drew near to Pylades. But Pylades seemed to him so near to death that he hardly dared to go on warding off the enemy, for fear of surviving the man for whom he lived. To see his eyes already filled with the shadows of death one would have said that he was trying to poison his friend's murderers with his own looks. Finally Pylades fell lifeless to the ground and his dear friend Orestes who, similarly, felt his own life hovering on the brink of his lips, clung fast to it until he had searched among the dead with a distracted gaze and found Pylades once more. Then, pressing his mouth against his dead friend's, he seemed to wish to expel his own soul into his friend's body.

'The younger of the two heroes died of grief upon the body of his friend and you must know that from the decomposition of their bodies which had doubtless impregnated the earth, there were seen to arise among the already whitened bones of their skeletons two young saplings, whose stems and branches, all intertwined together, seemed in haste to grow only so that they might become still further enlaced. It was recognized that they had taken on a new form without losing the memory of what they had been. For their scented buds leaned over one another and warmed one another with their breath, as if to make one another blossom more swiftly. And what shall I say of the loving exchanges which sustained their life together? Never did the sap, in which their nourishment resides, offer itself to their roots without their sharing it ceremoniously. Never was one of them undernourished without the other being weak for want of food. The two of them drank together at their nurse's breasts from within, just as you suck at them from without.

'At length these happy friends produced apples—but miraculous apples, which performed even more miracles than their fathers. No sooner had you eaten apples from the one tree than you became hopelessly in love with whoever had eaten the fruit of the other. And this occurrence took place almost every day, because all the offshoots of Pylades were always to be found near those of Orestes and *vice versa*. Their fruits were almost twins and could not bear to be parted.

'Nature had, however, defined the energy of their double essence with such care that when the fruit of one of the trees was eaten by another man, this engendered a mutual friendship. When the same thing occurred to two people of different sexes it gave rise to love, but to a vigorous love which always retained the character of its origin, for although the fruit made its effect proportionate to their strength, softening its virtue in the case of a woman, yet it still retained a certain quality of maleness.

'It should also be noted that the one of the pair who had eaten the most was the one most loved. This fruit took good care to be both very sweet and very beautiful, since there is nothing as beautiful and as sweet as friendship. Thus it was these two qualities of beauty and goodness, which are rarely met with in the same object, which brought this fruit into fashion. Oh, how many times over, thanks to its miraculous virtue, were the examples of Pylades and Orestes repeated! Since that time we have seen many a Hercules and Theseus,

Achilles and Patroclus, Nisus and Euryalus—in short a count-less host of those who, thanks to their more than human friendships, dedicated their memory to the temple of eternity. Offshoots were taken to the Peloponnese, and the exercise field where the Thebans trained their youth was ornamented with them. These twin trees were planted in a row and in the season when the fruit hung from their branches, the young men who went to the field each day, tempted by their beauty, did not abstain from eating them. Their hearts generally felt the effects of this at once. They could be seen swearing eternal friendships pell-mell, each one of them becoming half of another, living less in himself than in his friend and the most cowardly of them undertaking for his friend the most daring exploits.

'This heavenly malady fired their blood with an ardour so noble that, on the advice of the wisest men, they enrolled this troop of friends to fight in the same company. On account of the brave actions they performed they were later called the Sacred Band. Their exploits exceeded by far what Thebes had expected of them, for in battle each of these heroes ven-tured to perform such daring deeds, either in order to protect his beloved or to win his love, that antiquity has never seen the like of them. Thus as long as this company of lovers was in existence the Thebans, who had previously been considered the worst soldiers among the Greeks, always fought and con-quered everyone, even the Spartans themselves, the most war-like people on earth.

'But among the infinite number of praiseworthy actions of which these apples were the cause, the same apples, in their innocence, also produced some most shameful ones.

'Mirrha, a young noblewoman, ate of them with her father, Cinyrus. Unfortunately one of those they ate was of Pylades and the other of Orestes. Love at once overwhelmed nature and confounded it to such an extent that Cinyrus could swear: "I am my own son-in-law!" and Mirrha: "I am my step-mother." In short I think I can unfold to you the whole of their crime, by adding that at the end of nine months the father became the grandfather of the children he had begotten and the daughter gave birth to her own brothers.

'But chance was not content with this one crime and desired that a bull which had entered the gardens of King Minos should unhappily find there beneath a tree of Orestes several apples which it swallowed. I say "unhappily", because Queen Pasiphaë ate of this fruit every day. Behold the two of them consumed with a raging love for one another! I will not describe to you the enormity of its consummation. It will suffice to say that Pasiphaë sank to a crime for which there was no precedent.

'At precisely the same time the famous sculptor, Pygmalion, was carving a marble Venus at the palace. The queen, who liked good workmen, presented him, as a ceremonial treat, with a couple of these apples. He ate the finest of them and because he happened to lack water, which, as you know, is necessary for the cutting of marble, he moistened his statue with the other. The marble at the same time, penetrated by this juice, gradually grew soft and the energetic virtue of this apple did its work according to the artist's design, following within the image the features it had encountered on the surface. For it dilated, warmed, and coloured, in natural proportions, the parts it encountered in its passage. Finally the marble came to life and, moved by the passion from the apple, embraced Pygmalion with all the strength of its heart and Pygmalion, transported by a corresponding love, received it for his wife.

'In this same province the young Iphis had eaten of this fruit with the fair Ianthë, her companion, in all the circumstances necessary to cause a mutual friendship. Their feast had its usual sequel but because Iphis had found it extremely tasty she ate so much that her friendship, which increased with the number of apples she ate—for she could not have enough of them—usurped all the functions of love and, as this love gradually increased, so it became more male and more vigorous. For as her whole body, which was imbued with this fruit, burned to perform the motions which corresponded to

the impulses of her desire, it moved its own matter so powerfully that it constructed for itself much more powerful
organs, ones capable of putting her thoughts into action and
fully sublimating her love to its most virile extent. That is to
say, Iphis became what it is necessary to be in order to marry
a woman.

'I should call this occurrence a miracle if I had another
name left for the event which follows.

'A young and greatly gifted man called Narcissus had won,
by his love, the affection of an extremely beautiful girl whom
the poets have celebrated under the name of Echo. But
women, as you know, more than our sex, are never satisfied
with the way they are loved. Having heard the virtues of the
apples of Orestes being praised, she succeeded in obtaining
some from several places. And because she was afraid, since
love is always still apprehensive, that those of one tree
might be weaker than those of another, she wanted him to
taste two of them. But no sooner had he eaten them than the
picture of Echo was effaced from his memory—all his love
was directed towards the one who had eaten the fruit: he was
both lover and beloved; for the substance drawn from the
apple of Pylades embraced in him that of the apple of Orestes.
This twin fruit, distributed throughout the whole mass of his
body, aroused all the parts of his body to caress one another.
His heart, into which their double virtue flowed, directed its
warmth inwards, towards itself. All his limbs, animated with
his passion, sought to penetrate one another. Even his reflection, burning with passion amidst the cold of the pools, drew
his body close that they might be united. In short poor Narcissus became hopelessly in love with himself.

'I will not bore you by relating the sad end that befell him.
The past ages have spoken of it enough. But I have two more
adventures to relate to you which will take up the time better.

'You must know that the fair Salmacis was acquainted with
the shepherd Hermaphroditus, but on no more familiar
terms than the proximity of their houses would permit. Then
fortune, who delights in upsetting the most untroubled lives,

permitted that at a games where the prizes for beauty and for running were two of these apples, Hermaphroditus won that for running and Salmacis that for beauty. Although they had been plucked together they had grown on different branches, for these affectionate fruits mingled together with so much cunning that one from Pylades was always to be found next to one from Orestes and that was the reason why people generally picked one of each, since they appeared to be twins. The fair Salmacis ate her apple and the good Hermaphroditus thrust his own into his wallet. Salmacis was overcome with the passions inspired both by her own apple and by the young shepherd's apple, which was beginning to grow warm in his wallet. She began to feel attracted to him by the flow of sympathy between her own apple and the other.

'The shepherd's parents observed the nymph's infatuation and as they considered the match to be an advantageous one, they attempted to foster and increase it. For this reason, having heard the twin apples being praised as a fruit whose juice inclined people's spirits to love, they distilled some of it and taking some of the most purified quintessence of it, they found a means of making their son and his sweetheart drink it. They had concentrated its potency to the highest degree possible and it fired the hearts of these lovers with so violent a desire to be joined together that, at the first sight of her, Hermaphroditus became absorbed into Salmacis and Salmacis melted in Hermaphroditus' arms. They passed into one another and, from being two people of different sexes, they turned into a double I-know-not-what, which was neither a man nor a woman. When Hermaphroditus wanted to enjoy Salmacis he found that he was the nymph, and when Salmacis wished Hermaphroditus to embrace her she found she was the shepherd. Yet this double what's-its-name preserved its unity. It begot and conceived without being either a man or a woman. In short, nature presented in it a marvel that she has since been unable to prevent from being unique.

'Well now, are not these stories amazing? They are indeed; for to see a daughter coupling with her father, a young princess gratifying the passion of a bull, a man aspiring to enjoy a block of stone and another marrying himself; to see this girl celebrating as a maiden a marriage she consummated as a boy, and this man ceasing to be a man without becoming a woman, turning into a twin outside his mother's womb and the twin of a person who is no blood relation—all this is far removed from the ordinary ways of nature. Nevertheless, what I am going to tell you now will surprise you even more.

'Amidst the sumptuous variety of fruits of all kinds which were brought from the most distant climates to celebrate the wedding of Cambyses, he was presented with a cutting from a tree of Orestes, which he had grafted on to a plane tree. And among the other delicacies served him for the dessert were apples from the same tree.

'So tasty was this fruit that he was tempted to eat a great deal of it, and when its substance had been converted, after the triple ripening, into a perfect seed, he formed of it, in the queen's belly, the embryo of his son, Artaxerxes—for such were the peculiarities of his life that his doctors conjectured he must have been produced in this manner.

'When the prince's young heart was of an age to undergo the torments of love, he was never observed to sigh for his fellow humans. He loved only trees, orchards, and woods, but above all others to which he seemed susceptible, he was consumed with passion for the fine plane tree, on to which his father Cambyses had once had grafted that cutting of Orestes.

'His constitution followed so closely the progress of this plane tree that he seemed to grow even as the branches grew. Every day he went to embrace it. When sleeping he dreamed of nothing else and he conducted all his affairs beneath the spread of its green canopy. It was clear to all that the plane tree returned his passion and was entranced with his caresses. All the time, for no apparent reason, one could see its leaves fluttering, as if they were trembling with delight and its branches curving round his head as if to make him a crown and coming down so close to his face that it was easy to see

199

that this was more to kiss him than from any natural inclination to hang down. It was even observed jealously arranging and pressing its leaves one against the next, for fear that the rays of sunlight might slip between them and kiss him as well as itself. The king, for his part, no longer observed any limits to his love. He had his bed set up at the foot of the plane tree and the plane tree, which did not know how to repay such friendship, gave him what trees hold most precious, its honey and dew, which it distilled on to him every morning.

'Their caresses would have continued longer if death, the enemy of all beautiful things, had not brought them to an end. Artaxerxes died of love in the embraces of his dear plane tree and all the Persians, grieved by the loss of so good a prince, desired, in order to give him some further satisfaction in death, that his body should be burned with the branches of the tree—without any other wood being used for the pyre.

'When the faggots were lit, the flame from them could be seen entwined with the flame from the fat of the body and their blazing manes, curling upwards together, tapered away into a pyramid as far as the eye could see.

'This pure and subtle fire did not divide but when it reached the sun, which, as you know, is the ultimate destination of all innate matter, it formed the seed of the apple tree of Orestes which you see there to your right.

'But the strain of this fruit has been lost in your world and here is how this misfortune came about:

'The fathers and mothers of that world, who are only governed in the affairs of their families by motives of self-interest, were angry that their children, as soon as they had tasted of these apples, lavished on their friends all the wealth they possessed. They therefore burned all of these trees they could find. Thus the species was lost and that is why you can never find a true friend there any more.

'As these trees were consumed by fire in this manner, the rain falling upon them purified the ashes so that the congealed sap became petrified, in the same way that the humour of burnt bracken is metamorphosed into glass.[1] Thus were formed from the ashes of these twin trees in all the countries of the earth two metallic stones which are known today as iron and loadstone. Because of the attraction between the fruits of Pylades and Orestes, whose virtue they have still retained, the two still strive daily to embrace one another. And notice that if the piece of loadstone is bigger it attracts the iron, and if the lump of iron is greater it attracts the loadstone—just as formerly the miraculous effect of the apples of Pylades and Orestes was to make whoever had eaten the most of one of them more loved by someone who had eaten of the other.

'Iron is nourished by loadstone and loadstone by iron so visibly that the latter rusts and the former loses its strength if they are not brought together in order to repair the losses to their substance.

'Have you never observed a piece of loadstone pressed against some iron filings? In the twinkling of an eye you will see the loadstone covered with these metal particles. The amorous passion with which they cling to one another is so sudden and impetuous, that, when they have embraced one another all over, you would say that there is not an atom of loadstone that does not desire to kiss an atom of iron and not an atom of iron that does not seek union with an atom of loadstone. When iron and loadstone are separated they are continuously emitting from their mass the most mobile of their tiny particles in search of the one they love. But when the loved one is found and they have no further desires, all of these cease their travels and the loadstone spends its leisure in possessing the iron, just as the iron gathers all its strength for the enjoyment of the loadstone.

'It is evidently the humour which flowed from the sap of these two trees which has given birth to the two metals. Before that they were unknown and if you want to know what materials were then used for the manufacture of weapons of war, why, Samson armed himself against the Philistines with

[1] Potassium taken from the ashes of bracken was used in the making of glass.

the jawbone of an ass; Jupiter, King of Crete, with artificial fire, which he used to imitate thunderbolts and subdue his enemies; and Hercules, finally, conquered tyrants and tamed monsters with a club.

'But these two metals have yet another far more specific connection with our two trees. You must know that although our pair of inanimate lovers turn towards the pole, they never go that way except in one another's company. And I will reveal the reason for this when I have talked to you a little about the poles.

'The poles are the mouths of heaven, through which it takes back the light, heat, and influences which it has spread over the earth. Otherwise, if all these treasures from the sun did not return to their source it would long ago have been extinguished and would shine no more (for all its brilliance is simply a dust of blazing atoms which travel from its globe)—while the abundance of these little fiery bodies accumulating upon the earth without leaving it would already have consumed it in flames. There must therefore, as I have told you, be ventilators in the sky, through which the excesses of the earth can be disgorged, and others through which the losses of the heavens can be made good, so that the eternal circulation of these little living bodies may penetrate successively all the globes of this great universe. Now these ventilators in heaven are the poles, through which it feeds on the souls of all that die in its worlds, and all the stars are the mouths and the pores through which its spirits are exhaled once more.

'But just to show you that this is not such a new idea, when your ancient poets, to whom philosophy had revealed the innermost secrets of nature, spoke of a hero, of whom they wished to say that his soul had gone to dwell with the gods, they expressed themselves thus: "He has ascended to the pole," "He is seated at the pole," "He has crossed the pole." For they knew that the poles were the only entrances through which heaven admits all that has come from it.

'If the authority of these great men does not satisfy you fully, then the experience of your moderns who have voyaged to the north may perhaps content you. For they have discovered that as they approached the Great Bear, during the six months of night when it had been supposed that it was quite dark in that climate, the horizon was illuminated by a great light. This could only come from the pole because the nearer they drew to it, and in consequence the farther they went from the sun, the brighter this light became. It is therefore most probable that it proceeds from the rays of the daylight and from a great mound of souls, which as you know are simply made up of luminous atoms, returning to heaven by their accustomed doors.

'After that it is not difficult to understand why iron rubbed with loadstone or loadstone rubbed with iron will turn towards the pole. Being extracts from the bodies of Pylades and Orestes, and having always retained the inclinations of the two trees, just as the two trees had retained those of the two friends, they must aspire to be united with their souls. That is why they turn towards the pole through which they sense that these have ascended, with the proviso that iron will not turn away unless it is rubbed with loadstone nor loadstone unless it is rubbed with iron, because the iron will not leave a world without its friend the loadstone, nor the loadstone without its friend the iron. They cannot resolve to make such a journey deprived of one another's company.'

19

A conflict of opposites

THE voice was, I think, going to embark upon a fresh speech but the sudden noise of a great alarm prevented it. The whole forest was in uproar, echoing with the one repeated cry: 'Beware of the plague! Pass the word round!'

I begged the tree that had been addressing me at such length to tell me what had caused so great a disturbance.

'My friend,' it said to me, 'in this district we are not yet fully informed about the details of the scourge. I will simply tell you in a few words that the plague which threatens us is what is known among men as *conflagration*. And this is a good name for it, since there is no sickness among us so contagious. The remedy we shall apply to it is to draw breath and blow all together towards the source of the inflammation, in order to drive back the bad air. I think that what will have brought this raging fever our way is a fire beast, which has been prowling round our woods for several days; for since they never go anywhere without fire and cannot do without it, this one will doubtless have come to infect one of our trees with it.

'We have already sent for the ice animal to come to our aid: however, it has not yet arrived. But farewell! I have not time to talk to you now, I must think of the public safety and you must make your escape too, otherwise you run the risk of being involved in our ruin.'

I followed its advice, though without hurrying unduly, for I knew my legs. However, I was so unfamiliar with the geography of the country, that after eighteen hours' march I found myself in the depths of the forest I had thought to escape and, to crown my anxiety, my brain was shaken by a hundred terrible thunderclaps, while my pupils were blinded with the menacing and pallid brilliance of a thousand flashes of lightning.

The crashes redoubled from moment to moment with such fury that one would have said the foundations of the world were going to crack, yet despite all this, the sky had never looked more serene. Finding myself at my wits' end, I was ultimately tempted, by my desire to know the cause of such a strange phenomenon, to walk towards the place from whence the noise seemed to emanate.

I walked a distance of about forty-five miles, at the end of which I perceived in the middle of a very broad plain what appeared to be two balls, spinning noisily round one another, now approaching, now retreating; and I observed that it was when they collided that these great crashes could be heard.

But as I advanced further, I recognized that what from a distance had looked like two balls were two animals. One of these, although round at the bottom, was shaped like a triangle in the middle and its long head, with its red mane which floated upwards, was sharpened into a pyramid. Its body was pierced like a sieve and one could see little flames flickering through these fine openings which served it for pores, seeming to clothe it in a plumage of fire.

As I walked round about there, I met a most venerable old man watching this notable battle with as much curiosity as myself. He beckoned to me to draw near. I obeyed him and we sat down beside one another.

I was intending to ask him the purpose which had brought him to that country, but he silenced me with these words: 'Very well, I will tell you the purpose which has brought me to this country!' Thereupon he related to me at great length all the details of his journey. I leave you to imagine whether I was not left dumbfounded. However, my consternation increased when I was already burning to ask him what demon had revealed my thoughts to him and he cried: 'No, no, it is not a demon that reveals your thoughts to me.'

This new feat of mind-reading made me look at him more attentively than before and I observed that he was imitating my carriage, my gestures, my expression. He had arranged all his limbs and modelled all the parts of his face upon the pattern of mine: in short, my reflection in relief would not have counterfeited me better.

'I see,' he continued, 'that you are anxious to learn why I mimic you, and I shall be glad to give you the reason. You must know that, in order to understand your interior, I arranged all the parts of my body in a pattern similar to yours. For, being disposed like you in all my parts, I arouse in myself, by this arrangement of matter, the same thoughts that it produces in you.

'You will judge this effect to be possible if you have already observed that twins who resemble one another have generally a similar intelligence, passions, and will—to the extent that two twins were found in Paris that had never had any but the same illnesses and the same good health and married, without knowing each other's intentions, at the same time on the same day. They wrote one another letters in which the sense, the words, and the composition were the same and, finally, they made up similar verses on the same subject, with the same metaphors, the same turns of phrase, and the same sequence. But do you not see that since the composition of the organs of their bodies was similar, it was impossible for them not to act in a similar manner, just as two identical instruments, touched in the same way must give out identical harmonies? And that if I make my body conform completely with yours and become, in a manner of speaking, your twin, similar impulses of matter are bound to cause similar impulses of mind in both of us?'

After that he began to imitate me again and continued thus: 'You are now greatly exercised over the origin of the battle between these two monsters. I will teach you what it is. You must know that the trees in the forest behind us were unable to repulse the onslaught of the fire beast and have had recourse to the ice animal.'

'I have never before,' I said, 'heard tell of these creatures, except from an oak tree here, who was in a great hurry because he was only thinking of his own safety. I beg you, therefore, to instruct me on the subject.'

This is how he spoke to me: 'In this globe, where we are now, you would see the woods very sparsely scattered indeed, on account of the great numbers of fire beasts which ravage them, were it not for the ice animals, which come every day, at the behest of their friends, the forests, to cure the sick trees. I say "cure," for as soon as they have breathed upon the glowing coals of this plague with their icy mouths they extinguish it.

'In the world of the earth, where you come from, like myself, the fire beast is called *salamander* and the ice animal is known by the name of *remora* or *sucking-fish*. Now you will know that remoras live near the extremity of the North Pole in the depths of the icy seas, and it is the coldness of these fish, given off through their scales, which makes the sea water freeze in those parts, even though it is salt.

'The majority of the sailors who have made voyages of exploration to Greenland have come to experience that in some seasons the ice floes, which had stopped them at other times, were no longer to be met with. Now although they may have found this sea clear at a time when winter is at its most severe, they have not hesitated to attribute this to some secret warmth which had melted them: but it is much more probable that the remoras, which eat nothing but ice, had devoured all the ice floes for the moment. But some months after they have eaten them, you see, this terrible meal makes their stomachs so chilled that the mere breath they exhale freezes the whole Polar Sea once more. When they emerge on to dry land (for they live in both elements), they can satisfy their hunger only with hemlock, wolf's bane, opium, and mandragora.

'People in our world are mystified to know the origin of those chilly winds from the north which always bring frost with them. But if our compatriots knew, as we do, that the remoras live in that climate, they would understand, like us, that these winds come from their breath, when they try to blow back the warmth of the approaching sun.

'The stygian water with which great Alexander was poisoned, for the cold of it froze his bowels, was the piss of one of these animals. In short, the remora so pre-eminently contains all the principles of coldness that, when it passes under a ship, the ship is seized with cold and left quite benumbed by it, to the point of not being able to move from the spot. It is for this reason that half of those who have sailed north to discover the Pole have never returned, because it is a miracle if the remoras, which abound in those seas, do not stop their ships. So much for the ice animal.

'But as for the fire beasts, they dwell in the ground under mountains of flaming lava like Etna, Vesuvius, and the Red

Cape. The knobs which you see on the throat of this one, which are caused by the inflammation of its liver, are . . .'

But then we fell silent, in order to pay attention to this famous duel.

The salamander was attacking with great fury, but the remora was putting up an impenetrable defence. Each time they collided with one another there was a thunderclap, such as occurs in the worlds round there when a hot cloud encounters a cold one, which produces a similar noise.

With every glance of rage the salamander flashed at its enemy, its eyes gave out a red light, which seemed to set the air on fire, and as it flew it sweated boiling oil and pissed nitric acid.

The remora, for its part, was fat, heavy, and square, displaying a body all scaly with icicles. Its large eyes appeared like two crystal plates and their gaze transmitted a light so chilling that I felt a wintry shiver run through every limb of my body they alighted on. If I thought to put up my hand in front of me, my hand became numb with cold from it. Even the air round about it, stricken with its rigour, thickened into snow; the ground hardened beneath its feet and I could recognize the tracks the beast had made from the chilblains that greeted me when I walked upon them.

At the beginning of the fight the salamander had made the remora sweat with the intense heat of its first onslaught, but at length this sweat froze and coated the whole plain with a thin layer of ice so slippery that the salamander could not reach the remora without falling over. It became clear to us, the philosopher and me, that from falling and getting up so many times it had exhausted itself, for the thunderclaps produced by the shock of it striking its enemy, which had formerly been so frightful, were now no more than the dull sound of those muffled thuds which mark the end of a storm —and this dull sound, deadened little by little, degenerated into a hissing, like that of a red-hot iron plunged into cold water.

When the remora realized from the weakening of the

blows, which now scarcely shook it, that the battle was drawing to a finish, it reared itself up on a corner of its cube and let itself fall with all its weight upon the stomach of the salamander, to such good effect that the heart of the poor salamander, where what remained of its fire was concentrated, burst with such a terrible explosion that I know of nothing comparable to it in nature.

Thus died the fire beast beneath the sluggish resistance of the ice animal.

Some time after the remora had disappeared, we approached the battlefield and the old man, after first smearing his hands with some of the earth on which it had walked, to protect them from burns, grasped the carcass of the salamander.

'With the body of this animal,' he said, 'I shall not need to make a fire in my kitchen, for if I hang it from the pot hook it will roast and boil everything I put in the hearth. As for its eyes, I shall preserve them carefully. If they were cleansed of the shadows of death you would take them for two little suns. The ancients in our world were well aware of how to put them to use. These are what they called "ardent lamps" and they were only hung up in the grand tombs of illustrious men.

'Our moderns have come across them when ransacking some of these famous tombs, but thanks to their ignorant curiosity they have destroyed them, for, in trying to come at the fire, which they saw shining behind the membranes, they have broken them.'

The old man was walking all the time and I followed him, attentive to the marvels he related to me. And in connexion with the battle, I must not forget to mention the conversation we had concerning the ice animal.

'I do not believe,' he told me, 'that you will ever have seen a remora before, since these fish rarely rise to the surface of the water and, in addition, they hardly ever leave the Arctic Ocean. But without doubt you have seen certain animals which can, in some measure, be said to be of the same species. I told you just now that as one nears the Pole, this sea is quite full of remoras, which cast their spawn upon the mud, just like the other fish. You must know that this seed, which is an essence drawn from the whole of their mass, is so pre-eminently imbued with all its coldness that if a ship is driven over it and contracts one or several worms from it, which turn into birds, their blood will be quite devoid of warmth, and although they have wings they will be counted among the fish. So the Sovereign Pontiff, who knows their origin, does not forbid the eating of them during Lent. These are what you call *Barnacle Geese*.'

20

A walk with Campanella

I CONTINUED walking with no other plan than that of following him. I was so delighted to have found a man, that I dared not take my eyes off him, for fear of losing him.

'Young mortal,' he said to me, '—for I can easily see that you have not yet, like me, paid the fee which we all owe to nature—as soon as I set eyes on you, I saw in your face that indefinable something that makes us want to know people. If I am not mistaken about the circumstances of the conformation of your body, you must be a Frenchman and a native of Paris. That city is the place where, after dragging my shame throughout Europe, I brought it to an end.

'My name is Campanella and I am a Calabrian by birth. Since my arrival on the sun, I have spent my time visiting the various regions of this great globe in order to discover the wonders there. It is divided into kingdoms, republics, states, and principalities, like the earth. Thus the quadrupeds, the winged creatures, the plants, the stones—each have one of their own, and although some of them do not permit the entry of creatures of an alien species, particularly men (for whom the birds, especially, have a deadly hatred), I can travel everywhere without running any risk, because a philosopher's soul is fabricated of particles more rarified than the instruments which would be used to torture me. I was fortunate enough to be in the province of the trees, when the ravages of the salamander started those great thunderclaps, which you must have heard as well as me, and led me to their battlefield, where you arrived a moment after myself. And now I am returning to the Province of the Philosophers. . . .'

'What?' I said to him. 'Are there philosophers in the sun as well?'

'Are there philosophers?' replied the worthy man. 'Why certainly. They are the principal inhabitants of the sun and the very same of whose fame your world has its mouth so full. You will soon be able to talk to them, provided you have the courage to follow me, for I hope to set foot in their city before three days have passed. I do not suppose that you could guess how these great geniuses have found their way here.'

'No, indeed,' I cried, for have not so many other people up till now been too blind to find the way? Or do we fall after death into the hands of an Examiner of intellects, who grants or refuses us, according to our capacity, the right of citizenship to the sun?'

'It is nothing like that at all,' retorted the old man. 'Souls come to join this mass of light by a principle of affinity, for this world is formed of nothing but the spirits of all that dies in the surrounding orbs, as are Mercury, Venus, the Earth, Mars, Jupiter, and Saturn.

'Thus, as soon as a plant, a beast, or a man dies, its soul mounts to this sphere without being extinguished, just as you see a candle flame flying up towards it in a point—despite the tallow holding it by the heels. All these souls, united as they are in the fountain-head of daylight and purged of the gross matter which once hampered them, now carry out functions far more noble than those of growing, feeling, and reasoning, for they are employed to form the blood and vital spirits of the sun, this great and perfect animal. That is why you must not doubt that the sun operates intellectually—and far more perfectly than you do, since it is through the heat of a million of these purified souls, of which its own is the essence, that it knows the secret of life, that it injects into the matter of your worlds the power of generation, that it makes bodies capable of feeling their existence and, finally, that it makes itself seen and all things visible.

'It remains for me now to explain to you why the souls of the philosophers do not join the mass of the sun in essence, like those of other men.

'There are three classes of spirit in all the planets, that is to say in all the small worlds which move round this one.

'The coarsest of them serve simply to fill out the girth of the sun. The more refined ones insinuate themselves into the position of its rays. But those of the philosophers, which have not contracted any impurity during their exile, arrive on the sphere of daylight quite intact as new inhabitants of it. Unlike the others, they do not become component parts of its mass, since the matter of which they are composed at the moment of their conception is so nicely blended that henceforward nothing can decompose it (as with that which forms gold, diamonds, and the stars, whose particles are linked together by so many embraces that the strongest solvent cannot break their hold).

'Now these philosophers' souls are so much, in regard to other souls, what gold, diamonds, and the stars are in regard to other bodies, that the Epicurus in the sun is the same as the Epicurus who once lived on earth.'

The pleasure I derived from listening to this great man made the road seem shorter to me and I often quite deliberately broached abstruse and curious topics, asking him for his ideas about them, in order to be instructed. Indeed I have never seen kindness as great as his, for although he could have reached the kingdom of the philosophers by himself in a very few days, on account of the volatility of his substance, he preferred to weary himself for a long time with me, rather than abandon me among the vast solitudes.

He was nevertheless in a hurry, for I recall that when I took it into my head to ask him why he was returning before getting to know all the regions of that great world, he replied that his impatience to see one of his friends, who had recently arrived, compelled him to cut short his travels. I recognized, from the words that followed, that this friend was the famous philosopher of our time, Monsieur Descartes,[1] and that he was hastening for no other reason than to join him.

When I asked him, further, in what esteem he held the latter's *Physics*, he answered that it should be read with no less respect than that which the pronouncements of oracles are heard. 'Not that the natural sciences have no need, like the other sciences, to be examined critically for axioms they do not prove;' he added, 'but the principles of *his* are so simple and so natural that once they are supposed, there is no other system which fits all the evidence better.'

At this point I could not keep myself from interrupting him. 'But it seems to me,' I said, 'that this philosopher always denied the existence of vacuums. Yet, although he was an Epicurean, in order to have the honour of upholding the principles of Epicurus, that is to say of atoms, he established that the beginning of things was a chaos of completely solid matter which God divided up into an untold number of little squares, each of which He imbued with conflicting motions. Now *he* has it that these cubes rubbed against one another and so ground each other into particles of all kinds of shapes. But how can he reckon that these square pieces should have begun to turn separately, without admitting that a vacuum was formed between their corners? Would it not be bound to occur in the spaces left by the corners of these squares as they moved? Could these squares, which occupied a certain area before turning, have revolved in a circle if they had not taken up twice as much space when they spun? Geometricians teach us that such a thing is impossible. Therefore half of all this space must of necessity have been left empty, since there were no atoms yet in existence to fill it.'

My philosopher replied to me that Monsieur Descartes

[1] Descartes died on 11 February 1650.

would be able to explain that to us himself, for, being by nature as much of an obliging person as he was a philosopher, he would certainly be delighted to find a mortal man in this world whom he could enlighten on the subject of the hundred doubts, which he had been compelled to leave behind on earth when death surprised him. He did not believe that he would have great difficulty in giving me an answer in accordance with his principles—which I had perforce only scrutinized as far as the feebleness of my intellect would allow.

'For,' he said, 'the works of this great man are so comprehensive and so subtle that the study necessary to understand them calls for the soul of a true and consummate philosopher. This means that there is not a philosopher in the sun who does not hold him in veneration—to the point where no one would wish to deny him the first rank if his modesty does not restrain him from it.

'In order to cheat the pain which the length of the road may bring you, let us discuss this in accordance with his system which is certainly so clear, and, thanks to the remarkable enlightenment of this great genius, seems to fit everything so well, that one would say he has rivalled the beautiful and magnificent structure of the Universe itself.

'You will well remember how he said that our understanding is finite. Thus, since matter is infinitely divisible, one cannot doubt that this is something which our understanding cannot grasp and which it would be far beyond it to explain.

'But,' he said, 'although it cannot be observed by our senses, we can none the less postulate that this is so from our knowledge of matter; and we must not hesitate,' he said, 'to base our judgement on the things which we are able to postulate. Can we actually imagine the manner in which the soul acts upon the body? Yet one cannot deny or doubt the truth that it does. For it is a far greater absurdity to define as a vacuum a space which is actually a part of the continuous body of matter, since one would then be confusing the idea of nothing with that of existence and attributing qualities of its own to something which can produce nothing and cannot be the author of anything at all!

'But my poor mortal,' he said, 'I can tell that these speculations weary you because, as this excellent man says, you have never taken the trouble to distil your spirit thoroughly from the mass of your body, and because you have made it so lazy that it will not perform any functions without the aid of the senses.'

I was going to answer him when he pulled me by the arm in order to show me a valley of wondrous beauty.

'Do you perceive,' he asked me, 'that hollow in the ground we are going down to? One might think the tops of the hills which surround it had deliberately crowned themselves with trees, in order to invite passers-by to rest in its cool shade.

'It is at the foot of one of these slopes that the Lake of Sleep has its source. It is formed solely from the liquid of the five springs. Furthermore, if it did not mingle with the three rivers, dulling their waters with its heaviness, no animal in our world would sleep.'

I cannot express the impatience which pressed me to question him about these three rivers, of which I had not yet heard tell; but I was satisfied when he promised me that I should see everything.

We arrived in the valley soon afterwards and almost at the same time upon the carpet which borders this lake.

'You are very lucky indeed,' said Campanella, 'to be seeing all the wonders of this world before you die, and it is fortunate for the inhabitants of your globe that it will have carried a man who can teach them about the marvels of the sun, since, but for you, they would have run the risk of remaining in gross ignorance for ever and enjoying a hundred good things, without knowing their source. For you cannot imagine the riches that the sun bestows upon all your little globes, and this valley alone dispenses countless blessings throughout the universe, without which you could not live or see the daylight. It seems to me that once you have seen this country you will have to admit that the sun is your father and that it is the author of all things.

'Because these five springs flow into the lake, they only take fifteen or sixteen hours to run their course, yet they appear so exhausted when they arrive that they can scarcely move. They show their weariness in very different ways. Sight narrows as it approaches the Lake of Sleep. Hearing gets blocked up at its mouth, goes astray, and loses itself in the mud. Smell gives off a murmuring like that of a man snoring. Taste, jaded by the journey, becomes altogether insipid. And Touch, once so broad that it could accommodate all its fellows, finds its own course going underground.

'For her part, the Nymph of Peace, who makes her abode in the middle of the lake, receives her guests with open arms, puts them to rest in her bed and nurses them so tenderly that she even takes the trouble of rocking them to sleep herself. Some time after mingling thus in this broad ring of water, they can be seen at the other end, separating into five streams once again and resuming, when they emerge, the names they abandoned on entering. The ones most eager to leave, which tug at their companions to be on their way, are Hearing and Touch. As for the three others, they wait for these two to wake them up and Taste, in particular, always dawdles behind the rest.'

The dark hollow of a cave arched over the Lake of Sleep. A quantity of tortoises walked with slow steps along the banks and a thousand poppy flowers were reflected in the water and communicated to it the power to make one doze. One even sees dormice coming from fifty leagues away to drink there, and the purling of the water is so bewitching that it seems to be lapping against the pebbles in rhythm and trying to compose a lullaby.

The wise Campanella doubtless foresaw that I would feel some of its effects and therefore advised me to double my pace. I would have obeyed him, but the charms of those waters had already befogged my brain so much that I was barely able to hear these last words: 'Sleep then! Sleep! I will leave you. For the dreams one has here are so perfect that you will some day be very glad to remember the one you are about to enjoy. I shall amuse myself, however, by inspecting the curiosities of the place and then I shall come and rejoin you.'

I think that is all he said—or else the fumes of sleep had already put me in a state past hearing him.

I was in the middle of the most erudite and diverting dream in the world when my philosopher came and woke me up. I will tell it to you at a point where this will not break the thread of my narrative, for it is very important for you to know about it, so that you can understand how freely the minds of the inhabitants of the sun operate, while sleep holds their senses captive. I believe, myself, that this lake gives off an air which has the property of entirely purifying the mind of the encumbrance of the senses, for nothing enters your thoughts which does not seem to perfect and instruct you. This is what fills me with the greatest respect in the world for those philosophers who are called 'dreamers' and are ridiculed by our ignoramuses.

So I opened my eyes with a start and seemed to hear him saying: 'Mortal! You have slept long enough! Get up if you desire to see marvels such as could never be imagined in your world. Since I left you about an hour ago, so as not to disturb your slumbers, I have been walking continuously along the banks of the five springs which flow out of the Lake of Sleep. You can imagine with what attention I have observed them all. They bear the names of the five senses and they flow very close together.

'Sight resembles a forked pipe filled with powdered diamonds and with little mirrors which receive and reflect the image of all that presents itself to them. Its course flows round the kingdom of the lynxes.

'Hearing is equally double. It twists and turns like a labyrinth and one hears reverberating in the hollow depths of its bed an echo of every sound which is heard near by. Unless I am much mistaken it was foxes I saw there, washing out their ears.

'Smell is like the other two and divides into two little channels which flow under a single vault. It extracts from everything it encounters something invisible from which it composes a thousand kinds of scents, which take the place of its water. On the banks of this stream one finds many dogs sharpening their noses.

'Taste flows in spurts which generally only occur three or four times a day. It is further necessary for a great sluice gate of coral to be raised and beneath that one a number of little ones, which are made of ivory. Its liquid resembles saliva.

'But as for the fifth, that of Touch, it is so broad and deep that it surrounds all its sisters to the point of lying full length in their beds, and its thick humour spreads at large over lawns all green with mimosa pudica.

'You must know that I was almost petrified with awe as I admired the mysterious detours of all these streams, and I walked until I found myself at the mouth, where they flow into the three rivers. But follow me: you will understand the arrangement of all these things much better when you see them.'

I was aroused by what seemed such a firm promise. I offered him my arm and we followed the path he had taken along the dykes, which contain the streams, each in its channel.

At the end of two hundred yards something came into view that glittered like a lake. The wise Campanella had no sooner seen this than he said to me: 'At last, my son, we are nearing our destination: I see the three rivers distinctly.'

At this news I felt overcome with such enthusiasm that I thought I had become an eagle. I flew rather than walked, and ran about everywhere with such avid curiosity that in less than an hour my guide and I had observed what you are about to hear.

Three great rivers water the shining plains of this blazing world. The first and broadest is called Memory; the second, narrower, but deeper, is called Imagination; the third, smaller than the others, is called Judgement.

All day long on the banks of Memory one hears an importunate chattering of jays, parrots, magpies, starlings, linnets, finches, and all those species that twitter what they have learned by heart. At night they say nothing, for then they are busy drinking up the thick vapour of these watery regions. But their dyspeptic stomachs find this so hard to digest that in the morning one sees it all spilling out of their beaks again, in as pure a state as when it was in the river.

The water of this river appears glutinous and makes a great deal of noise as it flows. The echoes which are set up in its caves repeat a word more than a thousand times over. It begets certain monsters whose faces bear a kind of resemblance to those of women, and one also sees another wilder type there, which are blockheaded, with horns, and look more or less like our pedants. These spend all their time yammering, but only repeat what they hear each other say.

The river of Imagination flows more softly. Its liquor is light and brilliant and everywhere flashing. If one looks at this water it seems like a torrent of liquid sparks, which follow no fixed order as they flit past. But, having considered it more attentively, I noticed that the fluid travelling along its bed was pure potable gold and its foam was oil of talc. The fishes it supports are remoras, sirens, and salamanders. And instead of gravel one finds in its bed those stones that Pliny speaks of which make one heavy when one touches them one side and light when one touches the other. I also noticed there some of those others, from which Gyges had a ring made, that render one invisible. But above all there are a great number of philosopher's stones shining in the sand there. Along the banks were a multitude of fruit trees, particularly those which Mohammed found in paradise. The branches swarmed with phoenixes, and I observed seedlings of that apple tree from which Discord plucked the fruit she threw at the feet of the three goddesses. Cuttings had been grafted on to them from the garden of the Hesperides.

Each of these broad rivers divides into an infinite number of channels which merge into one another. I noticed that when a wide stream from Memory approached a smaller one from Imagination it immediately extinguished the latter, but if, on the other hand, the stream from Imagination was bigger, it dried up that of Memory. So as these three rivers, both in their main channels and in their tributaries, always run close beside one another, wherever Memory is strong Imagination is reduced and the latter swells as the former abates.

Nearby, with incredible slowness, flows the river of Judgement. Its channel is deep. Its liquid seems cold. And when one sprinkles it over something it dries it instead of wetting it. Hellebore grows in its mud, with roots that extend in long filaments and cleanse the water at its mouth. Serpents dwell there and upon the soft grass which carpets its banks a million elephants take their rest. Like its two sisters it distributes its waters throughout an infinity of tiny channels. It grows in stature as it travels and although it is ever returning upon its tracks it gains ground continually.

All the sun is watered by the moisture of these three rivers. It soaks up the fiery atoms of those that die in this great world. But that is something which deserves to be treated more fully.

The lives of the creatures on the sun are very long and do not come to an end except by a natural death, which only happens after seven or eight thousand years, when the arrangement of their matter is disordered by the continuous mental excesses to which their fiery temperament inclines them. For as soon as nature senses that it would take more time to repair the ruins of a body than it would to make a new one, the body tends to fall apart, so that from day to day one sees the creature not rotting, but disintegrating into particles resembling red embers.

Death hardly ever comes in any other way. Once the creature has expired, or, to be more precise, has been extinguished, the little igneous bodies of which its substance formerly consisted join the general stuff of this blazing world until they chance to be watered by the moisture of the three rivers. Their fluidity makes them mobile and in their haste to exercise the faculties of which this water has given them an obscure knowledge, they fuse into long chains. By forming a stream of luminous specks, they sharpen themselves into rays and scatter to the spheres round the sun. There they are not so much absorbed, but rather strive to arrange their matter as much as they can into the shapes suited to the exercise of all the functions, for which the water of the three rivers, the five springs and the lake has given them an instinct. That is why they allow themselves to be drawn into plants, in order to grow; plants allow themselves to be chewed up by animals in order to feel; and animals allow men to eat them, so that they can nourish the three faculties of memory, imagination, and judgement, of which the rivers of the sun had given them a foretaste.

Now, depending on whether atoms have been more or less soaked in the moisture of these three rivers, they bring to the animals greater or lesser powers of memory, imagination, or judgement; and depending on how much of the liquor of the five springs and the little lake they have absorbed, they will elaborate more—or less perfect senses for them and produce minds which are more—or less wide awake.

That is roughly what we observed, concerning the nature of these three rivers. One encounters little tributaries of them, scattered here and there, but the principal channels go straight to the end of their course in the Province of the Philosophers. Thus we could return to the high road without going farther from the water than the distance needed to climb up on to the causeway. We were still able to see the three great rivers flowing beside us, and as for the five springs, we could survey their whole length as they wound through the meadows. This road is very pleasant, though lonely. One breathes a free and pure air there, which nourishes the mind and makes it keep the passions under control.

21

A strange agony, a ticklish dispute, and a happy meeting

AFTER five or six days on the road we were feasting our eyes upon the rich and varied aspects of the landscape, when the sound of a languishing voice, like that of a sick man groaning, came to our ears. We approached the spot from whence we judged it to be coming, and on the banks of the River of Imagination we found an old man who had fallen upside down, uttering loud cries. Tears of pity came to my eyes at this and my compassion for the unfortunate wretch led me to ask what the matter was.

'This man,' Campanella replied, turning towards me, 'is a philosopher suffering the death agony. We all die more than once and, as we are only parts of this universe, we change our shape in order to go and take up life elsewhere—which is not a bad thing, since it is a way to perfect one's being and to arrive at an infinite amount of knowledge. His disease is the one which causes the death of almost all great men.'

His words made me consider the sick man again with more attention and from my first glance I observed that he had a head as large as a barrel, which was broken open in several places.

'Now! now!' said Campanella, pulling at my arm. 'Any help we might think of giving this dying man would be useless and would only upset him. Let us go on, for his sickness is incurable. The swelling of his head is due to his having used his mind too much; for although the elements, with which he has filled the three organs or ventricles of his brain, are very tiny images, they are still corporeal and in consequence occupy a large space when they are very numerous. Now you must know that this philosopher swelled his brain so much, by dint of piling image upon image, that, not being able to contain them any longer, it has exploded. This way of dying is that of the great geniuses and it is called "bursting with intelligence".'

We continued on our way, conversing all the time, and whatever came next to our eyes furnished us with matter for discussion. I should, in fact, have very much liked to leave the opaque regions of the sun and re-enter the luminous ones. For the reader will remember that the countries there are not all diaphanous: there are some which are shadowy, like those in our world, and which would be shrouded in darkness if it were not for the light of a sun which can be seen from there. As one gradually enters the opaque regions one becomes opaque oneself and, similarly, when one approaches the transparent ones, one feels oneself stripped of this dark obscurity by the vigorous irradiation of the climate.

I remember that, with regard to this burning desire of mine, I asked Campanella if the province of the philosophers was brilliant or shadowy.

'It is more shadowy than brilliant,' he replied, 'for as we are still very much in sympathy with the earth, our native country, which is by nature opaque, we should not be comfortable in the most illuminated regions of this globe. We can, however, make ourselves diaphanous by means of a vigorous effort of will power, when the fancy takes us, and it is even true to say that the majority of the philosophers do not use their tongues for talking. When they wish to communicate their thoughts, their flights of imagination purge them of the sombre vapour, beneath which they generally keep their ideas hidden. As soon as they have driven back to its seat the dark spleen which obscured them, their bodies become diaphanous and one can see the things they remember, imagine, and judge in their brains, and the things they desire and resolve in their livers and their hearts. For although these little images are more imperceptible than anything else we can think of in this world, we have eyes sharp enough to make out even the very minor ideas with ease.

223

'Thus, when one of us wishes to reveal to a friend the affection he bears him, one sees his heart directing rays at the image in his memory of the one he loves; and when, on the other hand, he wants to show his aversion, one sees his heart projecting eddies of burning sparks at the image of the person he hates and recoiling from it as much as it can. Similarly, when he is communing with himself, one can clearly observe the elements, that is to say, the images of each thing he contemplates, imprinting or projecting themselves and presenting to the eyes of the observer not an articulate speech, but the story of all his thoughts in pictures.'

My guide would have continued, but he was stopped by a hitherto unprecedented occurrence, which was that we suddenly observed the ground growing dark beneath our feet and the rays of light in the brilliant sky above our heads extinguished, as if a canopy four leagues wide had been unfurled between us and the sun.

I find it difficult to tell you what we imagined in this situation. All kinds of terrors assailed us, including that of the end of the world, and none of them seemed unlikely, because to see night on the sun, or the sky clouded, is a miracle that never happens there. This was not all, besides. Immediately afterwards a harsh creaking sound came to our ears, like the noise of a pulley turning rapidly, and at the same time we saw a cage falling at our feet. Hardly had it touched the sand when it opened and gave birth to a man and a woman. They were dragging an anchor, which they planted in the base of a rock. After this we saw them coming towards us. The woman was leading the man, pulling him along and threatening him. When she was quite close to us she spoke with some emotion in her voice.

'Gentlemen,' she said, 'is this not the Province of the Philosophers?'

I replied that it was not, but that we hoped to arrive there within twenty-four hours and that the ancient who suffered me to accompany him was one of the principal officers of that realm.

'Since you are a philosopher,' replied the woman, addressing Campanella, 'I must unburden my heart to you before I go any further.

'To explain the matter that brings me here in a few words, you must know that I am coming to complain of a murder committed against the person of my youngest child. This barbarian, whom I have here, killed it twice over, although he was its father.'

We were extremely puzzled by this speech and asked to know what she meant by a child killed twice over.

'You must know that in our country,' the woman replied, 'there is, among the other Statutes of Love, a law which regulates the number of embraces a husband may give his wife. That is why every evening each doctor goes the rounds of all the houses in his area, where, after examining the husbands and wives, he will prescribe for them, according to their good or bad health, so many conjunctions for the night. Well, my husband had been put down for seven. However, angered by some rather haughty remarks I had addressed to him as we were getting ready to retire, he did not come near me all the time we were in bed. But God, who avenges those who are wronged, permitted this wretch to be titillated in a dream by the recollection of the embraces he was unjustly denying me, so that he let a man go to waste.

'I told you his father had killed him twice over, because by refusing to make him come into existence, he caused him not to be, which was the first murder, but subsequently he caused him never to be able to be, which was the second. A common murderer knows that the man whose days he cuts short *is no more*, but none of them could cause a man *never to have been*. Our magistrates would have dealt with him as he deserved if the cunning wretch had not excused himself by saying that he would have fulfilled his conjugal duty, had he not been afraid (as a result of embracing me in the height of the rage I had put him in) to beget a choleric man.

'The Senate was embarrassed by this defence and ordered us to come and present ourselves to the philosophers and plead our case before them. As soon as we received the order to go, we climbed into a cage suspended from the neck of this great bird you can see, from which we come down to the ground or ascend into the air by means of a pulley which we attached to it. There are people in our province whose particular work it is to tame them when they are young and to teach them to perform tasks which are useful to us. What chiefly induces them to become tractable, contrary to their ferocious nature, is the fact that we abandon to their hunger, which is almost insatiable, the carcasses of all the beasts which die. Furthermore, when we want to sleep (for we need to rest when we are exhausted by the over-prolonged excesses of love), we let loose twenty or thirty of these birds at intervals over the countryside, each one on the end of a rope, and they take to the air with their great pinions and spread a night in the sky which stretches beyond the horizon.'

My attention was divided between listening to her words and the rapt contemplation of this giant bird's immense size: but as soon as Campanella had studied it a little, he exclaimed: 'Aha! To be sure, this is one of the feathered monsters, known as condors, that one sees in the island of Mandragora in our world and throughout the torrid zone. There the spread of their wings covers more than an acre. But as these animals grow more monstrous, the warmer the sun is where they are born, in the world of the sun they could not fail to be of a formidable size.

'However,' he added, turning to the woman, 'it is imperative that you should complete your journey. It is for Socrates, who has been given the charge of supervising morals, to judge you. But I beg you to tell us from what country you come, as it is only three or four years since I arrived in this world and I am still unfamiliar with the geography of it.'

'We come,' she replied, 'from the Kingdom of Lovers. On one side this great state is bordered by the Republic of Peace and on the other side by that of the Just.

'In the country I come from the boys are put into a Novitiate of Love at the age of sixteen. This is a most sumptuous palace which occupies almost a whole district of the city. The girls do not enter it until they are thirteen. Everyone undergoes a year of probation there, during which the boys devote themselves entirely to winning the affection of the girls and the girls to making themselves worthy of the friendship of the boys. When twelve months have expired, the Faculty of Medicine goes in a body to visit this amatory training college. It examines them all, one after the other, down to the most private parts of their persons, makes them copulate in its presence and then, according to how vigorous and well-built the male proves to be at this test, he is given ten, twenty, thirty, or forty girls as wives, from among those who are fond of him, provided that their love is reciprocal. However, the husband may only sleep with two at a time and he is not permitted to embrace any of them while she is pregnant. The girls that are judged sterile are only employed as servants and from the impotent men are recruited the slaves, who are allowed carnal intercourse with the barren women. In addition to this, when a family contains more children than it can feed, the State adopts them. But this is a misfortune which rarely occurs, for as soon as a woman gives birth in the city, the exchequer provides an annual allowance for the education of the child, according to its quality, which the State Treasurers themselves bring round to the father's house on a certain day of the year. But if you want to know more, come into our basket; it is large enough for four. Since we are all going in the same direction, we can while away the long journey with conversation.'

Campanella was of the opinion that we should accept the offer and I was equally delighted to avoid the fatigue. When I came to help them raise the anchor, I was quite astonished to see that instead of a thick cable to carry it, it was simply hung from a silken thread as fine as a hair. I asked Campanella how it could happen that a heavy mass like this anchor did not cause something so frail to snap under its weight. The good man replied to me that this cord did not snap because it had been spun so evenly throughout that there was no reason why it should give way in one place rather than another. We all piled into the basket and hauled ourselves right up to the top of the bird's throat, where we looked like no more than a bell hung about its neck. When we were hard against the pulley, we belayed the cable, from which our cage was hung, round one of the finest of its down feathers (which was, nevertheless, as thick as my thumb) and as soon as the woman made a signal to the bird to start, we felt ourselves cleaving the air with great force. The condor reduced or increased speed and went up or down as its mistress desired, her voice acting as a bridle. We had not flown two hundred leagues when over to our left we saw a night covering the ground, which resembled the one cast beneath it by our own living parasol. We asked the fair stranger what she thought it could be.

'It is another criminal, who is also going to be judged in the province we are bound for. His bird must be stronger than ours, or else we had dallied a great deal, for he did not leave until after me.'

I asked her what crime this unfortunate man was accused of.

'He is not merely accused,' she replied to us, 'he is condemned to death, because he has already been convicted of not being afraid to die.'

'How so?' said Campanella. 'Do the laws of your country command you to fear death?'

'Yes,' answered the woman. 'They command everyone to do so, except for those who have been admitted to the College of Sages. For our magistrates have discovered from painful experience that a man who is not afraid of losing his own life is capable of taking everyone else's.'

After some further exchanges which followed from these, Campanella sought to inform himself in more detail about the way of life of her country. He therefore asked her what the laws and customs of the Kingdom of Lovers were; but she excused herself from speaking about them, for the reason that, not having been born there and only half knowing them she was afraid of saying too little or too much about them.

'It is true that I have come from that province,' the woman continued, 'but I am, like all my forebears, a native of the Kingdom of Truth. My mother bore me there and had no other children. She brought me up in that country until, when I was thirteen, the King commanded her, on the advice of the doctors, to take me to the Kingdom of Lovers (from whence I have just come) so that I might be raised in the Palace of Love and receive a gayer and gentler education than that of our country, which would make me more fertile than she had been. My mother took me there and put me into that house of pleasure.

'I suffered a good deal before I had grown accustomed to their ways. At first these seemed very primitive, for, as you know, the opinions which we have imbibed with our mothers' milk always seem to us the most reasonable, and I had only just arrived from the Kingdom of Truth, my native country.

'I did not fail to appreciate that this Nation of Lovers lived much more gently and indulgently than ours, for although every man announced that the sight of me caused dangerous wounds, that my glances were deadly and that my eyes gave out a fire which consumed their hearts, yet the good nature of every one of them, especially the young men, was so great that they caressed me, kissed me, and embraced me, instead of taking revenge upon me for the harm I had done to them. I even grew angry with myself about the distress I was causing, so that, moved by pity, I one day revealed to them that I had resolved to take flight.

' "But alas! How can we save you?" they all cried, throwing themselves at my neck and kissing my hands. "Your house is surrounded with water and the danger appears to be so great that, but for a miracle, you and we should certainly be drowned already." '

'How so?' I interrupted. 'Is the Country of Lovers subject to flooding?'

'It must be said that it is,' she answered me. 'For one of my lovers (who would not have wished to deceive me—since he loved me) wrote to me that in his grief at my departure he had just wept an ocean of tears. A second I saw assured me that a wellspring of tears had flowed down his eyes for three days, and while I was cursing, for love of them, the fatal hour when they had first seen me, yet another of those that counted themselves among my slaves sent me a message to say that the previous night his eyes had brimmed over and caused a flood. I would have removed myself from this world, so as to be the cause of so many misfortunes no longer, but the messenger then added that his master had told him to assure me that there was nothing to fear because the furnace of his breast had dried up the flood. In short, you can imagine how aquatic the Kingdom of Lovers must be from the fact that they are only crying by halves there when nothing more than streams, fountains, and torrents issues from under their eyelids.

'I was very worried about what device I could employ to escape from all these waters, which must surely engulf me. But one of my lovers, who was known as Green-eyes, advised me to tear out my heart and embark upon it. I should not be afraid of it being too small, since I had found a place in it for so many others, nor of it sinking to the bottom, since it was so light. All I needed to beware of was fire, because the substance of this vessel was highly inflammable. I should therefore set sail upon the sea of his tears; the blindfold of his love would serve me as a sail and the favourable winds of his sighs, despite the storming of his rivals, would bring me safely to port.

'I spent a long time wondering how I could put this enterprise into operation. The timidity natural to my sex restrained my daring, but finally I decided that if the thing were not possible, no man would be so insane as to advise it, least of all a lover to his mistress, and I plucked up courage.

'I took hold of a knife and split open my breast and indeed I was already rummaging in the wound with both hands and identifying my heart with a fearless gaze, preparatory to snatching it out, when a young man who loved me appeared on the scene. He wrested the weapon from me and asked me the motive for this action, which he called "desperate." I told him the story of it and a quarter of an hour later I was very surprised to learn that he had taken Green-eyes to court. But the magistrates were perhaps afraid of paying too much regard to precedent or to the novelty of the case and passed it on to the Parliament of the Kingdom of the Just. There, in addition to perpetual banishment, he was condemned to go and end his days as a slave on the lands of the Republic of Truth, and his descendants, down to the fourth generation, were forbidden ever to set foot in the Province of Lovers. He was furthermore ordered never to use a hyperbole again upon pain of death.

'After that I came to have a great deal of affection for the young man who had saved me and, whether on account of this good office or of his passion for me, when his apprenticeship and mine were ended and he asked me to be one of his wives, I did not refuse him.

'We have always lived happily together and would do still, had he not, as I told you, killed one of my children twice over, for which I am going to ask vengeance in the Kingdom of Philosophers.'

We were very surprised, Campanella and I, by the deep silence this man observed. I therefore tried to console him, judging his profound taciturnity to be the offspring of a most profound sorrow, but his wife prevented me.

'It is not the excess of his grief which makes him keep his mouth shut,' she said, 'but our laws, which forbid all criminals whose case is *sub judice* to speak until they are before the judges.'

During this conversation the bird continued to make progress and I was quite amazed to hear Campanella shouting, with a look of rapturous joy on his face: 'A hearty welcome to you, dearest of my friends! Come gentlemen,' continued the good man, 'let us go and meet Monsieur Descartes. Let us go down. There he is, coming now, but three leagues away from here.'

This outburst left me quite perplexed, for I did not understand how he could know about the arrival of a person from whom we had received no news. 'To be sure,' I said to him, 'I suppose you have just seen him in a dream?'

'If you call a "dream",' he said, 'what you can see in your mind as clearly as you see with your eyes by day, when the sun is out, then I admit this.'

'But is it not day-dreaming,' I exclaimed, 'to believe that Monsieur Descartes, whom you have not seen since your departure from the world of the earth, is three leagues from here, simply because you imagined it?'

I was just uttering the last syllable of this, when we saw Descartes arriving. Campanella ran to embrace him at once. They talked together for a long time, but I found it hard to pay attention to the obliging things they said to one another, because I was so consumed with curiosity to learn the secret of Campanella's divination. This philosopher, who could read my passion in my face, told his friend the story of it and begged him to give him leave to satisfy me. M. Descartes replied with a smile and my learned teacher discoursed as follows:

'All bodies give off elements, that is to say, corporeal images, which hover in the air. Despite their movement, these images always preserve the shape, the colour, and all the other properties of the object they announce, but as they are very subtle and very refined, they pass through our sense organs without having any effect on them. They travel through to the mind, where they leave an imprint, on account of the sensitivity of its substance, and thus make us see very distant objects which the senses cannot perceive. This is what happens here, where the spirit is not imprisoned in a body made of coarse matter, as it is in your world.

'We will tell you how it occurs, when we have had sufficient leisure to satisfy our eagerness to talk to one another. For you certainly deserve to be treated with the utmost consideration. . . .'